I0614502

Sworn to Fly

by

Maria Imbalzano

The Sworn Sisters Series, Book 3

This is a work of fiction. Names, characters, places, and incidents are either the product of the author's imagination or are used fictitiously, and any resemblance to actual persons living or dead, business establishments, events, or locales, is entirely coincidental.

Sworn to Fly

Contact Information: info@thewildrosepress.com

Cover Art by *Diana Carlile*

The Wild Rose Press, Inc.
PO Box 708
Adams Basin, NY 14410-0708
Visit us at www.thewildrosepress.com

Publishing History
First Edition, 2021
Trade Paperback ISBN 978-1-5092-3698-5
Digital ISBN 978-1-5092-3699-2

The Sworn Sisters Series, Book 3
Published in the United States of America

"Why so quiet?" he asked after a while.

"I'm meditating."

"Really?"

She laughed—a welcome sound. "No. I didn't take the class yet. I thought I'd just let you do your thing."

"I can do my thing while talking." He pointed his camera in her direction and took a photo.

"Can you please give me some warning when you're going to do that? I can see my request that you not take my picture has fallen on deaf ears, so you can at least give me a heads-up." She pulled a stemmy reed from her hair.

"Sorry. Can't do. That's not the way I work. I like candid shots when the subject isn't prepared. They're the best."

"So I'm a subject now?"

Gabe headed over and sat down beside her, his leg touching hers. A shock wave coursed through him. He inhaled slowly, trying to take back control. When her arm brushed against his, the wave vied with sparks and heat.

Russet eyes held his for only a moment before she disconnected.

He cleared his throat, hoping to clear his head. "You're an amazing subject. The photos I took of you yesterday on our little walk were so natural. The intensity of your eyes when you were helping Missy, the sympathy on your face, even though you were the ultimate professional—portrayed a nurse in action, helping a patient. Beautiful."

Praise for Maria Imbalzano

Maria has received many honors for her work, including the ACRA Readers' Choice Heart of Excellence Award and the Wisconsin Romance Writers Write Touch Readers Award. She was also a finalist for the New England Readers' Choice Award, the NJ Romance Writers Golden Leaf Award, the RONE Award, and the Book Buyers Best Award.

~

SWORN TO REMEMBER:
"The romance between Samantha and Michael is slow burning but once they got together, they were electric."

~*N.N. Light*

~*~

"The author beautifully incorporated themes of love, loss and of course friendship! ...Highly recommend."

~*Leanne Treese, Author*

~

SWORN TO FORGET:
"Nicki and Dex have amazing chemistry and their heat is scorching, both in and out of the bedroom."

~*LJT, NetGalley*

~*~

"The emotions of the characters really tugged at my heartstrings. The pacing was quick, and the writing smooth."

~*Roni Denholtz, Author of* Meet Me at the Inn

Dedication

To my fabulous critique partners,
Kate Lutter and Kate Forest,
who encourage me to see the error of my ways.
And to my awesome daughters,
Alex Brady and Mackenzie Pyne,
who point out what my characters their age
would never do.

Chapter One

Do not let this be another mistake. Alyssa blew an annoyed breath at a strand of hair obscuring her vision. But the stray lock was not the problem. She scanned the reception area of Glenn Pines Mountain Resort, taking in worn, faded furniture, dark-paneled walls, and a floral carpet that might have been popular in the 1940s. A musty scent reminded her of her grandmother's basement.

The resort's website clearly omitted photos of this area, and understandably so. It would not have been inviting to the trendy clientele they'd marketed. Not that she fit into that group, but still, she had standards. She took a tentative step toward the check-in desk.

"Welcome to Glenn Pines." A perky twenty-something, sporting a name badge with Sharon etched in green, looked at her expectantly. "Name, please?"

"Alyssa Beckman." As she swallowed the dread that had crept up her throat, she watched Sharon leaf through dozens of manila file folders, a computer conspicuously missing.

When she booked this vacation two weeks ago, she'd been in a tailspin, grasping for something that would take her away from her job, her life, her comfort zone. She'd needed a change. Quick. So with little research, she jumped at the first site that caught her eye. "Live your best life with health, wellness, and balance."

Who could ignore a mountain retreat with a slogan like that?

Never one to fly to exotic locales despite her thirty-three years of living on this earth, she opted for something within driving distance. This Pocono Mountains retreat fit her requirements of not being too far, but far enough, not too expensive, but still making a huge dent in her rainy-day savings, and a definite change from her small-town environs. With any luck, it would cater to her specific needs—whatever they were.

At least that's what the website promised in promoting physical pursuits to challenge her, in addition to the softer undertakings like meditation, yoga, and mindfulness classes. Puncturing her bubble, trying something new, and clearing her mind of all its noise defined a tall order for one week, but if she could get away from the place where her latest bad decision had the potential to derail her career, she'd come back refreshed. And hopefully with a plan, or the seeds of one, for her future. Workwise, as well as personally.

Sharon finally pulled a folder from the masses. "You're in cabin thirty-five. I see you're signed up for the Adventure Program. Great package. Here's your itinerary for the week." A typed agenda with dates and times appeared before her. "There are ten physical activities and five classes already scheduled for you. The physical activities take two to three hours each. The classes are one hour."

"The Adventure Program?" Alyssa examined the proffered schedule. "Wait. This can't be right." Various hikes, mountain biking, rock climbing, ropes challenges, kayaking, and horseback riding were sprinkled throughout the week. "What about meditation, yoga…" She squinted, searching for those more relaxed endeavors.

"Any free time you have before, between, or after those scheduled can be used to participate in the other sessions our resort has to offer." Sharon continued her cheery welcome monologue. "If I were you, I'd sign up right now for the seminar on Dealing with Stress as well as Hot Yoga. Those classes fill up fast, and if you're interested, you don't want to wait until it's too late."

With three to six hours a day of straining her muscles, how would she be able to hobble to Hot Yoga? This was not going to work. Although her angst escalated, she kept her voice steady and added a hint of honey. "Perhaps we can adjust my schedule right now to replace some of these more physically challenging activities." Rock climbing would be the first to go.

"Excuse me." A man standing behind her interrupted, clearly impatient with the route her conversation was heading with Sharon. "Since this could take a while, I just need to ask a quick question." Without waiting for her consent, he jumped in. "Sharon, there's no problem if I join Eric's group this afternoon, right?" His question, although couched as a query, had an authoritative bent that left little room for a negative answer.

Sharon beamed. "Of course not, Gabe. Go right ahead."

"Great. See you later." A thumbs-up accompanied a wink.

Almost as an afterthought, he carelessly tossed a few words in her direction. "Sorry for the intrusion." He turned without waiting for a response.

Sharon's gaze followed him right out the door, her smile melding into a sigh.

Alyssa cleared her throat. "Can we get back to my dilemma?" Having witnessed firsthand how easily a scheduled activity could be adjusted, she felt more at ease with her request.

"Of course, Ms. Beckman." The smile disappeared. "We take great pride in reviewing your questionnaire and placing you in pursuits that fit your personal goals. The questions you answered were developed in conjunction with a psychologist trained in this sort of thing, and a lot of work went into developing the perfect program for you. Are you sure you want to change your goals at this point?"

She hadn't been aware she was setting goals with her candid replies. Whoever read her answers must have thought she needed to expend all that hostile energy by tackling nature hours a day and sitting through classes in stress relief the other part of the day. Maybe she did need that. Perhaps her placement in the Adventure Program was a blessing in disguise.

She exhaled her apprehension. "Since someone put so much effort into analyzing my questionnaire, I'll stick with the program."

"Great." Sharon's smile reappeared. "You'll notice that your first adventure starts in forty minutes. One p.m. sharp. It's a three-hour hike, about a thousand feet up. I hope you brought your hiking boots." She cupped her mouth with her hand as if to let Alyssa in on a little secret. "It's rated moderate, but it's pretty difficult."

The dull ache that had taken up residence in the back of her head upon arrival surged like a swarm of termites to her temporal lobe, pinching and stinging along their path. “Thanks for the warning.”

She massaged her forehead. Hiking boots? She’d congratulated herself for buying expensive sneakers with superior arch support, which cushioned on impact. Perfect for nature walks. Would they prove just as hardy on the mountain trail where she’d be in forty minutes?

Do not let this be another mistake.

Sharon whisked out a pamphlet. “Here’s the map of the property.” She circled the building where they stood. “Your cabin is in the back.” Her black marker asterisked it. “A fabulous spot, not far from the lake and the nature trails. Nice and quiet. And here’s the dining hall.” An arrow marked the spot on the other side of the property from her residence. “The walk will be great exercise right before a meal.”

Sharon’s take on everything Glenn Pines had to offer was bubbly. No wonder she’d been hired as a greeter. But despite her cheeriness, anxiety had taken root in Alyssa’s brain and sped through her blood. Breathe, she cautioned herself. This is what you wanted. Something different. Something physical. Something that would take your mind off the “issues” back home. Think positive.

Alyssa glanced down at her fully packed, oversized bag. Not knowing exactly what to expect, including varied weather conditions, she’d brought too many clothes ranging from swimsuits to sweaters, exercise togs to dressy jeans.

“Is there someone who can take my suitcase to my cabin? I only have one, but it’s heavy, and I don’t think the wheels will do well on the uneven ground.” Especially since her cabin looked to be about a half mile away through a wooded area.

"I'm sorry, Ms. Beckman, but we don't have a bellman. Everyone takes their own bags." Even when she delivered bad news, Sharon's smile never faltered.

"Okay, then. I guess I better get moving so I make that three-hour hike." Alyssa smiled through gritted teeth, took the map, and grabbed the handle of her trunk. "Thanks."

Sharon's ponytail bobbed enthusiastically along with her head. "Anytime. If you have any questions, just stop by. I can help you with anything."

Apparently not anything, but this was where she'd be for the next eight days. She'd better get into the spirit of things. Fast. Thankfully she was in fairly good shape from visiting her local gym three to four days a week. But rock climbing? Jeesh!

The autumn air was warm today, especially for the mountains, and as Alyssa struggled with her suitcase, beads of sweat trickled down her back. Yet she hadn't even encountered her first event. Glenn Pines was a little more rustic and no-frills than she'd anticipated. And a little more demanding. But the price was right, she had over a week off from work, and this was her time to self-reflect. Life was all about making adjustments and moving forward.

Arriving at her destination, she took the key—a real metal key, not a plastic swipe card—and unlocked her home away from home for the next eight days. It was small but functional, with a living room, bedroom, and bathroom. She didn't have to look hard to see the absence of a television, but a coffee maker and a small, dorm-room-style refrigerator sat in the corner.

Bare bones, but clean.

She quickly unzipped her suitcase, located her new sneakers and cushioned no-show socks, then slipped them on. Should she have bought hiking clothes—whatever they were? Her jeans, T-shirt, and pullover sweater would have to do. With only twenty minutes to get to the meeting spot, she'd unpack later.

Slinging her expertly organized backpack over her shoulder, she headed out the door and toward the Lodge, as the activities hub was called—another building at an enormous distance from her cabin despite Sharon's assurance she had the best accommodations at the place. She must use that line on everyone.

She pulled her cell phone from her pocket to send a quick text to her three best friends to say she'd arrived safely. They'd been a little wary of her vacation plan but attempted to hide their concern under words of encouragement. Alyssa's dread of travelling, especially alone, was no secret.

Undelivered popped up below her message. Not exactly a surprise. The lack of a computer at the reception desk should have given her a clue about spotty Wi-Fi service. Now the picture became clearer. Glenn Pines was a bucolic retreat where she could withdraw from civilization and become one with nature. Okay. She could deal with that. Forget pampering. Forget communicating with her friends or family. Forget catching up on senseless TV shows. She was here to escape and reboot. Something she desperately needed.

Passing through the game room to an outside courtyard, Alyssa headed to the location where the hike was to begin. Twelve others meandered near the appointed place, either talking or studying the trail map.

Alyssa stood off to the side, taking in her fellow hikers. A few had poles. Was that really necessary?

A woman about her age strode up and held out her hand. “Hi. I’m Edie Trent.”

“Alyssa Beckman.” She shook her hand. “I just arrived.”

“Very happy to meet you, Alyssa. I got here three days ago. It’s very…interesting. Sometimes I think I should have leaned toward the Mindfulness Program. This boot-camp experience is intense.” She whispered conspiratorially, “I ditched the rock climbing yesterday afternoon and went to a beginner’s yoga session. Later, I was told I shouldn’t do that. A great deal of thought went into my itinerary, and we’re expected to keep to the schedule.” She shrugged. “It felt so good to stretch and pose after mountain biking all morning. My muscles were killing me.”

So Alyssa was in boot camp despite the availability of a Mindfulness Program. Why hadn’t she paid more attention to the fine print? Or answered the questions with forethought rather than emotion. Not that she’d prefer to sit around and murmur mantras all day or listen to some spiritual guru talk about how she should embrace the universe. If she looked for a silver lining here, the physicality of her schedule assured she wouldn’t have time to dwell on her stupid mistakes twenty-four seven. She would embrace this experience with the goal of moving forward, not crying over the past.

Edie’s voice broke through her musings. “You’ll love the food. But get to the dining hall as soon as it opens. Breakfast is at seven, lunch at noon, and dinner at seven. If you get there later, everything will be picked over, and you don't want that. You'll be starving after all this exercise."

While Edie continued her monologue, Alyssa pictured grown adults pushing and shoving to get into the buffet line before they fell over from starvation. She glanced at an older couple who surely couldn't be doing all the activities scheduled on her agenda. But, of course, their itinerary would have been geared to the responses on their questionnaire as well as their age, ability, and physical health. She now remembered putting "excellent" next to every question dealing with her health and agility, not realizing she was setting herself up for the Adventure Program, a.k.a. boot camp.

"If you need any help finding anything," Edie continued, "I'd be happy to show you. Just look for me in the dining hall during meals since there's no cell service out here. Which is a good thing in my opinion. It's nice to unplug."

Alyssa had been hoping cell service was just spotty, not nonexistent. "I guess." She tried for upbeat but fell a tad short.

"Okay, ladies and gents, let's get started. As most of you know, I'm Eric, your hiking guide."

Several campers, as Alyssa now thought of them, waved and exchanged pleasantries.

"Welcome to Glenn Pines and to the best hiking trails around."

His warm baritone brought her into his fold. This place must require that all employees have a background as a former camp counselor or cheerleader. The two she'd already met radiated sunshine and perkiness.

"Just a few bits of advice." Eric became serious.

"Since it's been raining off and on the last two days, the trails are muddy and the rocks slippery. Take your time, watch your step, and help each other. There are several areas where the brush is low and you have to crawl on your hands and knees to get through."

Alyssa's mouth dropped open. She knew they were going on a three-hour walk, half of it uphill, but she assumed the trails would have been cleared. Crawling around in puddles and mud was never a considered possibility. Not that she'd ever hiked in the mountains before. The closest she'd come was walking up the hill to Bowman's Tower at Washington Crossing Park.

Eric kept going. "Some areas are fairly steep. You may get winded if you're not used to this type of exercise. Feel free to take a rest. I see all of you have backpacks. Hopefully, you've brought water and some protein snacks. We're following the orange trail markers up the mountain and the blue trail markers down. So if you get separated from our group, there's no need to worry."

Alyssa hoped that was all the bad news he had to deliver, but he held up his hand to stop the murmurings.

"We'll be crossing two streams. Because of the rain, they are higher than normal, and you'll be up to your knees in water. The good news is that you will see some amazing views along the ridgeline and once we reach the summit. There's also a beautiful waterfall about an hour into our hike. Enjoy."

Alyssa nudged Edie. "I thought this would be a nice walk in the woods on a perfect autumn day. It doesn't sound like that."

Edie laughed. "You're right about the perfect day. The rest remains to be seen. I'm a little worried I didn't buy a hiking pole before coming here. I did bring water, snacks, dry socks, and sneakers to change into."

Alyssa also had water and protein snacks, but no dry socks or second pair of sneakers. And it now sounded like her expensive new footwear would be ruined within hours of her arrival. A sigh escaped.

She shut down the disgruntled murmurings in her head as they began their trek on a meandering incline. She tried to appreciate the scenery while listening to Edie with half an ear. The woman could talk! But before long they were climbing steeper slopes, impeded by tree roots, fallen trunks, and skittering stones making it difficult to breathe, much less talk, and the hikers now formed a single line as they individually navigated the treacherous terrain.

The distinct clicking of a camera caught Alyssa's attention, and she turned to see who had the sure-footedness to walk and click.

It was the guy behind her at the reception desk. At the time, she hadn't taken in his features—too focused on her mission to adjust the Adventure Package. Chestnut brown hair inched over his collar and curled slightly. A neatly trimmed beard highlighted a strong jaw. Eyes the color of pale emeralds caught on hers. He arched a brow as if to ask what she found so interesting.

Her cheeks burned, and she strode over to Edie, needing a conversation to conceal her self-consciousness.

"Eric is the best guide," Edie gushed. "He's very knowledgeable and handsome. Don't you think? I wouldn't mind getting to know him better, but I think he may be interested in Sharon at the front desk. I see them flirting with each other. Besides, I live five hours away. In Pittsburgh. Long-distance relationships never work out. At least not for me. How about you?"

After a few seconds, Alyssa recognized silence. Edie had stopped talking and surprisingly asked her a question.

"I don't know. I never had a long-distance relationship."

"Of course you probably have a gorgeous boyfriend who couldn't accompany you here. It seems everyone I meet is in a relationship—either married, living together, dating for years. It's hard for me to find someone available who is smart, employed, and nice. Maybe it's me. I don't know." She shrugged, not inviting comment.

Alyssa feared her problem with men might have something to do with talking too much, but she shouldn't pass judgment too soon. She was certainly a friendly sort, but even Alyssa had distanced herself from Edie over the past hour, needing quiet to deal with this challenge.

She laughed to herself as she pictured Charlie Brown sitting in a classroom as the teacher's words came out as a nasal whaugh, whaugh, whaugh. Edie's discourses were beginning to sound like that.

As promised, they stopped on a rickety bridge, and a rushing waterfall crashed into a pristine pond. It was pretty, maybe even spectacular, but all Alyssa could dwell on was getting her breathing under control and dropping the heavy backpack at her feet for a much-needed rest. Those aerobics classes had not prepared her for this. Would it be rude to suggest they turn around here and head back? She glanced at her colleagues, and none of them were struggling like she was. They were all taking photos or pointing at some special tree or bird or whatever.

Her gaze stopped on the guy from reception. He moved easily, fluidly, as he cradled his camera with professional ease, keeping his distance from the others. Sharon had called him Gabe. Cool name. He squatted to capture some natural phenomenon, but her eyes focused on his thighs, his butt.

Her analysis of the male form was interrupted by the older couple whom she had glimpsed earlier. "I'm Missy," said the woman, smiling at her. "This is my husband, Conrad."

"Nice to meet you. I'm Alyssa, the newbie here." She shook out her legs to keep the blood flowing. "I seem to be having a harder time than anyone else on this hike."

"You'll get used to the challenges. It just takes a couple of days," Conrad volunteered.

Alyssa inwardly groaned. Sooner would be better. "What brings you here?" she asked instead of why in the world would you have signed up for this?

"We're celebrating our thirtieth wedding anniversary this week." Missy grinned as if this anniversary getaway were the best thing ever.

Conrad jumped in. "Not exactly a romantic getaway for two, but we love it here. We're doing something good for our bodies and souls." His chuckle was contagious.

"Thirty years. Wow. That's…quite an accomplishment. I never made it to…" Alyssa stopped, halting herself from sharing her pathetic history with strangers. She waved it all away. "Never mind. I'm here celebrating my freedom—a new beginning."

"This is a good place for that, too." Missy patted her on the arm. A sympathy pat, no doubt.

Too soon for Alyssa, they continued their upward hike. She concentrated on slowing her pace and shifting her weight forward to alleviate some of the strain on her back. Her new sneakers were caked with mud, and the lower half of her jeans were now drenched and stiff from having crossed two streams.

When they finally arrived at their destination at the top of the crest, Alyssa sank down on a patch of grass overlooking a gorge. Now that she could rest for a while, the scenery came into focus. And as promised, the view was magnificent. Mountains reaching for the heavens across a divide surrounded by an azure, cloudless sky looked picture perfect. She inhaled the earthen energy surrounding her, hoping its restorative qualities would revitalize body and soul.

Despite nature's beauty, her unused muscles started to tighten, and her wet clothing sent a chill through her system. So much for the pleasure part of this trip.

Time for the descent.

Not so bad, at first. But when the group headed toward a steep decline, Eric cautioned them. "Be careful of the roots and rocks. It's easy to trip or slip. Look down."

The photographer passed her, continuing to snap away as they made their way down through the wooded landscape. His focus veered from trees to foliage to candid shots of the hikers. Maybe he worked for Glenn Pines. That would explain why he cut in on her conversation with Sharon and why they seemed to know each other better than a receptionist and a guest might otherwise. Although he was missing the chipper gene. Would they end up back at the activities center facing a wall of photos to purchase like at an amusement park?

Alyssa made sure she stayed out of his camera's eye. She looked a mess, felt worse, and didn't need to see the evidence on a five-by-seven glossy.

Clickety-click.

She looked up to see the camera's lens pointing in her direction. "Hey. Don't do that. I don't want to buy any photos."

"Good, because they're not for sale." A smirk insinuated itself on his mouth.

"Don't you need my permission to take my picture?" Her hands went automatically to her hips—her "meaning business" pose.

"Only if I want to sell it." He snapped another picture. "But that scowl on your face would never sell."

She was about to give him a lesson in tactfulness, but a thump and crash behind her hijacked her attention. Missy lay face-planted on the ground, her arm underneath her body.

Alyssa rushed to her side, then crouched on the ground. "Are you okay? What happened?"

"I tripped." Confusion furrowed Missy's forehead. "I guess I wasn't paying enough attention."

"Stay still for a moment. Let me help you. I'm a nurse." She shrugged off her backpack, then gently positioned Missy to make it easier for her to sit up.

As Missy used her hands to push herself to a more comfortable spot, she squealed. "My wrist."

Alyssa examined it. "I don't know if it's sprained or fractured, but hold it against your body with your other hand. Like this." She dug into her backpack and pulled out an ice pack. "This will help any swelling but not the pain." She gingerly laid it against Missy's wrist.

Eric appeared beside them, assessing the situation. "I'll call for help." He took a walkie-talkie from his backpack. Thank goodness for that.

"I'm so embarrassed," cried Missy.

Conrad knelt beside her. "Don't be, honey. It could have happened to any of us." He massaged her back as he spoke quietly to her.

A pang of jealousy spiked through Alyssa as she wrapped Missy's wrist with an ace bandage for stability. No one had ever cared about her like that. Grudgingly she acknowledged it was because she'd never been with the right guy.

Eric cut into her bleak thoughts. "The EMTs at the clinic are bringing a wheelchair. They won't be long. We're not too far from our starting point. We'll get you to the hospital for X-rays as soon as we can."

"Just what I need to ruin our week." A tear slipped down Missy's face.

"Honey, don't worry." Conrad kissed her forehead. "We'll get you checked out at the hospital. Maybe it's just a sprain."

Alyssa kept to herself that many times a sprain was as bad as a fracture.

"What if it's broken?" Missy's face contorted.

Edie chimed in as if she worked there. "Conrad can take you for a boat ride, or you can join classes in meditation or spiritual wellness. Maybe you can volunteer to be the ref for volleyball games. You'd be in charge, and the players would have to abide by your calls. Such power!"

Encouraging Missy to look on the bright side was

sweet of Edie.

"That's right." Alyssa's voice filled with compassion. "Once your wrist is stabilized, you'll be able to move around." She didn't share that the swelling would be painful and set her back a few days. "Mountain biking will be impossible, but as Edie said, there are so many other things to do here. And you have a great husband to help you." She placed her hand on Conrad's shoulder.

She guiltily thought if it had been her who had fallen, she wouldn't have to go mountain climbing or do the ropes challenge. Was she that worried about trying new skills to think breaking a bone would be better than participating in those events?

Once the EMTs arrived, they helped Missy into the wheelchair, and everyone headed back to the Lodge.

"I'm so sorry to all of you," Missy stated. "I'm holding you up."

Eric spoke for the group. "You're not. We'll be back to camp in less than fifteen minutes. Just hold tight and don't worry about the rest of us."

Twelve bedraggled hikers agreed and followed in Missy's wake.

Alyssa held back, waiting for Edie. "Thanks for chiming in with things Missy will be able to do. She needed to hear that."

"I feel bad for her. A whole week ahead with dozens of activities she won't be able to participate in. But thank goodness there are a host of others that don't require physical force. I should know. I've studied the entire brochure in case I have to substitute despite their suggested schedule. After today's hike, I have a feeling my legs won't want to mountain climb tomorrow morning."

Alyssa's thighs cramped in recognition. Her agenda was taking her to the lake tomorrow morning, but just in case, she'd better study that brochure as well. "What brings you to Glenn Pines?"

Edie sighed. "I want to find my best life." Apparently, that slogan worked on Edie, too. "I was laid off from my job as a program manager last month. I had worked at the same company for the past ten years. Since right after college. It was my first job, and I assumed I'd be there my entire career. I loved it. Loved my co-workers, the job was interesting, challenging."

"I'm really sorry to hear you were laid off. That's awful." Alyssa couldn't imagine being let go from a company that defined her career. Although, she might be in a similar position if she was transferred out of the ER where she'd been for ten years. "With all your experience, you should be able to find another job. Maybe even somewhere in the same company."

"They're experiencing difficulties due to overseas competition. And even though my skills transfer to other companies, I can't quite figure out my next step. There are thousands of people in the Pittsburgh area who have lost jobs. The market is saturated with unemployed middle-management associates."

Alyssa had no information or knowledge to add to this conversation, so she walked quietly beside her.

Edie turned the discussion around to Alyssa. "I heard you tell Missy you're a nurse. Do you like it?"

"Yes, I love it. For the most part. I work in the ER at a hospital in Princeton. It's busy and fast-paced."

"Why did you come to Glenn Pines?"

"I needed a vacation. Feeling a little off at my job." She inwardly cringed at her understatement. "I wanted to try something I've never done before. I tend to do what's comfortable, easy. This place seemed like a good first step. Until I got here and saw my proposed schedule."

Edie chuckled. "We're both here now and should make the most of it. Hopefully, we'll leave feeling refreshed and ready to take on our challenges. There's a really good class called Bring Happiness to Your Life. I plan on attending sometime this week after my scheduled activities. Maybe you should, too."

Alyssa nodded. She'd been holding on to seething anger for the past three months as if it were a shield while armoring herself in outward indifference. Peppered with antagonism. It was time to consider her options, make a decision about her future, and be at peace with whatever that decision would be. Perhaps she could bring contentment to her life if she couldn't get all the way to happiness.

"Tonight I'll see what I'm already signed up for, then plan any downtime. Since there's no television or wireless reception, I'm guessing there's not much else to do but go to bed early."

Edie shook her head. "There's a game room, and most of us go there after dinner. If you're not into playing pool or ping-pong, there are board games like Trivial Pursuit and Monopoly. Jigsaw puzzles, too. And sometimes we play charades."

"Really?" Although Alyssa had never gone to summer camp, this was exactly how she would have imagined it.

"It's fun to get to know everyone. There's much

more talking and sharing after dinner when everyone can relax." She paused briefly. "By the way, who's the guy with the camera? I saw you talking to him before."

Alyssa shrugged. "I don't know. And if you don't, I guess he doesn't work here."

"This afternoon is the first time I saw him. I like that brooding, quiet type, don't you? We'll have to get to know him. Which won't take long in a place like this."

Maybe a good thing. Maybe not. The jury was still out.

Chapter Two

Gabriel Sutton pulled the camera strap over his head and sat on the nubby, bisque sofa in his cabin. He peered at the LCD screen of his favorite Nikon and scrolled through today's photos. While the foliage was beautiful in the afternoon sunlight, he was much more interested in his human subjects—one in particular.

He should have gotten her name—the woman who scowled and frowned. A photo with her hands on slim hips made him chuckle. But the photos of her holding an ice pack as she tended to the lady who had fallen were really beautiful. Long brown hair cascaded over one shoulder, and the concern etched on her face was so real, so emotional.

Her dewy skin glowed flawlessly from the distance, but when he zoomed in, a trace of freckles ran over the bridge of her nose, and the rosy glow came from a sheen of sweat, more apparent on her brow. Full lips slightly ajar were frozen in mid-sentence, and sympathetic, chocolate-brown eyes studied her patient's face as she cradled the woman's wrist tenderly in her hand. She was kneeling, bent over at the waist, a discarded sweater in a heap beside her.

As though drawn to his human subject, a ray of sun shot through leafy branches, casting a filtered column of light right behind her.

If he had been working on one of his photo shoots,

he would have taken hours to set this shot up and wait for the right moment to capture what he'd captured in an instant.

He sat back and exhaled. He was here to take a break from the rat race of his international travel schedule—a break foisted upon him by his agent—yet he could never stop taking photos. In addition to supporting his livelihood, it was in his blood. Photographing nature at its finest was for pure pleasure, although not quite as interesting as when he added the human effect. In those, he saw determination, friendship, caring, perseverance. Real life. Raw emotion.

So different from his career as a high-fashion photographer.

Usually, he was tethered to some palatial garden, ancient ruins, or edgy architectural wonder, albeit in Paris, Athens, or Singapore. Models posed in designer duds that cost thousands while draping their bodies over marble balustrades, standing precariously atop crumbled stone walls, or posing against winding steel and curved glass buildings. Over-the-top makeup and hair were the norm. Smiles. No smiles. Vacant eyes. Eyes that spoke. Whatever the ad agency or marketing department or high-concept engineer wanted. He was an expert in his field. Sought after by the best. Paid top dollar.

So why had he been so testy lately?

He laid his camera on the couch and stared at the worn carpet.

The answer to that was a little more complicated than he wanted to contemplate right now. Hopefully, a week away would give him the break he needed, and his agent would get off his back and stop threatening to pull jobs from his schedule.

At least that was his intended mission for this little vacation. Unfortunately, his agent's harsh question interfered with his goal. *Are you going to start coming in on budget, or are you going to allow your stubborn adherence to perfection kill your career?*

The obvious answer to anyone of sound mind would be to fall in line and do what was demanded. Yet adhering to the ad agency's or editorial director's strict schedule tied his hands where his art was concerned. He was a perfectionist—perhaps too obsessive when it came to his photography. In his mind, why even submit photographs if they weren't the best they could be?

He had no control over the weather, other countries' rules and regulations, or glitches with flights for whomever needed to be present for the shoot. So why not give him a break and let him do what he needed to do with the time he needed to do it in? Surely the powers that be could shift some funds in their budgets to accommodate unforeseen circumstances. Especially if it would mean acquiring the perfect photographs.

Just thinking about his dilemma put him in a foul mood—not the objective for this foray into the mountains of Pennsylvania. He needed to relax, kick back, clear his head, and focus on the activities Glenn Pines had to offer.

And if the woman who summoned the sun's beam crossed his path, he might be open to focusing on her, too.

****

At seven that evening, Alyssa hobbled to the dining

room, her heels blistered, calves tight, thighs screaming, and stomach grumbling. Despite her aching body, she took in her surroundings—floor-to-ceiling windows encircled the open, airy room, its exposed wooden beams grounding it. White linen tablecloths and napkins added elegance along with autumn floral centerpieces bursting with color.

Even though dinner went from seven to nine, the line at the buffet table was as long as the checkout line at a buy one, get one free sale at her favorite shoe emporium. Having burned an extraordinary number of calories today, she contemplated cutting in near the front of the line to stave off her irritability. But she figured her fellow campers were all in the same position, and she wasn't the type to create a mutiny. However, this line had better move fast because she couldn't swear her best behavior would last.

The line inched along at a mud turtle's pace, and when she finally got to the food, she was less than thrilled to see no fried chicken, mac and cheese, or hearty chili. Her rumbling stomach craved comfort food to ease her sore muscles and starving body. Having no choice, she piled on several salads, salmon, poached chicken, and steamed vegetables—a balanced nutritional diet she sometimes aspired to at home but rarely achieved. Maybe she'd learn something about healthy eating this week in addition to how best to strain her muscles.

When she could no longer fit another thing on her plate, Alyssa looked around the room for a friendly face—maybe an acquaintance from this afternoon's excursion. As if radar detectors, her eyes honed in on the photographer, and her stomach did a triple flip.

Interesting.

And unacceptable.

She wasn't here to meet a man that turned her head. She was here to clear her head. Eyeing Missy and Conrad, who sat by a window overlooking a fountain ringed by chrysanthemums, she headed to join them, a much safer choice given her goal. "I see you made it back from the hospital. How are you feeling?"

A cast covered Missy's wrist. She motioned for Alyssa to sit. "I'm fine. Sort of. My wrist is fractured in two places. And my fingers are so swollen right now it hurts to even wiggle them."

Alyssa sat and gave her a sympathetic smile. "I'm sorry this happened. The best thing to do is to ice them so the swelling goes down. And hold your hand up over your elbow once in a while."

"Thanks for your help today, Alyssa. You got right in there and took charge. You set me at ease." She looked over to her husband. "You, too, Conrad."

"For better or for worse." He chuckled.

But the sparkle in his eye told Alyssa their entire relationship fell on the better side of the spectrum. Even after thirty years.

They ate and talked easily, but Alyssa couldn't keep her glance from straying toward the corner where the photographer sat alone reading while eating. Who could ignore someone who looked like him even if she didn't want to connect? Tall, gorgeous, emerald-green eyes. Clearly he was not as social as the other people here, given the noise level in the room.

She dragged her focus away from him and made a concerted effort to concentrate more on her dinner mates. She learned that Missy and Conrad were both lawyers from Chicago who'd met at work, married, and had two daughters who were now grown. Missy practiced estates and trusts and Conrad corporate law. Although they worked at different firms, they weren't far from each other, which allowed them to commute together. They also served on various charitable boards.

"It sounds like the two of you have really figured it out. You have such a satisfying life, combining high-powered careers with volunteer work and time for each other. I would love to have a relationship like that."

"I'm sure you will, dear." Missy patted her hand. "You just have to find the right person."

As if that were an easy task. Alyssa was obviously clueless when it came to men, and she'd experienced enough heartache in these past two years to convince herself to steer clear of the male species. The time had come to work on being happy in her own skin.

At the end of the meal, Missy pushed her plate away. "I'm going back to our cabin to take some ibuprofen. My hand is starting to throb." She studied her fingers peeking out from the cast. They had turned a bruised shade of purple.

Conrad stood and helped her up, encouraging her to hold on to him. "Oh, I almost forgot." He turned to Alyssa. "I found this camera lens cap on the ground near where Missy fell. That photographer must have dropped it. Could you take it to him, please?" He put the cap on the table in front of her and started walking away. Before they got to the next table, he called over his shoulder. "I'm sure we'll see you tomorrow, Alyssa. You should head on over to the game room. That's where everyone congregates after dinner."

"Thanks for the tip." *But not for the chore.*

Alyssa didn't want to engage in a conversation with the photographer. His unsettling gaze earlier today seemed to study her with amusement, and she was not here to amuse. She inhaled, then stood. Might as well get this over with. With singular purpose she headed to his table by the window.

"Hi. I'm Alyssa Beckman." She stuck out her hand to shake his, as if this were their first encounter.

Sage eyes twinkled. "Gabe Sutton." He stood and took her hand. A gentleman. Who would have thought, given their encounter on the trail. "Why don't you join me?" He pulled out the chair across from his.

"No…thanks. I already ate. Conrad Griffin asked me to give this to you." She held out the lens cap. "He found it on the ground near where Missy fell today."

His intense gaze roamed over her face. Was he studying her again?

Having the need to fill the void, she continued while he took his seat. "Missy is the woman who broke her wrist on our hike. She and her husband, Conrad, got back from the hospital a little while ago." Why was she babbling? "Anyway, he thought this might be yours."

"It is. Thanks."

Finally. He speaks.

"You were great with her this afternoon. I got some terrific action shots of you."

"What? When?"

"When you were helping Missy."

"I'm sure my hair was a mess, and I know I had dirt on my face. And everywhere else for that matter. So they couldn't be that terrific." She had spent the better part of a half hour washing the caked-up mud off her new sneakers and the bottom of her jeans.

A slow smile inched over his lips. “I love photos like that. Raw, pure. Not staged with perfect hair and makeup, perfect sets. Although I did get some great angles. And the light filtering through the trees added a whole other dimension. One I don’t often get on shoots.”

Confusion marred her brain. “On shoots?”

“I’m a professional photographer. High fashion.”

“You mean you take the photos in all those fabulous places where the models are dressed in over-the-top clothes?”

“Yep. That’s me. Well, I’m one of them.”

“That must be so interesting. I love the scenery in those photos. Like Tahiti or Ecuador or Bermuda.” Seeing photos of those exotic locations was the closest she’d probably get to them.

He laughed. A nice laugh. “I’m told most people don’t notice the background. They’re looking at the fashions.”

“I’m not much of a fashionista.” She glanced down at her brown tweed pants and orange V-neck sweater. “I’m an ER nurse. I wear scrubs every day. The dressiest clothing I have are black jeans and a few silk blouses.” Could she be any more boring? In seconds he’d be yawning. But why should she care? He was a man. And men were off limits.

“I noticed you were limping. Did you get hurt today?”

When did he notice that? “My sneakers were rubbing against my heels, so I have a few blisters. I’m also not used to hiking up and down mountains. My thighs are killing me.” She massaged them to keep the stiffness at bay.

"You have quite a few days ahead of you to tackle different sports. Are you sure you're up for it?" An eyebrow cocked as if challenging her.

"Of course I'm up for it. I'm here, aren't I?" She didn't intend to come off so huffy, but something about his tone goaded her.

He shrugged a shoulder. "The right clothes and equipment go a long way in making things easier. Hiking boots, for example, would have prevented blisters and kept your feet drier. They wouldn't have helped your thighs, though."

The superiority in his voice jolted her out of their friendly banter. Was he being condescending, or did he simply feel the need to educate her? Either way, she didn't like his arrogance. "Too late for clothing advice." She turned to go, but his question stopped her.

"If this isn't really your thing, what brings you to Glenn Pines?"

Not wanting to be rude, she gave him a terse answer. "I needed a vacation. And a little time to think."

Both objectives seemed laughable after her indoctrination today. Given her grueling schedule, this week would be no vacation. Even thinking could very well go by the wayside.

His gaze held hers. "We have something in common."

She doubted that.

He stood. "It was nice to meet you. I'm sure I'll see you around." Instead of shaking her hand, he placed his warm palm on her arm, sending zings through her bloodstream. A gorgeous smile melted the previous discomfort provoking her.

Maybe he wasn't being arrogant. She might have misunderstood. But it didn't matter.

With a quick wave, she murmured a "see you" and proceeded toward the door, trying with every ounce of willpower to avoid limping. What difference did it make how he came off? She was here to focus on herself. No distractions. Especially from members of the opposite sex.

Edie waved to her from across the room, so she went over and slid into an empty chair.

"I saw you talking to that photographer. Is he single? Employed? I know he's hot. Did he ask you out?"

Alyssa chuckled at her run-on questions. "I didn't see a ring, so I assume he's single. Definitely employed. A high-fashion photographer who assuredly dates models. And he categorically did not ask me out."

"He was taking pictures of trees and some of the hikers. Why would he want to do that when he can photograph beautiful women?"

Alyssa shrugged. "He's here for vacation, but I guess taking photos is something he enjoys." Sweaty and mud-caked hikers were his only option. "Maybe he's immune to beautiful women."

"Perfect. My new career can be as a photographer's assistant. I wouldn't mind hanging out with him all day, carrying his equipment."

Although Edie was surely kidding, a tinge of jealousy stabbed Alyssa. "How do you go from project manager to photographer's assistant? I think you should be moving up the ladder, not down. In my humble opinion."

Edie laughed. "Jeez, Alyssa. Lighten up. I was only

fantasizing."

Alyssa shook her head. "I know. I'm tired and not thinking clearly. It's been a long day. I'm going back to my cabin to see what's in store for the rest of the week." She rose, testing her screaming thighs, which were getting tighter by the minute. "Have a nice night, Edie. See you tomorrow."

"You're going to miss out on charades in the game room." Edie widened her eyes, clearly appalled at Alyssa's decision to call it a night.

"I'll join in some other time."

Fun and games would have to wait. She only had eight days to clear the slate of the past and come up with a plan to assure a happy future. Not easy subjects to tackle in one week.

But she could start.

Chapter Three

The alarm shattered her unconsciousness, and Alyssa jumped up at the invasion, knocking the clock to the floor before grabbing it and slapping the off button. Wanting to attend a class and breakfast before the games began, she had set the old-fashioned clock the night before for six thirty. She eased out of bed, testing her legs. Her entire body was stiff and in need of stretching from the previous day's exertions.

Her morning scheduled activity didn't start until nine thirty—plenty of time for yoga at seven, the perfect antidote for tight muscles. She'd never done yoga before, but how hard could it be? She'd tried Pilates, Zumba, spinning, and Jazzercise. Whatever new studio opened up in her area, she joined. Until she got bored and moved on to the next thing. Yoga looked far more sedate than any of the other exercise classes she persevered through, and the stretching should relieve some of the soreness in her legs.

Surprisingly, ten other people were already there—men and women, none of whom she'd met. After obtaining her mat, she followed the instructor's cues and assumed a lotus position before inhaling and exhaling slowly. She performed the moves satisfactorily until they got to the garland pose.

She squatted as directed with her feet as close together as possible while keeping her heels on the floor, not an easy maneuver. The instructor then told them to separate their thighs slightly wider than their torso.

Fire burned through her muscles as the instructor continued in that calm, easy voice. "Exhale and lean your torso forward to fit snugly between your thighs."

Okay, she could do this for maybe a second.

"Press your elbows against your inner knees, bringing your palms together. Keep that resistance going while holding the position for thirty seconds."

Alyssa listed to the side and toppled over in slow motion. A giggle escaped.

The instructor peered in her direction but continued in her serene monotone. "Some of these positions may feel uncomfortable at first, but the more you do them, the easier they'll become."

Uncomfortable? Try impossible, painful, awkward, burning, excruciating. She could go on. Alyssa moved back onto the center of her mat and did a simple squat so she wouldn't disrupt the class again, but even that had her thighs quivering. So much for easing those muscles for today's adventures.

The hour passed much slower than she'd anticipated, and her stomach growled while doing the savasana—the final pose where she lay on her mat, breathing in and out and taking all unnecessary thoughts from her mind. Unfortunately, she couldn't remove the stubborn notion that she was starving, and the minute class was over, she dashed toward the dining hall.

With a full plate she scanned the room, and a flurry of hands got her attention. She followed the hands to Edie and sat.

"Where are you coming from?" Edie dipped her spoon into a yogurt parfait.

"Yoga. What was I thinking? It was hard. And so not relaxing." Alyssa gulped some orange juice, then dove into her eggs. "It must be the mountain air. I could eat a house. Or a horse. Or something big."

Edie chuckled. "It's everything. The air, exercise, eliminating stress. The food is incredibly good, but it's healthy. Did you see they have several cooking classes? I want to take the one on Greek cuisine. Join me. It's at four today. There's another one tomorrow on the health effects of spices. Not that I cook much at home, but maybe I'll get into it when I get back."

Alyssa was getting used to Edie's incessant talking, and right now it worked to her benefit. She could eat without the interruption of having to respond.

Out of the corner of her eye, she saw Gabe walk in, his ever-present camera in hand. Her entire body buzzed at his mere presence. He strode over to talk to Missy and Conrad, but her focus fixated on broad shoulders and toned pecs stretching his black T-shirt to perfection. After a few minutes, he left them, got some food, and went to sit by himself. Clearly a loner who must cherish his own space, since he could have sat with any number of people with open chairs at their tables, including Alyssa and Edie.

"Alyssa, are you listening?"

She brought her attention back to Edie. "Sorry. Did you ask a question?"

"What are you doing next?"

Alyssa glanced at her watch. "Kayak races on the lake. Are you going mountain climbing?"

She sighed. "It's on my schedule. I guess I'd better

go. I don't want to upset the agenda gods."

"How are your legs holding up?"

"Great. Since this is my fourth day, my body's getting used to the exercise."

Good to know Alyssa would be able to walk without cringing at every step in a few days. Tomorrow it would be her arms that wouldn't work after kayaking all morning.

She finished her breakfast and stood. "I need to go back to my cabin and change out of my yoga attire. See you later. Have fun mountain climbing."

"I don't know about fun, but it will be a challenge. Wish me luck."

Alyssa fist bumped her. "Good luck."

She took her plate to the appointed area and hightailed it out of there, eager to get outside into the sunshine and unseasonably warm October air. The leaves on the trees had started to turn, and the yellows and reds were rich in hue, made brighter by the sun's rays filtering through the foliage. She should take some pictures. Of course they wouldn't be of the quality of Gabe's, but she'd preserve this memory of shifting outside of her comfort zone—taking the first step to a better future.

Quickly she donned her bathing suit and covered it with jeans shorts, a T-shirt, and a sweatshirt before wrestling her feet into damp sneakers. By muscle memory, she braided her long, brown ponytail to keep it under control before grabbing her well-stocked backpack in case of an emergency. All in four minutes flat.

As she approached the lake, colorful kayaks painted the shoreline where the races were to begin. Her shoulders tensed. They were all single-person crafts. So much for her plan to choose a partner who knew what he or she was doing. Now her lack of skill would be on full display.

She introduced herself to Tim, the person in charge, who asked each participant as he handed them a paddle whether they had ever kayaked before. About a third of her colleagues had never had the pleasure, so at least she wouldn't be the only rookie. The tightness in her shoulders eased a bit.

"You'll notice we are on a flat lake." Tim waved his hand toward the water. "No rapids, no obstructions."

A few in the crowd chuckled, but Alyssa wasn't totally at ease yet.

"I'll show you the basics—how to paddle to keep going straight, how to turn, and what to do if your kayak rolls over."

The tension came back with a vengeance, and Alyssa rotated her shoulders to distribute the stress to other parts of her body. She took in every instruction as if her life depended on it—although really, she should lighten up. She could swim. This was only a boat ride on a calm and serene lake, not a white-water rafting trip in the rapids of Idaho Springs.

Tim ended his lesson with wise words surely said to every group at many of these activities. "This is not about winning. It's about conquering the challenge. And having fun." He pumped his fist in the air. "Let's get to it."

Alyssa gingerly stepped into her appointed boat and lowered herself onto the seat in the cockpit, not wanting to be the first to send it into a roll before they even got started. They were all encouraged to paddle out onto the lake and try their hand at the skills taught. She dipped her paddle tentatively into the water to the right, then to the left, spinning in circles. Tim came over and coached her one-on-one, which helped enormously but sent heat to her face when she spotted Gabe gliding past her, smirking—or at least that's how she interpreted his grin.

After some time spent practicing, they were ready for the races. With twelve kayakers, two groups of six were formed, and unfortunately, Alyssa and Gabe ended up in the same group. The fastest three kayakers from each group would then compete, first winnowing the group down to four, then two, then a winner. The losing teams, or B teams as Tim called them, would also compete. Alyssa shook out her arms to get the blood pumping for competition. This would be fun even if she was ousted from the A team in the first heat.

She glanced to her left as Gabe maneuvered his boat next to hers.

"Hey, Beckman, are you going to win this race?"

Ray-Bans covered his eyes, so she couldn't see the teasing mirth that was surely evident.

"I'm going to try, Sutton."

His chuckle grated on her nerves. The gloves were off.

When Tim blew his whistle to start the race, Alyssa dug in with everything she had. She was determined now to at least make it to the next round.

Gabe paddled beside her, his powerful shoulders propelling his boat slightly ahead. He called out, "Make your strokes longer, reach forward more."

She followed his instructions, despite bristling at

his arrogant lesson, and before long she was gliding toward the front of the pack, along with Gabe and another guy, his name a mystery. When they reached the buoy designating the finish line, she was third.

Euphoria rushed through her, and she high-fived Gabe, temporarily forgetting her annoyance over his coaching.

"You follow directions well, Beckman." His megawatt smile did little to eclipse those irritating words.

"I'm a quick learner. No need to coach me next time. I can do it on my own."

"A woman taking control. Very sexy."

Was he flirting with her? Probably not. Praise must come easy to him as part of his job. Saying how beautiful or smart or talented a model was so he'd get the best poses out of her. Ignoring his statement, she turned her boat and headed back to the starting area where the next group of boats was preparing for their contest. She came to a stop in the shade of some oak trees as she rooted around in her backpack for sunscreen. Her sweatshirt long abandoned, she peeled off her soaked T-shirt. Thankfully, she'd had the forethought to wear her bikini under her clothes. The raw denim of her shorts clung to her butt, clammy and wet against the tops of her thighs. She slathered sunscreen over all of her exposed areas and prepared for the next race. Energy zapped through her system, and she briefly enjoyed the endorphins slamming within as she pushed away all thought that in an hour or so, she wouldn't be able to move her jelly-like limbs.

After the three winners from the second race arrived back, Tim gave a short lesson on the flora and fauna in and around the lake, providing the second team with a chance to rest before competing again. Not a bad idea, given the exertion forced on unused muscles, tendons, ligaments, and bones.

When it was time for her next race, Alyssa paddled to the far side of the competitors, staying away from Gabe. He confused her. One minute he was taunting her, the next helping her, and the next flirting with her. She didn't need or want any of it.

Tim blew his whistle, and the kayakers were off. Gabe's instructions replayed in her head as she pulled her paddle through the water. Missing was Gabe's boat next to hers, guiding her, pushing her to catch up. She shouldn't have been so rash in steering clear of him.

And of course Gabe came in first. She was fifth.

"Hey, Beckman." Gabe paddled toward her. "I guess you still needed my coaching expertise in order for you to final."

She rolled her eyes and paddled away.

"Aren't you going to congratulate me?" His voice followed her, its teasing comradery slipping through her resolve.

Her lips inched up into a smile, and a chuckle escaped, but she didn't turn around.

****

When the last of the races was over, Tim encouraged the kayakers to go off, on their own or in groups, to explore the rest of the lake. That had been Gabe's intention anyway. Group activities were fine for a while, but the privacy of the woods on the opposite side of the lake beckoned.

Tim's voice floated behind Gabe as he headed out. "The more familiar you get with the strokes and maneuvering your boat, the more it will become second nature. You'll be looking for lakes in your area to kayak on when you get home."

Gabe laughed. Would Alyssa ever pick up a paddle again?

A temperate breeze tousled the cool waters, and as he got closer to shore, the leaves—mimicking the vibrant color of chrysanthemums—rustled in the wind. The sun hovered high in the sky, warming the air, but the tall cedars and pines still cast long shadows over the fringes of the lake.

He drew his kayak onto the shore and dug his Nikon out of its waterproof sack. Before heading into the woods, he pulled out a pamphlet on native trees and studied it for a few minutes. A splash hijacked his attention, and he turned. Alyssa struggled with some reeds a few yards from the shore before her paddle slipped from her hands and into the water. She leaned over to get it, and it teased her, moving slightly beyond her reach. He couldn't help but chuckle. She tried once more, and her kayak listed, so she leaned toward the other side—*uh-oh, too far*. As if in fast forward, the kayak rolled, callously dumping her in the muck of the lake's weedy sludge.

A scream escaped as she pushed herself upright in the shallow water, mud and debris covering her hair and face. She swiped at the offending muck, attempting to dash it away from her eyes. Laughter bubbled in his chest.

As she tried to stand, her feet must have gotten sucked into the mud, and she panicked, slapping her arms against the water in a crazy, freestyle swim stroke.

Heaving a sigh and an eye roll, Gabe sprinted into

the water. “You’re okay. Calm down. Stop fighting.” He clamped his hands around her forearms and pulled her up into a standing position before sliding behind her, snaking his arm around her bare midriff, and pulling her farther up out of the trap that had bound her feet.

His hands splayed across her toned stomach, smooth as silk and a little slippery from that sunscreen he’d watched her apply over an hour ago. At the time, his fingers had twitched as he momentarily thought of offering some help.

Breathing in quick gulps, she squirmed against him, causing a riot within.

“Are there snakes in this water?” She kicked as he unceremoniously carried her from the lake and deposited her onto solid ground.

“Probably.” Slithery creatures didn’t bother him, especially a slithery sexy woman.

Alyssa shivered before shrieking. “My backpack!” It was floating near the overturned kayak.

Gabe shook his head to dislodge erotic thoughts of Alyssa’s toned and half-naked body writhing against him. With determined focus, he trudged into the water to retrieve her backpack—also righting her kayak and pulling it partly onto shore.

“What’s in this thing?” He hefted her backpack up and down. “It weighs a ton. I’m surprised it didn’t sink.”

She glared at him. “Provisions.”

“What kind of provisions? It feels like you have a ton of rocks in here.”

He tossed it on the ground next to her, and she unzipped the pack as if needing to check its contents for water damage.

She pulled out her "provisions" one by one, taking inventory. "Band-Aids, antiseptic cream, bug spray, scissors, sterile wipes."

Her brow unfurrowed as she methodically placed each item on the grass.

"Aspirin, aloe, ice packs, superglue."

"Superglue?" He looked down at her, confusion taking up residence. "What do you need that for?" Without waiting for an answer, he stooped and gathered the items on the ground and tossed them back in their sack. His uncharacteristic irritation was an obvious attempt, at least to him, to bury his physical attraction to her. "You don't need any of this. Are you a hypochondriac?"

She closed her agape mouth. "I am not a hypochondriac. I'm a nurse, and that was very rude. I had all of these items in here in an organized fashion. Have you no manners? I carefully packed that bag so I'd be prepared for any problem. Thankfully I had it with me when Missy fell yesterday."

He exhaled, conflicting emotions running amok. "I'm sorry." He avoided her flashing eyes and sexy curves while searching for appropriate words to make him less of an ass but still provide distance between them. "Eric had a first aid kit. All the guides do. You don't need to carry an extra fifteen pounds around. Maybe your kayak wouldn't have flipped if you didn't have *that* unbalancing the boat."

He dared a glance to see if his lukewarm apology worked, but she was busy rearranging her provisions, ignoring him.

He couldn't help himself. "Did you bring a dose of

antibiotics to ward off the parasites invading your nose and mouth when you fell into the sludge?"

Her eyes widened. "No. Do you think I need it?"

A laugh escaped. "I was kidding."

He sat on the ground beside her, his cargo shorts and T-shirt sopping from his act of heroism. If he dwelt on his discomfort, his mind wouldn't stray to his erotic save.

Her gaze darted to his neck. "Oh no! What happened with your camera?" She jerked her head from side to side, surveying the ground around them. "You didn't lose it in the water, did you?"

"Of course not. When I saw you reaching over the kayak to get the paddle, I knew you'd end up in the lake. I set my camera down near that log." His chin jutted in the general direction before he started laughing. "It really was a funny sight. I should have taken a few shots before plunging into the water to save you from those pesky reeds."

"You would have let me drown to get a few good photos?" Her nostrils flared as she threw eye daggers.

"You were in two feet of water. You wouldn't have drowned."

"People can die in a few inches of water, you know."

He wisely stopped laughing. "You're right."

She scowled at him, quelling any future sarcastic comments about her uncalled-for panic.

Still, he couldn't keep from pushing the envelope. She was adorable when provoked. "Now that I saved you from death, I believe you owe me. After I determine an appropriate repayment, I'll let you know."

Something close to a *harrumph* escaped. "You're

awfully high-handed." Although her words criticized, they were softened by the slightest of smiles.

"I'm accustomed to making the rules. Being in charge."

"Yes. I learned that during our race today. Are you always this bossy?" She reached into the bottom of her reorganized backpack and drew out a towel to wipe her face and arms.

He took the towel and poured water over it from his bottle. "Yes. I am." He gently brushed her face with the wet cloth, rubbing in places caked with dirt. He was so close her breath whispered over his cheek as he discovered flecks of amber in her brown eyes. He swallowed, holding on to her questioning gaze as his fingers caressed her cheek. He gently turned her face to inspect his work. "I'm used to directing everything on my shoots." His voice was raw, husky, affected by her nearness. He cleared his throat. "If I ever asked for an opinion, I might get one."

She sat up straighter, cutting him off from stroking her soft skin and studying her stunning eyes. "Maybe that's why you needed a vacation. You take on all responsibility all the time. At the hospital we work in teams. Everyone's opinion is considered."

"The doctors listen to the nurses?" His aggravating remark, which would surely be followed by her irate response, should dissipate the sexual tension building within.

Her brow creased and her eyes flashed, as expected. "We're right beside them, working together. Sometimes we have a better understanding of the situation or the patients' needs."

"My assistants occasionally give me a heads-up

about the personality of one of the models or whether we're on schedule. But I don't see that as teamwork. I make the decisions and expect everyone to comply." A little more needling seemed in order.

"Of course you do." She shook her head as if ready to give him up as a lost cause. "What about with your friends? You must be more open to their opinions."

He shrugged. "There's not much time to get together with friends. They have their lives. I have mine."

"How sad. Although if you're as domineering with friends, you probably lost them all."

"Did you mean to say that out loud?"

The telltale sparkle in her eyes gave him the answer. A woman who didn't use filters. Interesting.

"What about you? Do you have a lot of friends?"

"I still see my best friends from high school. Even though none of them live in the same town anymore, we're not that far away from each other. We get together at least once a month. They're all very important to me."

"Why?"

"We're there for each other. If one of us has a problem with a boyfriend or spouse or child, we're there to help her through. And they're there for me, too."

"Do you have a boyfriend, spouse, or child?" Best to find that out up front before his uncontrollable attraction steamrolled over his brain.

"No. Not at the moment. I had a fiancé. We split almost two years ago."

"Ahhhh."

"What does that mean?" Her sharp tone advised

him her annoyance was back, although if truth be told, it had probably never totally left.

"Last night, you said you needed time to think. Anyone who takes a week off to think has something major going on. Now I get it."

"What is it exactly that you get?" She crossed her arms and gave him a bold stare.

"You were part of a couple. Now you're alone. Trying to figure out how to be alone. So you came to Glenn Pines to look for answers. I knew you couldn't have come here for vacation as you said."

She narrowed her eyes at him, showing strong disapproval of his analysis. "You're wrong. David was two years ago—in the past. Another…" She waved away the rest of that sentence.

He laughed softly. Maybe she wasn't as open as he'd initially thought.

Silence followed, marred only by the birds calling to each other.

After several minutes, Gabe broke in. "Would you like to walk with me? I want to take some photos."

What was it about her that had him craving her company? He could have easily ended their conversation and went on his way without her—his original plan. And smarter plan. Even more surprising than his invitation was her agreement to tag along.

Alyssa followed him as he trekked into the woods, stopping when he did. He pointed his lens upward and fired off several shots, moving here and there to capture the sunlight playing off the multihued leaves. She sat on a fallen tree trunk, looking at the foliage.

"Why so quiet?" he asked after a while.

"I'm meditating."

"Really?"

She laughed—a welcome sound. "No. I didn't take the class yet. I thought I'd just let you do your thing."

"I can do my thing while talking." He pointed his camera in her direction and took a photo.

"Can you please give me some warning when you're going to do that? I can see my request that you not take my picture has fallen on deaf ears, so you can at least give me a heads-up." She pulled a stemmy reed from her hair.

"Sorry. Can't do. That's not the way I work. I like candid shots when the subject isn't prepared. They're the best."

"So I'm a subject now?"

Gabe headed over and sat down beside her, his leg touching hers. A shock wave coursed through him. He inhaled slowly, trying to take back control. When her arm brushed against his, the wave vied with sparks and heat.

Russet eyes held his for only a moment before she disconnected.

He cleared his throat, hoping to clear his head. "You're an amazing subject. The photos I took of you yesterday on our little walk were so natural. The intensity of your eyes when you were helping Missy, the sympathy on your face, even though you were the ultimate professional—portrayed a nurse in action, helping a patient. Beautiful."

Alyssa's face reddened as she turned her head away from him.

"I have one of you laughing, too. That woman, Edie, was talking your ear off, but you let her."

That brought out a chuckle.

"My goal is to capture emotion, raw and undetected by most others."

"Can I see the photos you just took of the tree branches?"

He flipped his camera over and leaned toward her, scrolling slowly through the shots. Sun glinted off the upper branches while casting shadows and darkness on the lower ones.

"These photos don't look like real scenery. They look like paintings." She peered up into the trees, then back at the LCD screen. "You have a gift. You see things that most of us humans don't."

"Thanks."

He stood, needing to get away from the heat she generated in him, but the second he moved, his body yearned for more contact. He strolled a little farther into the trees, working his magic with the camera to get his mind off more carnal thoughts. While he wasn't opposed to hooking up with an interesting woman for a week before getting back to his reality, he feared Alyssa was too vulnerable, working through more than she'd let on.

He returned to the log where she still sat, holding his hand out to pull her up. Warmth spread through his veins and ricocheted to his core. Something he hadn't felt in a while.

She was completely different from the women he met—New York City women who were sophisticated in their perfectly put-together appearances and mysterious in keeping their inner selves hidden so he never quite knew who he was dealing with. He played their game, and it worked for him—not getting too close to anyone to call it a relationship. Yet lately he'd been desiring something more.

Maybe he shouldn't put her on the off-limits list too quickly.

Chapter Four

"What are you going to do with all these photos you're taking?" Alyssa shook the warm tingles from her hand when Gabe let go, but the fuzzies inched up her arm. Not good on any level. She needed to stay away from men for the time being. She couldn't afford another mistake emotionally. As they walked back toward the lake, she kept at least three feet between them.

"I'm not sure." Green eyes turned serious, holding secrets.

"Do you like photographing trees and birds instead of models?"

A grin escaped. "It's a nice change from my normal routine." He stopped to inspect a leaf on a low-hanging branch but didn't take a photo. Must not have been impressive enough—poor leaf. "But it's not something I would do professionally." He meandered through the woods toward the lake. "This is the first vacation I've taken in two years. It's nice. I didn't expect to enjoy it so much."

"I wouldn't think a world traveler would vacation in a place like this. I picture you somewhere more exotic."

"Why aren't you on an island in the Caribbean or experiencing the culture of a European country?"

"This is the first trip I've ever taken by myself. It

was within driving distance from my house, and the price was right." She avoided his searching eyes, wishing she hadn't accompanied him.

Spending alone time with a man, any man, was not part of her "fix Alyssa" agenda. And feeling this little tug of attraction should have sent her running in the opposite direction. But here she was, sharing a piece of herself with this handsome, sometimes annoying, sometimes engaging photographer who was probably a player to the hundredth degree. His life had to be one big, beautiful party attended by models and other arty types who worked with him in dozens of glamorous locations.

His words cut into her fantasized version of his reality. "This is hardly your typical vacation spot. People come here to learn something about themselves. What is it you want to learn about yourself, Ms. Beckman?"

His grin told her she didn't have to take his question seriously, and his statement highlighted his intent for being here.

What did she want to learn? Other than how to stay away from the wrong men, she didn't quite know. She hoped the experience itself would shed some light.

"I'm feeling unsettled in my life right now." An understatement of epic proportions.

Not only did David, her ex-fiancé, cheat on her, she'd chosen to assuage that pain by having an affair with a married colleague who dumped her because his wife was getting suspicious. Then he'd suggested it might be better for both of them if she switched departments at the hospital. Because of course, working together was becoming problematic, punctuated with quarrels and prickly sarcasm. Mostly sprouting from her mouth. She shivered at her belligerence.

While Dr. Cole Peterson—her former lover and boss as head of the ER—held a major role in turning her life upside down, once she started to take some of the responsibility for her predicament, she'd begun contemplating a change. Working side by side with the man she had fallen in love with but couldn't have was not working for her. "I've been at the same hospital for the past ten years, and although I love working as an ER nurse, I have to transfer to a different department. I've been thinking about what area in the hospital I'd want to move to, if any. Or maybe I should interview at a different hospital as an ER nurse. Or get an additional certification so I can make more money." She shrugged. "Not that I expect to get those specific answers here."

If things had worked out with Cole, she wouldn't have even considered any of this. But ever since their strained conversation a few weeks ago where he suggested it might be better for her to transfer departments, her brain had been on overload.

"If I were you, I'd focus on why you're feeling unsettled first. Is it simply boredom with your job, or is there an underlying problem?"

Intense green eyes studied her face, as if to see through her and discover her secret.

Heat flooded her cheeks. "You sound like a shrink."

He laughed. "I've been to enough counseling sessions to qualify. I'm a master at trying to analyze why I make the choices I make."

"Your life sounds pretty glamorous to me. Working in different countries, surrounded by gorgeous women all the time."

He nodded. "I am lucky to do what I do. But apparently I need to chill a little. I've been getting cranky lately, taking out my frustrations on my co-workers and sometimes my employers. My agent demanded that I take a break before I bite off some of the hands that feed me. Which, of course, also feed him, given his commissions." While he spoke with some humor, underlying ire sharpened his tone.

"What are you frustrated about?"

"I've been told I've been going over budget. The art director at one of the magazines I do editorial spreads for put me on a short leash. If I come in one more time over budget, she's cutting me from their go-to list of photographers."

"What's the reason you've been over budget?" Keeping the questions focused on him gave Alyssa some comfort that her private woes would stay private.

"A few of the shoots took a little longer than anticipated in order to get the right shot. She doesn't understand that this is art I'm creating for their magazine, not something that should be rushed to stay under budget."

Definitely more of a control freak than he let on. "What does your agent say?"

"He's been in my ear for the past few months, grousing that budgets aren't suggestions. They're etched in stone. If I don't do my part to rein in expenses on these shoots, the magazine won't make a big enough profit to stay in business, and then no one will have a job there. Unless I get with the program, I'll be history."

"Do you plan to fall in line?" Somehow she

doubted it.

His sigh was heavy. "I have to. The magazine pays a big part of my income, and it's steady work. Recently, I invested a huge chunk of savings in a friend's business. Now is not the time to mess around with my earnings."

"What magazine hires you?"

"*StyleSelect.*"

She stopped mid-stride, impressed with his connection. "That has a huge circulation, doesn't it? Two of my girlfriends have subscriptions." She wasn't one to waste time or money on a fashion magazine showcasing expensive designer clothes she could never afford.

"Glad to hear it. Now I know my job is secure."

She glanced at him to see if a teasing smile accompanied his cutting remark. None. "There's no need for sarcasm." She began to walk away from him, but he grabbed her hand.

"Wait. I'm sorry. I didn't mean to take it out on you. See what I mean? I'm cranky." He gave her a lopsided smile that reached his eyes, and her resolve to leave melted in an instant. He tugged on her hand, pulling her down to sit on a trunk beside him. "I'm pretty good at helping others analyze their issues. I'm just no good with my own. So let's talk about your quandary."

She inwardly groaned. She should have escaped when she had the chance.

"Sticking with the physical as opposed to the emotional dilemma, I have some questions," he continued, as if she agreed to his suggestion. "Do you still want to be an ER nurse, or are you looking for something different?"

"I love being an ER nurse. I just can't do that at my hospital any longer."

"Is the hospital where you work too small? Is the ER too political? Or are there personality conflicts? What's the reason you're contemplating a transfer?"

She sighed. Cole was the reason, the personality conflict, the person who unmoored her, sending her into turmoil mode. But she had no intention of sharing that piece of intel with him.

Unless she should. If she ripped off the Band-Aid and told him what had sent her into this tailspin, he'd never act on what little attraction might exist between them. He'd run in the other direction. A good thing. Since, with her history, she couldn't rely on her strength to stay away, despite her good intentions.

Anxiety stomped through her like angry fire ants, and she stood, needing to move, to get the blood flowing toward her brain. And to dissipate the angst. She started back into the woods. He followed.

"The reason I'm in such turmoil is because I had an affair with a doctor I work with. He's in charge of the ER." Her ears burned with embarrassment. "It's not a good place for me to be anymore."

"Ahhh. A little more of the truth."

She studied the ground to avoid eye contact.

"If it was an affair, then the good doctor is married. I guess he's not leaving his wife for you?"

"No." Her voice rasped as mortification pricked her brain. She shouldn't have disclosed this humiliating information.

"Do you still care about him?"

Really? Was she really having a therapy session

with a photographer?

"Your silence answers my question."

"No. You're wrong. I hate him. But I hate myself, too. When we started out, it was fun. A salve to treat my ego over my broken engagement. There was no thought of a relationship developing. We didn't date. We just…" She didn't need to say the words. "I never had a conversation with Cole about anything significant. Religion, cultural heritage, our early years, who we voted for." She grimaced. "It was…I don't know what it was. We had stolen moments in his room at the hospital."

She shouldn't go into the other places they'd had *moments*. She couldn't even believe she was confessing this lewd behavior to a stranger. Being an open book had its negatives, yet she didn't stop her sad saga. "But things changed. We began seeing each other on days off if he could get away. He would tell his wife he was working overtime. The deceit was awful, but it was exciting to be with someone who had the same interests. Especially after my broken engagement… I thought he cared."

She was running off at the mouth without filter and wanted to stop herself. They were walking side by side along a dirt path, and thankfully, she couldn't see Gabe's face without turning toward him. Which she avoided.

"After a while, I started to fall for him. Maybe he knew it and needed to back away. He told me we had to stop seeing each other because his wife was becoming suspicious."

Gabe finally chimed in. "That was probably true. Did you not believe him?"

"I did. But I also saw it as an excuse. Although what did I expect? He had never talked about leaving her to be with me. I don't even know if that's what I wanted. But once I couldn't have him… You know how it goes."

Alyssa thought back to several cautionary conversations with her girlfriends, Sam, Nicki, and Denise. "My friends warned me. They told me I should end it with Cole. They knew the affair would never last. I'd be the one left behind. But I ignored them.

"I felt nauseous every time I saw him at work. I had cared about someone who didn't love me. Someone who was married to someone else. But honestly, I think I was more upset about being rejected. Again. My ego couldn't handle it." She sighed. "That was three months ago. I still work with Cole because I don't know what else to do."

"So you came to Glenn Pines to escape."

"I needed time away so I could think more clearly."

"That's good. You've taken action."

"A little too much action. My legs still ache from yesterday's hike, and I'm sure my arms will fall off by tonight."

He chuckled. "Physical adventures will keep you from dwelling on emotional problems—at least while you're engaged in them. In my book, that's a good thing."

It probably was. She hadn't thought about Cole once during their grueling hike up and down the mountain yesterday, and not today either until Gabe started his inquisition.

"This place is a good sanctuary to work through the

hard stuff when you're alone."

His soothing voice eased some of her angst—not only over the whole sordid situation with Cole, but with sharing that piece of herself with Gabe.

"I came down here to the lake last night. There were a million stars in the sky. When you see something like that, troubles melt away, seeming extremely small in the vast expanse of the universe."

Alyssa turned to face him. "Thank you for keeping your judgment of me to yourself."

"We all make mistakes. It takes courage to see them and learn from them."

His kind words wrapped her in a warm blanket of understanding. So very comforting. "Maybe we can help each other figure out our next moves." *Ugh.* Why did she say that? It sounded like she was offering to monopolize his time when all he wanted to do was take a break from his job and figure out how to make everyone, including himself, happy. And that's exactly what she wanted to do as well. Alone. "I don't know where that came from." Her cheeks heated, and she stammered in an attempt to backtrack. "I…I need to figure out my next steps by myself, and I'm sure you do, too."

Their trail had looped around, and they were back at the lake. She grabbed her backpack. The sooner she got away from him the better so she didn't resort to her old ways of filling a hole in her romantic life with the next hot guy who came along.

She tried to make light of the awkward moment she foisted upon them. "I'd better get back. I'm starving, and I have a team challenge this afternoon." She rolled her shoulders and shook out her arms. "Hopefully, I'll have some strength left in these limbs to toe the line. The schedulers here really should take pity on the newbies. Two strenuous workouts in one day. I won't be able to move tomorrow."

"Why'd you sign up for such a rigorous program?"

"I didn't know I was. It wasn't clear to me that the answers on my questionnaire would dictate my activities. I thought I'd be able to pick and choose when I got here." She dared to look at him, afraid of inviting another sarcastic comment about her shortcomings—this time in the reading-of-the-small-print department.

He surprised her and kept his mouth shut.

"Thanks for helping me out of the water before." She'd die before thanking him for the psychology session.

"You're welcome." He pushed her kayak from the shore and held it for her to get in. "I'll head back now, too. I need to change before lunch." He looked down at his muddy and water-logged cargo shorts before turning his eyes on her. "You could use a clean set of clothes yourself."

She chuckled. "I'll start with a shower to get this gunk out of my hair."

After carefully climbing into her kayak, she grabbed the paddle and summoned all of her athletic abilities so she wouldn't humiliate herself again. It worked. Her strokes kept her in a straight line heading for the area where they'd begun earlier this morning. Gabe caught up to her, and they paddled in tandem, not talking, just being.

When they reached the opposite shore, he jumped out of his kayak and helped Alyssa out of hers. "We don't want a repeat of your last encounter with the reeds."

She rolled her eyes but decided against commenting further.

Although all she wanted to do was get away from him and the shame of her true confession, she was strangely disappointed she wouldn't be seeing him the rest of the day. His ability to listen without judgment was very appealing. And those mercurial emerald eyes—from light to dark to light again—weren't a bad depth to fall into.

She gave him a half-hearted wave as she headed in the direction of her cabin. "I hope your week here is successful."

He smiled, a genuine, gorgeous smile. "Yours, too." He turned to go in the opposite direction but called over his shoulder. "Maybe I'll see you around. We can talk more."

Her heart pounded against her ribs.

She needed to stay far away from that temptation.

Chapter Five

Gabe hiked alone that afternoon, taking an easy, sloping trail through the lush landscape. A fleeting thought crossed his mind that Alyssa would like this trail. *Why am I even thinking about her?* She had enough baggage to weigh down not only herself, but anyone who came near. He didn't like baggage. He travelled light and kept his relationships casual and at arm's length.

Yet something about her drew him in. Sure, she was pretty. Chocolate brown eyes that showed a myriad of emotion—which she didn't try to hide. The angles of her cheekbones photographed beautifully. Thick, long, brown hair, highlighted by the sun, had him itching to unleash her braid this morning—before it was mired in muck and reeds. He chuckled at the picture in his head.

He should be running in the other direction. She had a broken engagement for reasons unknown and tried to assuage her pain with an affair. With a superior no less. A clear violation of corporate policy everywhere. Not to mention the morals of it all. Sure, she'd been vulnerable and possibly not thinking clearly, but despite that, her bad decisions led to bad consequences. She was obviously adrift.

He wasn't here to fix someone else. He had his own damn problems.

Even so, she had some very nice qualities.

Refreshingly open and honest, she wasn't one of those fake women trying to make herself appear better to him than reality. She didn't hide her flaws. She was real. And engaging. And empathetic. Maybe being at Glenn Pines opened his eyes when he usually forced them to remain closed.

But enough about Alyssa. He was here for a reason. To relax and enjoy free time without the stress of budgets and the pressure of deadlines.

Needing to get out of his head, he directed his attention outward. Hundreds of fall flowers lay before him in a carpet of majestic reds, purples, golds, and oranges. He stopped and studied them before taking photos from afar at first, then coming in closer and closer until only an individual petal filled the frame. Away from the canopy of the trees, the sun shared its warmth, and he removed his pullover before stuffing it into his backpack. A warm breeze blew through the fields, bending the blooms this way and that—a synchronized dance of willowy stems decorated in colorful bonnets.

Hours passed as he played with light and shadow, color, and black and white. Anytime he had a camera in his hand, he was happy. And the quiet solitude of the afternoon lifted his mood. He was at peace. With no one having tantrums or getting angry because he was shooting past deadline. This could be a whole new avenue for him, but it wasn't exactly what he'd been pondering recently.

He stowed his camera and walked toward a winery one of the guides had told him about. With nothing to take his attention away from himself, he skidded back to part of the conversation he'd had with Alyssa this morning. The part about being cranky with his employers over budgets.

Possibly his surliness surfaced over more than a simple creative disagreement. Until recently, he'd been more than happy to traipse the globe at his employers' whims. But now, he started to wonder if he should change paths. Settle down. Not that he had anyone to settle down with, but he'd never find that person by flitting from city to city, country to country.

Maybe his peevishness had something to do with his younger brother getting married and seeing how happy he was. Gabe needed more stability in his life. He always pictured having a family—a wife and maybe two kids. At thirty-five he should at least start to move away from his bachelor ways.

Listening to Alyssa talk about feeling unsettled in her current job and coming up with options for change had him questioning whether he should consider his own options. He could take fewer international shoots and do more studio work in New York City. Maybe even balance his magazine and ad jobs with the artistic photography he dreamed about.

Interesting thoughts which had his attention despite that this time off wasn't meant to send him in a different direction. The week away was intended to get him to fall in line.

Neither was it his aim to complicate his life any further. Yet, inexplicably, Alyssa kept popping up, ruining his inner therapy session. Spending time with a beautiful, complicated woman who was also trying to figure out her next step had the potential to muddy his future, not clear it.

He would just have to shut it down.

****

After the team challenge, Alyssa's achy and rubbery arms vied for attention with her growling stomach, and dinner wasn't for another three hours. A cooking class was the perfect antidote for both of her issues. No strenuous physical activity and surely, they'd let her eat what she made in the class.

"Over here, Alyssa," Edie called to her over the din of vacation chefs.

She took up residence at a high counter next to Edie. "What are we making? I didn't focus on the menu." Alyssa pulled the white apron assigned to her over her head and tied it around her waist.

"I'm glad you took my advice. This will be fun. We're making chicken horiatiki."

"And what exactly is that?" Alyssa was not adventurous when it came to food. Or anything else for that matter. Hamburgers, salads, eggs, pasta. That about covered her cooking repertoire.

"It's a Greek dish with yogurt, feta cheese, kalamata olives, and some other ingredients. You'll love it."

"Maybe. I don't like olives."

"You can pick them out when it's finished, but it really does add to the overall flavor."

On the counter before them was a myriad of ingredients, most of which Alyssa recognized. A cucumber, some grape tomatoes, a lemon, and an onion. Next to them sat bunches of green herbs, their identity a mystery. But she'd soon learn.

Their instructor, Betsy, owned her own restaurant in the next town over and had that glow about her, proving she loved her job.

"Okay, class. Today we're going to make one of my all-time favorite salads with a few special touches. We are going to toss cucumber, tomato, red onion, pickled pepperoncini, and kalamata olives in a red wine vinaigrette to create the classic Greek horiatiki. Then we'll make a creamy sauce of Greek yogurt, feta, and lemon. Of course, we will add chicken and homemade pita chips to finish it off." Her broad smile told the class they were going to love the outcome. "Since there are nine of you, let's break up into groups of three to cook the chicken. No use in each of you doing one breast."

Betsy looked the part of a professional with her large white chef's hat and apron showcasing her stitched name on the top left pocket.

"I want a chef's hat," Alyssa whispered to Edie.

"I don't think you get one of those until you graduate from culinary school. That might take you a while."

No kidding.

Edie folded the woman to her right, Frannie, into their little group of three. They followed Betsy's step-by-step instructions for searing the chicken, skin side down, over medium-high heat before flipping it to sear the opposite side. This was easy and much more fun in a group. In the future, Alyssa should invite her girlfriends over for dinner, and they could all help in the preparation.

As they each took a vegetable and either chopped, sliced, or diced, Edie filled in the narration part of the program whenever Betsy stopped talking. "I love how Betsy makes a meal like this seem easy. And it's healthy. She has a cookbook out that I'm definitely going to purchase so I can try her recipes at home."

"It won't be as much fun, though," Alyssa piped in. "Here we're doing it together so we can collaborate. When I'm home by myself, anything that takes longer than fifteen minutes is not on my dinner list. I don't want to spend an hour on something I'll eat in five minutes."

"But part of the fun is turning raw ingredients into an amazing dish."

Alyssa shook her head. "If I want something homemade, I head over to my parents' house. They only live a few miles away, and my mom cooks every night. I don't know why, but she seems to think it's her job as a wife. Even though she still works full time as a teacher." She didn't add that her mom was on medical leave for a year, and pushed the thought aside before it had time to bring her down.

"That's the way it is for some couples." Edie apparently found it necessary to explain Alyssa's mother's role in her parents' relationship. "I'm going to be that woman when I get married. If that ever happens."

Alyssa's sympathy kicked in. "Of course it will if you want it to." She was a firm believer that an acceptable mate was out there for everyone. If they didn't sabotage their own fate as was her expertise.

By the time they finished their masterpiece and ate their small portion, class was over.

Alyssa surprised herself. "This was really fun. And it will tide me over till dinner." It also kept her from dwelling on more serious thoughts. Like the reason she was here, and her goal to figure out a plan for going forward.

A win-win-win in her mind.

****

She arrived at the dining hall at seven thirty, a full day of experiences behind her. Seeking Edie out had become second nature to her.

"How was the rest of your day—other than our fantastic cooking class?" asked Edie as she ate a forkful of salmon.

Alyssa joined her with a plate filled with roasted chicken, whole wheat pasta, and several vegetables she had never seen before. "Good. Actually great." Gabe's long shadow still clung to her, even if he did dive too deeply into her personal life.

Edie's eyebrow inched up. "What made it so great?"

"This morning I went kayaking, and I came in third in the first heat—which put me in the next race. It was a lot of fun." The glee over her accomplishment seemed a bit much, but then again, this was all new to her.

"Had you ever kayaked before?"

"No. Tim, the aquatics director, gave us lessons, and Gabe coached me during the race."

"You got to spend time with Gabe all morning?" Edie's mouth dropped open.

"A little. Not much during the races, since I didn't make it into the finals, and he ended up winning the whole thing. But after, I ran into him on the other side of the lake where I was practicing my strokes." She kept her mortifying deposit into the lake and Gabe's rescue to herself. "He was taking photos of some of the trees and stuff, so I tagged along for a little while."

"Did he take you into the woods and have his way with you?" Edie's eyes were huge as she egged Alyssa on to share all the sordid details.

"Of course not. Really, Edie. Even if he wanted to, do you think I would do that?" Alyssa added some indignation to her words for effect. Yet she couldn't seem to pull it off given her history of sexual encounters at the hospital.

"I would. And I'd remember it forever as one of the best experiences in my time at Glenn Pines."

Edie's somberness tugged at Alyssa's heart. "When was the last time you had a serious boyfriend?"

"Never." She kept her head down and continued eating. "I go on dates here and there, but they never turn into anything."

Alyssa toyed with giving her advice, not at all sure it should be coming from her. Perhaps full disclosure would give it the appropriate weight. "I know I'm not the best person to be handing out relationship advice. I pushed for an engagement from my long-time boyfriend because I thought it was time to get married. Then he cheated on me because he didn't really want to get married. So we broke up, and I had an affair with a married man to get over David's rejection. Are your insides screaming yet?"

Edie's eyes widened, but she said nothing. Surprising for her. Alyssa's pathetic history must have shocked the voice right out of her.

Alyssa put her fork down, contemplating how best to say this. "I don't know you well, but you're a very friendly person, which is really nice. But sometimes you talk too much, and that can turn a guy off real fast. In my opinion, you should take some time to listen in between sentences." She softened her criticism with a head tilt and a rueful smile. "It might help."

Edie adjusted her utensils, patted her mouth with

her napkin, and sighed. "I know I talk a lot. I do that when I get nervous. Especially when I'm meeting someone new. Like when I got here and met new people. Or sometimes it has nothing to do with that. Like when things weren't going well at work. I would fill the empty air with words. I guess I think that puts others at ease. Then they don't have to talk. Today, in Alternative Approaches to Health and Wellness, I met a few new women. After class, I invited them to go to the juice bar for a smoothie, but they didn't want to. I assumed they just didn't want a smoothie. But maybe they didn't want a smoothie with me."

Alyssa felt Edie's rejection to the core, but no use sugarcoating the problem. If she'd learned anything from having four biological sisters and three best friends, it was to say what she meant and not talk in circles trying to spare feelings. It just confused people. Or sent the wrong message.

"Edie, when I told you your problem is that you talk too much, your response contained at least ten sentences without a breath. I know you heard me. I know you understand what I'm saying. You simply need to work on it. It may take time, but I'm willing to help. At least this week."

"So you're not going to desert me, too?" Tears shone in her eyes.

"Of course not." Alyssa smiled, hoping to set her at ease. Her candid criticism that Edie turned people away solely by talking couldn't be comfortable to hear.

"I'm really going to try. I'm a quick learner. You'll see."

"Are you going to the game room tonight?" asked Alyssa.

"Yes. You're coming, too, right? You can elbow me every time I get too chatty."

"I can't. I'm sorry, but I need to do something."

Edie's smile faded. Alyssa couldn't let her think she didn't want to hang out with her because of her talkativeness. That would be cruel.

"Since we're so busy all day, I have to start working on my employment plan tonight. I didn't mention it to you earlier, but I'm thinking of transferring to a different department in the hospital. Or maybe switching hospitals. I only have six nights here to figure out all my options and determine the best one for me."

"I should probably be doing that, too, but I'll have a lot of time once I get home. While I'm here, I want to enjoy every minute."

Alyssa had procrastinated long enough. Complacency would keep her rooted in Cole's orbit or at his mercy if he decided to transfer her without her consent. He was head of the department and could do whatever he thought best. She needed to stay ahead of the situation and determine her own destiny.

After dinner, Alyssa excused herself and ambled back toward her cabin, inhaling the clean mountain air to clear her mind for the task ahead. The scent of pine needles hung on the breeze, reminding her of Christmas—always a happy time with her family. Darkness shrouded her, and she looked up at the sky. Millions of stars dazzled the inky dome. Recalling Gabe's words about the view of the heavens by the lake, she took a detour and wandered to a spot where the trees had been cleared.

"Incredible! Absolutely beautiful," she whispered

to herself.

"I agree." His voice came from behind and sent shivers to her extremities.

She turned, and Gabe was a few feet away, blankets in hand. "Are you cold?" he asked.

"A little." She rubbed her hands up and down her arms to cover the real reason for her tremors. "I came here for a few minutes to experience the view. It's magnificent."

"I told you. I'm glad you did. We can stargaze together." He laid one blanket on the ground and rolled another as a pillow. "I see you ditched your backpack. Smart choice."

His smile and teasing remarks warmed her, but his nearness had her insides jumping. *Noooo.* She didn't want to feel butterflies or elephants or anything beating or trampling around in her chest. "I…I have to go."

He reached out and took her hand, pulling her down to the blanket with him. "You can leave in a few minutes. It's a much better view when you're relaxed."

What could she do but comply? A few minutes wouldn't kill her. Gabe assuredly had no romantic intentions. He hadn't invited her here. They both happened to show up at the same time. Besides, how could he have any amorous thoughts after hearing her true confessions this morning? She was surprised he hadn't jumped in his kayak and sped away without a backward glance.

Amazingly he had listened. And asked probing questions. He didn't come up with a solution like many men were prone to do. As if they had the answers to everything.

Maybe all he wanted right now was to share a

beautiful night sky with someone who could benefit from seeing the insignificance of her problems in the vast scheme of the universe. No ulterior motive—no chance for a bond to be made. He travelled the world taking pictures, and she worked in a small-town hospital in central New Jersey. Their worlds would never mesh, despite their collision here.

"I brought some wine. I don't know if you drink or if you even like wine." He held up the bottle and two plastic cups.

"Were you expecting to meet someone else here?" She started to rise, not wanting to ruin his romantic date.

"No. I was hoping you'd show up." He concentrated on removing the cork, so she couldn't see whether he was teasing or serious.

Confusion rattled her brain, and a pervading shyness stole her words.

He looked over at her. "What's with the silence? I'm used to you either putting me in my place or working through your issues." He handed her a half-filled cup. "It's from a local winery. I ended up there today while I was hiking through some meadow trails."

She took the offered wine with the goal of turning the conversation away from her "issues." "Did you take more photos?"

"Yes. I got some great shots."

"Didn't you have a scheduled activity this afternoon?"

"Nope. I only have one group activity per day, which allows me to wander around, take photos, think about how to handle my career."

He must have filled out his application in a much

more reasonable and sane manner than she.

"What about you? What did you do after we parted?"

"I ate." She laughed. "I'm always starving here. But I'm sure the exercise I get will ward off any extra pounds. I had a team challenge after lunch. Then I took a cooking class and ate some more. Before I had dinner. I may need to add to my schedule tomorrow. Do some kickboxing or Zumba."

"You may not find those activities here. But you will find hiking, canoeing, horseback riding. And stargazing."

The sky had gotten even darker since she arrived, and the stars tripled, making a magnificent, glittery canopy over their heads.

"It's absolutely amazing. I've never seen this many stars in my life." Alyssa lay back on her elbows and raised her face to the sky. "Even in the park near my house, there are too many lights from the town interfering."

She looked over at Gabe who had assumed the same position on the blanket as she.

"Over there is the square of Pegasus." He pointed to the southern sky. "See the four stars? Pegasus is a winged horse that was born from the blood of Medusa when she was beheaded by Perseus."

"I don't remember much about Greek mythology. Why was Perseus so violent?"

"Medusa was a monster with snakes covering her head. Whoever looked at her turned to stone."

"In that case, I suppose Perseus had to do what he had to do."

"If you look to the left of the square"—his finger

traced a path—"that W-shaped constellation is Cassiopeia."

His arm was close enough to touch, and his deep voice, hushed as if in church, surrounded her in warmth.

She needed to break the spell he was spinning. "How do you know so much about astronomy?"

"I studied it a bit."

"Thanks for inviting me to join you. This is the best show ever. And I'm very impressed with the lecturer."

She connected with his eyes, and they drew her in, so close she could see his pupils, large and round, surrounded by beautiful green irises. His lashes were thick, a perfect frame. Her gaze moved to his lips, full and oh so sexy.

She blinked and turned her head to stop from falling into his abyss.

"I'm glad you were here when I arrived." His voice curled around her like a hug, but she refused to look at him. Too tempting. Too dangerous.

Sitting up straighter, Alyssa crossed her legs lotus style and took a sip of wine. Hopefully the cool liquid would douse the fire starting a slow burn in her gut.

He studied the sky and continued to share his knowledge of constellations, stars, and planets. She welcomed the distraction, asking questions, making comments—being the perfect student.

Before she even realized it, they were both lying back next to each other, a spare blanket covering them for warmth. Quiet enveloped, and the power of the universe surrounded her while the power of Gabe lay mere inches away. She sensed his gaze and turned toward him, watching in slow motion as his mouth descended on hers. His sweet kiss fluttered over her lips, teasing, instigating, making her want more. His tongue brushed against the seam of her mouth, and she opened it, just slightly, allowing for the barest of tastes, a fizzy sensation. Warm fingers caressed her cheek, her neck, and she brought her hand up to trace the planes of his jaw. Playful kisses turned passionate, and she swirled in his orbit, snaking her arms around his neck, bringing him closer, feeling the heat of his chest against hers.

His kisses floated from her mouth to her cheek to her ear to her throat. Heaven and earth collided as she buzzed with life, energy, and sexual yearning. She found his lips with hers, devouring him with a passion she hadn't experienced in months. So, so good. And so, so bad.

That one slip of reality entered her consciousness, and she broke their connection. "We should stop." Her voice was husky, raw with need. She lowered her eyes. "I'm sorry. I don't think this is a good idea."

First and foremost, she had met him only yesterday. But a few other reasons surfaced that were more important, like she made terrible choices when it came to men. And she needed to stand on her own before she even thought about getting involved with another. But no need to get into those right now.

Gabe exhaled and rolled away from her. "Okay."

Immediately, the chill of the night replaced his heat.

They sat up in awkward silence as the moments stretched on. Alyssa couldn't let this continue. "Let's talk for a while. Do you have any more wine?"

He smiled. “Of course.” He took her cup and poured some in, as well as in his. “Cheers,” he said, holding his cup up. “To making new friends.”

“We spent way too much time on my reasons for being here this morning. I’m sorry I was so talkative.” And open. Yet her transgressions didn’t scare him away. “I don’t understand why you would come to a place like this. It’s hardly one of the natural wonders of the world. You must be slumming it this week.”

“I like rustic. And getting away from the craziness of New York City. It’s such a beautiful setting not far from home. Tranquil when I need it to be, and adventurous when I want comradery and a physical outlet. A good place to de-stress. And to think about the future.”

“I’m surprised Glenn Pines appeals to you when you’ve experienced so many exciting spots in the world through your job.”

He chuckled. “I do get around when I’m working, but I don’t always get a chance to act the tourist. I’m too busy creating a fantasy, usually in only one location. Behind the scenes, people are running around perfecting sets, applying makeup, fixing hair, coordinating wind machines. The models are like mannequins, holding poses, unable to talk, smile, or move until they’re told to.”

“At least when you’re done, you can spend some downtime with your colleagues and explore whatever city you’re in, right?” Alyssa only dreamed of visiting such exotic venues. Her fear of actually going somewhere new kept her firmly rooted on the East Coast.

“You’d think that. But it doesn’t work that way. I

have to be on location a few days early to check the area for lighting, weather conditions, logistics. I work with the people from the magazine if I'm doing an editorial spread, or with the creative team from an advertising agency if I'm doing a commercial ad. Then there's usually two to three full days of shooting, just to get a few perfect shots. Next thing you know, I'm onto my next gig."

"You must be in demand if you have no time between assignments."

"I have a good reputation in the business. But as I told you, I've run into a problem with one of my main employers. Unfortunately, in the last conversation I had with the editor of *StyleSelect*, I blew up and told her what she knew about fashion photography could fit in her espresso spoon."

Alyssa almost choked on her wine. "Not the best way to react when she holds the power over hiring."

"I don't understand why she can't see that the end product is worth it. She's seen the transformation over this past year with my more arty shots. Sure, I spent extra time prepping and incorporating the flow of the outfit into the surrounding natural beauty of the setting. Making the model an extension of the background, and the background an extension of the model. It's the blend of nature or architecture with the human element that's so special. I'm not interested in selling clothing. I'm interested in eliciting an emotion. It takes time to set up that ultimate shot, get the ideal light which casts the perfect shadows, and then coax the human body to embrace the symbiotic connection which brings it all together."

Wow. She hadn't realized he was that passionate

about his job.

He continued. "That time has paid off. The photos have been spectacular. Not that she gives a hoot."

"It sounds to me like you're no longer satisfied with being a high-fashion photographer. You said yourself in our first conversation that most subscribers to the magazine don't look at the scenery. They're interested in the clothes. You're now at odds with your livelihood. You either have to give her what she wants or move on."

"In my mind, staying stagnant isn't an option. In order to stay at the top, I have to add to my talents, become newer, edgier. Which takes more time and effort."

"But if you do that, you'll lose jobs and won't be at the top."

"I agree it's a catch twenty-two."

"If your ideas are no longer conducive to magazines, or vice versa, what do you see yourself doing?"

"In my fantasy world, I would create the emotions I've been talking about. It's called fine art photography. It's like painting a picture for a gallery, only doing it with a camera. The photographer decides what image or images he wants to convey. It's not created to sell a product or support a piece of journalistic writing. It's created to be enjoyed, to hang on a wall in a museum or someone's home. You may know of Peter Lik who takes incredible landscape photos of active volcanos, mountains, the sky, water, flowers."

"I don't know of him, but why can't you do that?"

"I could, but I don't know if I'd be able to make a living. My reputation is in fashion photography, not fine art. If and when I do try it, my view would be a little different. I'd use a landscape or architecture or a piece of furniture, but I'd also use a model."

Alyssa chuckled. "Of course."

"It's not for the reason you're thinking. I'd want a live person to be the focal point as well as an extension of the background."

He was out of her league here. She'd never taken an art course in college and didn't know the first thing about photography other than point and shoot. "Give me an example."

"Let's say I chose a waterfall in Hawaii as the background, and I have a model standing behind the deluge in a flowing gown. With my current job I'd be selling the gown, but I also see a story there. The woman could either be waiting for her lover to join her in this beautiful, natural setting where the two of them will fall into each other's arms. Or she and her lover might have recently broken up, and she is hiding her tears as the falls crash around her. I decide what the story will be, depending on the light, the shadows, the atmosphere—sometimes the model's personality."

His vividly descriptive scenarios allowed her to picture both. She'd love to know which one he would see through his lens. "If you want to tell a story, why don't you take photos and write about them?"

"Words aren't used in fine art photography. The picture tells the story. And it may be a different story to different people, depending on their backgrounds, their personalities, their experiences. My interpretation might be the opposite of yours. Similar to a painting."

Interesting. She understood how he could make a living photographing for magazines and ads. But taking photos to sell in a gallery seemed like a pipe dream. Yet who was she to be the naysayer? It was his life. His career. If he was that talented as a high-fashion photographer, then he could assuredly leverage that talent to another area.

As if he heard her thinking, he answered her. "I don't know if it would be enough to sustain me. Would anyone want to buy my work? Could I go from 'lights, camera, shoot' with dozens of assistants, project managers, and set designers to being on my own to create my artistry?"

"Maybe you can balance fashion photography with your art photography. It doesn't have to be one or the other, does it? You can move slowly from fashion to fine art, and if it works out, the balance will change."

They sat in silence for a while, and she wondered if he was taking her idea into consideration or writing off her advice as coming from someone who hadn't a clue what she was talking about.

"What are you thinking?" Gabe slid her hair behind her ear. "I want to see your face."

Her entire body heated at his intimacy.

"It's nice to sit out here in the quiet of the night and talk. But I don't know enough about your business or your art to be of any help."

"Just talking is helpful. And your ideas are worth consideration. Until today, I haven't thought much about changing course, but now that you've forced me to talk about my vision of an ideal career, there's a lot to contemplate." Gorgeous green eyes trained on hers. "I thought I was here to take a break, talk myself into following the rules, and then return to my life as I know it. But our conversations today have been eye-opening."

He reached out and threaded his fingers through her hair, setting little cherry bombs off in her veins.

The heat he generated couldn't be ignored, but deep within she knew it wouldn't make much of a difference what type of photography he did as his career. He would still be living in a different world.

Those emerald eyes reached into her soul and mended some of the cracks. "Let's not dwell on either of our issues anymore tonight. I don't want to ruin the aura here." He took her hand in his and massaged her palm with his thumb before raising her fingers to his lips and brushing a kiss over them. "Maybe tomorrow we can continue to analyze our respective futures."

A riot coursed through her bloodstream. So he intended to see her tomorrow. Happy feet danced in her stomach, kicking away whatever warning her conscience heaved in her direction.

Chapter Six

Alyssa used every ounce of willpower to end her time with Gabe. Once back in her cabin, she pushed all thoughts of him aside and pulled out the notebook she had purchased for this very reason. She was much better at thinking when she could write down her thoughts.

The time had come to focus on her professional life. She'd been an ER staff nurse for ten years at Nassau General. It was fast paced, challenging, and she liked her job. Even used to love it. But these past few months had been difficult at best, and after Cole's pronouncement that she should think about transferring, she'd been at sea. Alyssa didn't like change. She required stability, security in knowing everything was in order, every personality known.

She liked monotony! Not the best label to adhere to her choices, but appropriate.

A change would be good for her growth and her confidence.

She titled the page in her notebook *Job Options*. Anytime she faced a dilemma, she would write down the pros and cons—everything that came to mind whether viable or not. Once she had a list, she could go back and eliminate what was out of the question, and narrow that list to a few options she would consider. Then she would rank them.

She began to write.

Easy Changes. Move to another area of the hospital (check with human resources to see what areas are hiring). Change hospitals to another in central NJ (check ER nurse positions/other opportunities on local hospitals' websites).

Harder Changes. Move to another hospital outside of central NJ. Take a certification course to increase skills and/or add skills. Look at jobs outside of a hospital that require nurses (i.e. schools, nursing homes, social services, nonprofits, corporations). Go back to school to obtain a master's degree in nursing (get into management or teach).

Hardest Changes. Look for a job out of state. Join the army/navy/marines as a nurse. Consider a stint outside of the country (i.e. Doctors Without Borders).

She laughed at the options under *Hardest Changes*. She might as well add *win an Emmy*, for that was just as likely as the last two she'd written down. A job out of state could work if she chose Pennsylvania or New York, and not anywhere farther. Pennsylvania was right across the Delaware River, a mere twenty minutes to the Yardley/Newtown area. New York was more of a challenge. Manhattan would be a brutal commute—at least two hours door to door if she took the train, then a subway—and she couldn't see herself living there. Big cities were overwhelming.

Alyssa reviewed the list several times with the new goal of coming up with a short-term and a long-term plan. As soon as she got back to work on Monday, she'd check with human resources to see what jobs were available at Nassau General. No use changing hospitals while she worked toward her long-term plan.

She knew the politics at Nassau General as well as the systems. Baby steps.

What intrigued her the most under *Harder Changes* was getting a certification in another area of nursing. Ever since her mom was diagnosed with breast cancer a few months ago, she had periodically thought about working in oncology, specifically for a breast cancer program.

She'd let this percolate a while, keeping it tucked in her brain while she hiked or kayaked or sat quietly this week. Maybe she'd bounce her ideas off Edie. Or Gabe.

That thought made her smile. And her stomach whirl.

Within seconds she was back on the blanket under the stars, Gabe's lips on hers, sending every cell and molecule in her body whizzing and bouncing and flying. Warm fingers caressing her face, her neck. His solid body pressed against hers.

No, no, no. Do not go there. A relationship is off limits to you, Missy.

She only hoped her rash instincts would be tamed by her reasonable self.

****

The alarm clock buzzed, loud and insistent as Alyssa slapped at it with eyes closed. Six thirty. When she finally silenced the offensive device, she pulled the sheet over her head and slid easily back into dreamland, only to wake with a start at eight.

Unable to rush, despite the lateness of the hour, she shuffled to the bathroom, every muscle and corpuscle making its presence known. She would have stood in the shower longer if the spray was more than a light trickle and the water steaming. A lukewarm soft rain did nothing to massage those aches and pains from yesterday's events, made worse by her dead sleep. After gingerly dressing for the day's events, she raised her arms to braid her hair. A huge mistake since her shoulders screamed in protest.

She twisted from side to side, then stretched her arms overhead in an effort to get the blood moving and the muscles warmed. Today's torture was the low ropes course.

How bad could that be? Maybe the Glenn Pines tormenters had devised her schedule to give her a break on her third day here.

Running late, she arrived for breakfast and scooped up the last bit of scrambled eggs in the bin. Edie had been right. She needed to get to the dining hall soon after it opened. With only a half hour to eat and get to her appointed activity, she scanned the half-empty room and saw no one she knew, so she sat by herself.

Last night, by the lake with Gabe, had been amazing, but she wouldn't think about it or him anymore. It was a one-time experience that could not happen again. Nothing positive could come from starting something with him when it would end next Monday, with each of them going their separate ways. She pushed her eggs around her plate. Not a good sign. Food and energy were a must at this place, and she needed the fuel to embark on her next event.

Once she put her mind to it, Alyssa finished her meal in record time. She then strode to the low ropes course, fortifying her lungs with the crisp mountain air infused with the earthy scent of fallen leaves. This place lived up to its motto, and she intended from here on out to live her best life with health, wellness, and balance. An added bonus was the opportunity to meet new people at each activity, and she'd met some really nice ones over the past two days.

Kevin, their leader, called the group over to a log a few inches off the ground. "There are seven activities on this low ropes course. It's a great place to master these challenges before we do the high ropes course later in the week."

A few groans echoed around her as her colleagues took in Kevin's meaning—especially since some of these supposedly low activities had bridges at least eight feet high.

"I'm going to break you up into three pods with six people each. Some of these challenges are solitary, and some are done in teams. The entire exercise this morning is meant to give you opportunities to push your risk tolerance, perform under pressure, and collaborate with your team members. Let's get started."

Kevin grinned as if knowing that some of these seemingly simple activities had hidden traps. She didn't doubt that, given her experiences thus far. Ropes, cables, a cargo net, bridges, and a trapeze-like structure populated the area.

She scanned the group of eighteen, and pinpricks of pleasure shot through her when her gaze rested on Gabe. She bit her lower lip and scolded herself. *Stay away. There will be no romance here.* Thankfully, she was on the other side of Kevin, and they were not assigned to the same pod. At least fate was looking out for her.

Her pod started at the low log, similar to a balance beam but round. They were each to walk across it forward and then come back side-stepping like a crab. The others in the pod stood on either side of the log to steady the participant in the event he or she lost their balance. Easy, peasy.

Alyssa had taken gymnastics as a kid and been a cheerleader in high school. Balance was not a problem for her as she took the log with confidence and speed. Some of her teammates were not as coordinated, needing the rest of the group to encourage and give a hand when necessary. Since the log was only a few inches from the ground, no one was in danger of getting hurt if they toppled off.

Next came the cargo net. A vertical contraption strung up between two poles about twenty feet apart.

Alyssa pushed her shoulders front and back to get the blood flowing, knowing they'd be aching even more once she had to paw up the net. Two people at a time would climb the netting like a spider—or maybe a monkey—hands gripping and feet positioning for balance as they climbed to the top, then down. Each winner got bragging rights and the chance to do it again against the other winners—until one remained. Although it looked simple enough before anyone started, the net shifted under the weight and maneuverings of both participants. Alyssa held no fantasy of winning this competition, but she'd try her darndest.

Laughter, mild curses, and taunts flew through the air as the team members on the ground encouraged or teased their new friends.

Alyssa's turn came too quickly, but she might as well get this over with. She positioned her hands in holes in the net above her head, waiting for her competitor to get in place, and for someone to shout "go."

"Hey, Beckman, fancy meeting you here."

Her blood warmed—or did it freeze?—as she turned her head left to encounter laughing, green eyes accompanying Gabe's gorgeous, wide smile.

She shook her head to dispel the image. "What are you doing here?" she hissed. He was not assigned to her pod.

"Joe wanted to switch with me so he could spend time with Tara. Romantic, isn't it?" His voice dripped with teasing sarcasm.

Someone shouted "Go," immune to the conversation going on between them. Of course, Gabe spidered up with ease while Alyssa's body jerked with each of his movements.

"Come on, Beckman. Get moving."

Her teeth gritted so hard her jaw ached, but those words unclenched her fingers, and she grabbed for a higher hole in the net as her feet scrambled for a new foothold.

"That's it. Keep coming." Gabe hung where he was without climbing higher.

"You don't need to wait for me." Ire punctuated her words as she climbed almost level with her nemesis.

"You always do much better when I'm coaching you."

That did it. She pulled all her energy into her core and worked her way to the top, refusing to give Gabe even a glance. Then she dug her feet in to climb back down, calculating that the drop was only about six feet. She let go and landed on the ground in a crouch position to soak up the shock mere seconds before

Gabe.

"Hey, that was cheating." His brows V-ed over flashing eyes.

"Says who?" Her tone was sugar sweet.

Having grown up with four sisters all competing at some level for something, Alyssa had walked the edge of the rules to beat them out whenever possible.

Kevin happened by at that moment and clapped her on the back. "Great job, Alyssa. You're onto the next round."

"Validation from the chief." She smiled at Gabe before turning to ignore him.

That was stupid. Now I have to do this again against someone else.

If she gained nothing more this week, she'd be a lot stronger physically than when she'd started. She might have to take up kickboxing or CrossFit when she got home to keep the momentum going.

She didn't win the next heat but came damn close. Now that she had the hang of it, she'd do even better if a similar challenge was on the high ropes course.

Alyssa followed her group over to the pipe bridge—a span of eighty feet between platforms and eight feet off the ground, according to Kevin.

A nudge at her elbow had her turning. Gabe stood right behind her, looking up. "That does not look like it belongs on the low ropes course." The edge in his voice clued her in to his anxiety.

"Are you afraid of heights?" Bemusement tickled her words.

The serious set of his jaw and the shadows haunting his eyes gave her the answer.

Her first thought was to tease him, but none of

these activities were as simple as they initially looked. She'd better take her turn before razzing him.

Alyssa scaled the ladder easily to the platform, grabbed hold of the ropes on either side, and placed her foot on the first pipe to test its stability. The bridge seesawed with her weight. She placed her other foot on the next pipe, keeping her feet wide toward the sides for balance. It worked, and the bridge calmed down. Perfect. She moved with caution from rung to rung, holding tight to the ropes on each side while moving agilely, but with core strength, across the span.

An added benefit to this challenge was the fresh pine scent of the woods surrounding her as well as the cool breeze whispering against her face, all while droplets of sweat trickled down her back from previous exertions. Kevin was right. These risk-taking activities gave her the opportunity to learn that she could do it, despite misgivings, despite aches and pains. She was strong and smart and open to new challenges. And hearing the cheers from her teammates as she approached the far platform gave her even more confidence.

When she climbed down the ladder and approached her team, the next woman started to cross. Interestingly, the guys held back with Gabe the farthest away.

"Don't worry, I'll coach you. I'm sure you'll do much better."

His mouth inched up into a smile. "I guess I deserve that." Sparkling eyes held hers, and he nodded. "Let's do it."

Those three little words held a host of meaning—bringing her into his orbit as a duo, showing his vulnerability in needing help, and of course the ever-present sexual undertones that accompanied some of his remarks. But her self-imposed mission was to focus on the plain meaning of his statements, not any hidden implication.

"Come up with me. I need you close by."

Her throat tightened, and she couldn't swallow as her heart spun and dipped in her chest.

Her brain begged her to run, but her soul soared. She couldn't run if she were flying.

She would have preferred to follow him up the ladder, but his courteousness had her scrambling up ahead of him.

"Nice ass, Beckman."

She stopped mid-climb and turned to glare at him. "Keep your eyes off my butt, or I'll leave you up here alone."

"I thought part of all this was to enjoy the view." His impish grin did nothing to douse the heat from her cheeks. What part of staying away from him didn't her psyche understand?

On the platform, she motioned for him to move in front of her. He brushed by without even trying to evade her space. He caressed her arm as his chest came into the briefest of contacts with hers. Tiny champagne bubbles fizzed from her toes to her head, the effervescence almost making her giddy. She hid her smile, trying her best to ignore the tempest he started deep in her belly.

"Hold on to the ropes on both sides of the bridge." She kept her voice even and encouraging despite the storm within. "Put your right foot on the closest pipe while keeping your left on the platform. Feel how your weight affects the motion of the bridge?"

He followed her direction, and the bridge undulated with his step.

"Whoa." He pulled his right foot back onto the platform. "I don't think I can do this."

"Don't look down. Look ahead. Enjoy being up in the pines. Take a deep breath and try again."

He did as she suggested.

"Good. Now move your left foot off the platform to the second pipe. Keep your feet wide, your core centered."

The bridge swung from side to side before settling, as his hands strangled the side ropes.

"Good. I'm going to coach you from here because if I come onto the bridge behind you, I'll upset the balance."

"Okay." He agreed through gritted teeth.

Her smile burst over her lips. Finally, she was in a superior position to him.

He took at least five minutes to get to the other side, pausing between steps to allow the span to stop moving altogether before inching forward. She'd have to get him to keep moving the next time, but their colleagues were patient and encouraging from the ground, clapping when he eventually reached the other side. Instead of following him across the span, which would have taken her thirty seconds, she descended the ladder and met him on the ground.

"You didn't want to show me up, huh?" His face was pale and that gorgeous smile missing.

She shrugged. "No need." She yanked his arm. "You should be proud of yourself. You tackled your fears and made it to the other side."

"You're right. Thanks for helping."

Despite his pallor, the gratitude in those gorgeous green eyes zinged to her heart.

She swallowed, hoping to dislodge any warm, fuzzy feelings instigated by Gabe's mere presence, before turning her attention to Kevin.

The next few activities—a low zip line, twisted climbing tower, and power-leap bar—were fun and a lot less threatening.

While her muscles still ached and she faced many more activities which would take her out of her comfort zone, today's challenges were fun instead of daunting. Maybe day three was her turning point.

Chapter Seven

The canoe activity for the afternoon was by some miracle not a race and not an obstacle course. It was a simple how-to lesson, and Gabe made sure Alyssa was planning to attend before he signed up. Once there, he maneuvered himself so they'd share a canoe.

She sat up front as the bowman, and he took the rear as the steersman. The only thing that marred this arrangement was that they couldn't face each other. After they were schooled on the basics, they were set free to paddle around on their own. Getting the hang of their rhythm, they skirted the perimeter of the lake, working on syncing their strokes, with one paddling on the left and one on the right, to keep them straight until they had to turn.

The afternoon temperatures were in the high seventies this entire week, wonderfully warm for late October in the mountains. The sun shone bright with not a cloud in sight. The sky was such a stunning blue that he couldn't come up with the right hue, other than perfect.

"Can we stop for a while?" Alyssa glanced over her shoulder, her large brown eyes flashing amber in the reflection of the lake.

She had on a bikini under her shorts and tee, and anticipation over her getting hot enough to remove those impediments almost encouraged him to deny her request.

"Sure. Let's paddle to the middle where we'll be warm under the sun." Was he too obvious?

When they reached the perfect spot, they pulled their oars into the canoe, and she gingerly turned around to face him. He removed his tee, and raking eyes took in his chest.

"Your turn." He couldn't hide his lascivious smile.

With a sly grin, she pulled her shirt up and over her head, giving him another glimpse of that toned and tight midriff he'd had his hands wrapped around the other day. His fingers itched to be back there.

She remained quiet for a while, basking in the warm afternoon sun. His head spun with need as he regarded her studying their surroundings. His entire being ached to touch that smooth, silky skin, feel her body heat against his. He should have had the foresight to bring a blanket. They could have docked and found a place out of sight to make his fantasies real. Just thinking about what he wanted to do sent fire to his extremities—one in particular. That seductive kiss they'd shared last night had begun a slow burn that heated up fast. Unfortunately, she'd pulled away. Clearly afraid of starting something with him.

Her sensual voice broke into his carnal thoughts. "Where are you going after you leave here?" A question out of the blue.

"Paris, for some designer shows. Then Rome. I have a photo shoot for a multi-million-dollar ad campaign."

"When will you be back in New York?"

Was she hoping to get together with him after they left? Lawrenceville was only sixty miles from New

York City. It could work. Of course, it was probably not a good idea.

She'd naively expect him to be her boyfriend, not a guy who came and went with each job. Unless he changed course fast. Which wasn't likely. He needed the magazine income to not only pay the exorbitant mortgage on his Central Park West co-op, but also to replenish his investment account, which had been nearly wiped clean when he invested in *American Traveler* magazine, owned by his friend Adam Conroy. That in itself would keep him firmly handcuffed to his crazy schedule for the foreseeable future and nix the idea of a change.

Yet instead of shutting down the notion of seeing her after this week, he fueled the idea. "In four weeks, I'll be joining my parents for Thanksgiving in New Jersey. My mom is thrilled since I miss so many holidays."

"That's nice." She wasn't biting. "Where do your parents live?"

"Morristown." Even easier to travel to Lawrenceville from there than New York City.

"Is that where you grew up?"

"Yep. My father needed to be near an airport for his work, and my mom was against living in Manhattan."

"Why did your dad need an airport close by?"

His stomach bunched as it often did when talking about his father. "He's a well-known nature photographer. He spanned the globe to get incredible shots that are not only in the most prestigious nature magazines, but museums and galleries."

"Wow. Impressive. Two artists in the same

family."

"I suppose." A distinct chill ran through his core. "But he wasn't a great dad."

Her eyebrow arched. "Did he teach you what he knew about photography?"

He squinted at the lake as if seeking the answer from its depths. "He tried. But I didn't want his help." Anger tinged his words, and he surprised himself by sharing this glimpse into his personal life. He needed to kill this discussion and try for something less personal. They'd been having such a nice conversation, and this thread was a definite mood changer.

But Alyssa's curiosity wouldn't be contained, and astonishment marred her brow. "Why not?"

His jaw tightened, and he gripped the side of the canoe to transfer some of his tension. "I didn't want to replicate his life. He was never home when my brother and I were growing up. He missed every important event in our lives from tournaments to graduations." His teeth clenched, sending a sharp pain to the top of his head. "Although I visit on holidays if I'm around, it's really to see my mom. I have nothing to talk about with him." He tried replacing his resentment with a tight smile. "Sorry. Sore subject."

They sat in silence, and Gabe felt Alyssa's eyes studying him. Surely she could read the resentment in every facial nerve and strained muscle that could not be neutralized despite his attempts.

"Will your brother be there on Thanksgiving?"

By the change in subject, she probably thought she was averting a minefield, but this new topic had the potential to explode as well.

"Yes. He and his wife also live in Morristown."

"Are you close to your brother?"

His conscience kicked at him. "We used to be growing up. Since I've been away a lot over the last six years, I don't see him—them—often. Not that he's talking to me much these days." Maybe it would be good to let her see how his job affected this relationship. That way, she wouldn't expect anything from him.

Uncertainty floated over her face as she possibly searched for a safe subject. Yet she dove in. "What happened?"

No use sugarcoating the issue. He'd been brutally honest thus far. "He got married last year, and I missed the rehearsal dinner the night before the wedding. I barely made it to the wedding itself, even though I was the best man. A photo shoot ran over by two days, and it was hard to get connecting flights coming from Tanzania." Of course the shoot running over had been his fault. One of those perfect shots he was going for hadn't come together until the fourth day. "My brother didn't talk to me at all for six months. But things have gotten a little better. His wife has been our mediator. I adore her."

She leaned forward, a frown furrowing her forehead. "Did you explain why you almost missed the wedding?"

"Of course. His response was that I should never have taken the job so close to their big day. He called me arrogant and egotistical and a few other choice names."

She nodded, as if accepting his brother's description of him. Not good.

"Getting back to your dad."

She paused, and he toyed with shutting her down. But he didn't.

"I know that slights incurred when you're younger can shape your relationship. But you're older now and have a career of your own, which takes you to every corner of the world. Maybe if you opened up to your dad about how you feel about the past, the two of you could develop a better relationship. You may find you have a lot more in common than you'd like to think."

He didn't respond, afraid of what he would unleash on an unsuspecting Alyssa.

She continued in the void left by no comment. "It seems your mom sees you a lot less than she'd like because of the way you feel about your dad. Yet she was the one who stayed home and supported you and your brother through all the events your dad missed. You may regret it if you don't mend fences. Someday it might be too late."

She was picking at the scab, and he wanted to bat this conversation away, but the truth of her statement gave him pause. Although he called his mom every few weeks, it wasn't the same as an in-person visit. And she wasn't—they weren't—getting younger. "You sound like you've experienced something like this firsthand."

She shook her head to deny his assertion. "I've always been close to my parents." She stared at the bottom of the canoe. "Recently, my mom was diagnosed with breast cancer."

A chill ran down his spine, despite the heat of the sun. "I'm so sorry, Alyssa."

"Thank you." She blinked back tears. "She's strong. She'll beat this. I hope. But I'm grateful for every hour I spend with her. I've been involved in her decisions, along with my dad, every step of the way. I've been taking her to some of her chemo treatments when I can." She swallowed. "All I'm saying is that you might want to consider fitting your family into your schedule before it's too late."

Her beautiful eyes were shiny and full of emotion.

"Thank you for sharing that." His throat clogged at the pain she'd resurrected for his benefit. "It's something to think about." Although he'd need to have a hard conversation with his father before he could move on.

He inhaled a cleansing breath. Talking to Alyssa was harder than going to therapy. He had laid out his issues under her dogged questioning, and she had given him a very good reason to repair his strained relationships. But he was wiped out from talking about himself. Besides, he needed to determine this next step on his own—after he had time to reflect on it.

"What about you? Where did you grow up?"

"A few blocks from where I currently live. My ex-fiancé and I bought a small Cape Cod not far from my parents. When we broke up, I agreed to buy him out if he would give me two years to come up with his half of the equity. I've been working overtime at the hospital every chance I get to sock away that money. Hopefully, I'll be able to save enough by the due date, or I'll have to sell the house."

"Maybe he'll give you a break if you're a little short."

She snorted. "Yeah. Right." Her gaze floated to an egret standing on a rock by the side of the lake.

Good to note no love lost between her and her ex-fiancé. "Do you have siblings?"

“Oh, do I. I have four sisters. Not to be confused with my three best friends from high school who I also call my sisters. My biological sisters all live within twenty minutes of my parents. I see them on every federal and religious holiday, someone’s birthday, and any day they deem special.” Her smile told him she didn’t mind in the least. Here he travelled the world barely seeing his family, and she saw hers on a constant basis.

“That’s a lot of togetherness.”

“I love it. During our summer gatherings, we play volleyball, croquet, badminton. Of course, there’s always arguing over the rules and who made a point or didn’t, but it’s all in good fun.”

“It must have been interesting growing up with four sisters.”

“I like your choice of words. I’m the middle child. We all get along now. Not so while we were growing up. We’d steal each other’s clothes or take too long in the bathroom. Any little infraction could set one of us off, and the other four would choose sides. My poor mom.”

Alyssa laughed while recalling the memories. “Flying brushes, hair pulling, loud arguing, and a thousand tears. But they were also my confidantes, advice givers, and comforters.”

“I’d think your father was the odd man out. Six women in one house!”

“We had two female cats, too. But he survived. He actually loved it. He’s very proud of all of us.” She stared out over the lake. “I’m the least impressive of my siblings. The average kid of the bunch.”

“What makes you say that?”

"My oldest sister, Jessica, is a college professor, Heather's a CPA, Ashley is an actuary, and Stephanie is the executive director of a nonprofit."

"And you're an experienced and well-respected ER nurse."

"I suppose. I don't always feel as accomplished as my sisters. Being the middle child, I felt ignored most of the time. In order to get noticed by my parents, I'd do things like not turn in my homework or botch a test. My grades weren't great. Until I got to college and applied myself. By then, I was away from my siblings and making it on my own. But those old feelings never truly die."

So true. The minute he started talking about his absent father while growing up, the anger came back with a vengeance.

She focused her attention on the far side of the lake. "It must be interesting to see places around the world you've never seen before. When you go to Paris and Rome the next few weeks, will you sightsee after you're finished with business?"

"I thought about adding a few days onto my trip in Rome. Although I've been there before, there's so much I haven't seen. No matter how many times I visit a place, I can always explore a new area if the timing works out. Although I'd much prefer to share that experience with someone special instead of doing it on my own. But it's never practical."

"Why not?"

"Anyone I've dated had her own career and couldn't get away at the drop of a hat. Anyone I date in the future will have the same issue."

"Unless you can schedule it ahead of time."

"While I'd love to, our shoots are never that predictable. Rain, snow, windstorms, sandstorms. Any of the above, and more, can play havoc with the schedule, and although I may think I have three to four days on my own to explore, any or all of those days can be cancelled due to an extension of the shoot. It wouldn't be fair to whomever was meeting me."

"That's too bad, but I can see how it wouldn't work out. At my job, we have to put in for vacation days at least two weeks ahead of time, preferably more, and they can't coincide with any of the other ER nurses' vacations. I'd never be able to jet off at a moment's notice." Her face reddened. "I don't mean to insinuate that we'd meet up after one of your shoots. I'm just…thinking out loud."

"I like your thinking." He'd love for Alyssa to meet him in Rome. But dare he even suggest it?

She ignored his positive reaction. "What are your favorite cities, countries?"

"My favorite places to go now are not the capitals of the world, but the small towns surrounding them. When I was in Stresa on Lake Maggiore in Italy a few months ago, I took a side trip to a tiny village called Oiva. It was in the foothills of the Alps, not far from Switzerland, with a population of one hundred twenty people. Can you imagine?" He smiled at the memory. "I met the mayor, who also owned a winery, a dairy, and a restaurant in town—which town was made up of all his relatives. He also had the key to the church and took me on a tour. I loved photographing the vineyards while the laborers worked, with the sun coming up over the snow-peaked Alps in the background. While outdoor shots were my favorite, I also got some wonderful photos of his family in the dairy making cheese and the wine cellar filled with barrels of fermenting wine. Those little side trips fuel my creativity for fashion shoots."

"I've never been to a foreign country."

Surprise caught him up short. "Really?" How could that be possible? Travel was so easy.

"I've only been on a plane once—when I was twelve—when our family went to Disney World."

"Did something happen to keep you from travelling again?"

She shrugged. "It's going to sound silly, and it's not the only reason why I've never been anywhere." She pulled at a thread on her shorts.

"I promise I won't judge." He hoped his words would curl around her like a soft, warm blanket and make her feel safe in opening up to him.

"We were at the airport." She started hesitantly but picked up momentum. "Being the middle child, I was usually the odd kid out. My two older sisters were walking together ahead of my parents, looking in all the store windows, and each of my younger sisters was with one of my parents. I was always trying to tag along with my older sisters, wanting to be included as well as to feel more grown-up."

She squirmed on the hard wooden seat as if trying to get more comfortable. "I lost them somehow, too focused on the souvenirs being sold in the shops. When I turned to go back with my parents, I couldn't find them either. People were everywhere, streaming by, but none of them were my family. I started to cry as I rushed into store after store, looking for my sisters, my parents. I didn't know what to do, where to go. It was probably only five minutes before I saw my dad, panic on his face. Of course, he yelled at me to pay attention and stay with them. He must have been scared, too, and he hugged me hard as I buried my runny-nosed, sob-choked words of apology against his chest. I clutched him as if I'd never let him go, and he stood there with me, letting me run out of tears. Just thinking about those few minutes when I was lost makes my heart race."

He let her words breathe a sigh of relief. "I'm living proof that things that happen when we're young take root and form a part of who we are today. Your fear is real, and memories come bursting out to tangle with us when triggered. I think you need to travel with someone you trust, someone who will guide you, until you feel comfortable exploring on your own without worrying about getting lost."

She nodded. "You'd think I would have outgrown my fear, but instead of pushing it away in favor of experiencing other countries, other cultures, I continue to live in my own little world—the world I'm comfortable in. And it's been okay." She shrugged. "Besides, I don't have the money to travel."

Money was a convenient excuse, but low-cost trips abroad with tour companies abounded. No need to go there with her. He'd love to be the person to help her over the hump, for that's all it would take before her small world could expand. If he invited her to meet him in Rome, would that hurdle be too high to jump?

She broke into his thoughts. "Now you know why I'm such a homebody. And a scaredy-cat. And lacking the adventure gene. Even this inconsequential trip kept me awake nights worrying about who I'd talk to, what

I'd do twelve hours a day." She laughed. "In retrospect, I needn't have lost sleep over that one."

"You're incredibly sociable and outgoing. I'm surprised you'd be worried about making friends. Maybe if you signed up for a ten-day tour of a country you've been enamored with, you'd see how easy it could be. The tour operators plan everything from picking you up at the airport to your hotels, meals, and entertainment." While he'd love to be the one to show Alyssa the beauty of other countries, his current career would interfere with that plan.

"This was my first trip away alone. A baby step. But this isn't a foreign country where I don't speak the language or know the culture. This is a little mountain resort in the Poconos—a mere two and half hours from home."

"Now that you've taken this step, it might be easier to consider a bigger one."

"Maybe." Doubt shadowed her face. "What did you do with the photos from Oiva?"

"Nothing."

"That's too bad. Maybe seeing them in a travel magazine would inspire me to take a step off the East Coast."

They sat in silence for a while, and all Gabe could think about was the completely different lives they led.

****

At five thirty Wednesday morning, Alyssa realized she'd been staring at the shadowed ceiling for over an hour, but she couldn't turn off her brain and stop replaying the previous day.

She'd helped Gabe inch by inch across the pipe bridge, encouraging his halting steps, advising him where to place his feet, and always telling him to look ahead and not down. In the end he had made it, triumphant gratitude in his eyes.

During their afternoon canoe trip, they'd shared pieces of themselves through their family dynamics. Although their conversation was sometimes hard, the hours they'd spent together were magical. Getting to know each other on a deeper level intensified their connection.

And then he disappeared.

No Gabe during dinner. No Gabe in the can't-miss game room at night. Had she said something to turn him away or scare him off? Was her admission about being a homebody and travel neophyte a complete turn-off to the world adventurer? Or had she pushed him too hard with her unrequested advice to build a better relationship with his family?

Reflecting on Gabe's kiss from Monday night sent shivers from the root of her hair to the soles of her feet. Luckily, she had found her wits and put an end to what could have led to a more physical intimacy. But oh, how she fantasized about taking it further. Especially after making even more of a connection through their camp activities as well as their conversations. Or at least she thought they had.

After throwing the sheet aside, she quickly dressed in discarded jeans and a sweater from the day before. She had to talk to at least one of her girlfriends. Relationship analysis wasn't her strong point. She was more of a spontaneous, "do what felt good at the moment" kind of gal when it came to men. Which had gotten her in the predicaments she ended up in with David and Cole.

No cell service meant sneaking off to her car, driving down the mountain a bit, and hoping for the best within a reasonable amount of time. Why she felt guilty about leaving the premises she didn't know. Perhaps it was because Glenn Pines touted their technology-free zone in favor of experiencing face-to-face conversation as well as spirituality—whether with nature or her inner self.

Alyssa quietly left her cabin and tiptoed over a blanket of fallen leaves, wet with dew. The chill of the pre-dawn mountain air cut through her sweater, but she didn't want to lose time by backtracking to get her jacket. Hopefully, no one else was out and about at this time of morning to catch her in the act of escaping.

Her brisk walk became a jog, and by the time she reached her car, she was no longer cold. In fact, a few drops of sweat rolled down her back. As if a spy, she turned her head from side to side, surveying her surroundings to assure no one else witnessed her betrayal.

The coast was clear.

With heart racing, she jumped into the driver's seat, then inhaled before turning on the ignition and backing out of her spot. The crunching gravel under rubber sounded like a freight train zooming through the quiet of night. Holding her breath, she drove out of the parking lot and onto a country road barely visible with pre-dawn light filtering through the trees.

The dashboard clock displayed *5:52.* While calling one of her friends was a great idea in theory, she deliberated over which to contact at this hour. All three of them might be awake, feasibly sitting at their kitchen tables having cups of coffee in peace before the craziness of their days descended. Which one would be the least bothered by her intrusion? Her plan to seek early morning advice now seemed ill-advised, but she had come this far. She would carry through.

Denise, the most even-tempered and reasonable of them all, would be too busy getting three kids prepared for the school day. Her husband, Ben, would already be on his way to New York City, and she could picture Denise packing lunches, making breakfast, and getting herself organized before waking the kids, who would probably ignore her prodding.

No. Denise was not the person to bother this morning with her dilemma.

Nicki might be good. But then again, maybe not. Her philosophy had always been to date whom she wanted, when she wanted, with no regard for a possible commitment. Not until Dex turned her head had she even considered settling down. Her advice would be to have fun, great sex, and stay in control of the situation.

Since Alyssa's track record was the opposite of keeping control, Nicki's words of wisdom would be pointless.

Sam was a great choice. Her analytical lawyer brain would allow her to observe and give advice without getting pulled into the emotions of it all. At least that's how she was able to not only practice divorce law, but become a star in her field. Alyssa, on the other hand, sympathized with her patients' pain due to injuries or illnesses and often worried about them, even when she wasn't working.

Approaching a general store, she pulled into the lot and checked her phone for service. Three bars. Success.

She called Sam without dissecting her decision

further.

"Alyssa. Is everything all right? It's six ten in the morning. Aren't you on vacation?"

Alyssa laughed. "Yes, I'm away for the week. And Glenn Pines is not the vacation I thought it would be with a lot of pampering and slothfulness. It's more like summer camp with a boot-camp philosophy. Boating, hiking, mountain climbing, ropes course challenges."

"That sounds…interesting. I guess you don't get to sleep in?"

"No. Well, I could have slept a little longer. But my mind wouldn't turn off. I'm sorry to call you this early, but I need your advice. Do you have a few minutes, or do you have to get ready for court or something?"

"I have time. I'm sitting out on the deck having my coffee."

Alyssa pictured Sam relaxing on one of the lounge chairs overlooking the ocean, the sun inching over the horizon as fishing boats heading out for the day dotted the view. Late October at the beach was such a perfect time. No crowds, beautiful fall weather, and sunshine. She should have rented a house down the shore for her week off.

"Great. I'll dive right into the reason for my call. I met someone." She let her statement sink into Sam's conscious. When she didn't hear an "oh no," she continued. "I know I came to Glenn Pines to work on myself. To figure out why I choose the men I choose. The wrong men. And I also came here to determine what I want to do with the next chapter of my career. My intent was to stay to myself, think, get a massage, think some more, get a facial." She chuckled. "But since Glenn Pines is not that type of place, I've been meeting people while hiking and kayaking and taking classes."

"That's great, Alyssa. I know it was hard for you to go on this vacation by yourself. It was a big step. I'm glad to hear you're embracing the experience and you're not holed up in your room, meditating or something."

"I am going to take a class in that. Not sure it's for me, but I'll find out. Anyway…I met this photographer. His name is Gabe. He's all wrong for me, but I'm smitten."

"Smitten? I love that word. Go on." Caution marked her words.

Alyssa gave her a condensed biography of Gabe as the fashion photographer, world traveler, and adventurer, omitting the personal bits about the schism between him and his dad. She also added in his musings about changing his focus from fashion photographer to fine art photographer. Almost full disclosure was a must for a thoughtful response.

Several seconds of silence on Sam's end had Alyssa holding her breath. "You're thinking this will never work, right?" As she said the words, all light and air disintegrated from her body, and a heavy sigh escaped.

"I didn't say anything. Yet. But it's hard to imagine that dating a man who travels the world would make you happy in the long run. We both know you're a homebody. The opposite of your photographer." Sam's words contained a heavy dose of caution. "I don't want to see you get hurt. Again."

Her lungs squeezed and her chest burned. Calling

rational Sam had been a bad idea. "Maybe he'll find a way to balance his schedule. He might end up being in New York City more of the year than not if he transitions." At least that was what she chose to think, although she didn't have a clue if it were true.

A choked laugh came through the phone. "You hate New York. When I lived there, I had to beg you to come in for a weekend, which you did maybe once a year. As I recall, I had to meet you at Penn Station because a subway was out of the question, and you weren't aggressive enough to fight New Yorkers over a taxi."

"That was a few years ago. I can learn to like it. But…I don't think I could live there. Besides, I wouldn't leave my mom right now. She has a tough road ahead of her, and she relies on me and my experience as a nurse."

"As she should. Anyway, isn't it a little too early to think that far ahead?" Analytical Sam was taking over. Possibly a good thing. "You met Gabe three days ago. You don't know now that you're still going to feel the same way about him at the end of the week. You don't know him yet. He doesn't know you. Maybe you should see how the rest of the week plays out. Spend time with him, but not all your time. Have fun with him, but have fun with others, too."

Logical and sage advice. Alyssa nodded. "That sounds good. But what if I keep running into him and he wants to spend time together?" More like what if she kept seeking him out and encouraged a rendezvous.

"Be polite. Friendly. And tell him you have other plans at that moment. You'll see him later. Then make sure you leave."

Sam knew Alyssa too well. She understood that Alyssa craved attention from the opposite sex to make her feel secure. Especially an attractive man who made her melt. "But I can spend some time with him each day?"

Sam chuckled. "Alyssa, you don't need permission from me. You can do whatever you want. I'm simply giving you some advice on how to deal with your concern over getting too close too quickly. Then getting hurt. That is what you're afraid of, right?"

"Yes. I've been thinking about my stupidity in having an affair with Cole. It was a distraction, the perfect diversion after a bad breakup. David had done such damage when he cheated on me that I didn't want a relationship. I thought I knew what I was getting into and I wouldn't be foolish enough to fall in love. Until I did. In my convoluted reasoning, I believed that because he was married, I was safe."

"I can understand why you didn't want a relationship after David. Eight years is a long time to be with someone. A long time to learn to trust that person who then ruins everything."

Alyssa realized that Sam could have been talking about her own marriage. Although she'd only been married to Tom for three years, they had dated for several years before that. Tom's betrayal with his co-worker had devastated Sam.

She blew out a breath that ruffled her hair. Men were impossible. "I came here to work on myself. To get away from everything so I could breathe. And think. And learn how to make good decisions going forward. Cole is in the past. David is in the past." She dropped her head against the steering wheel and left it there, seconds ticking by without her saying more.

"Are you still there?" asked Sam, concern in her voice.

"Yes. I clearly shouldn't be thinking about another guy right now. Especially one who is the total opposite of me. I don't know what I was thinking. I need to focus on myself before I dive into anything further."

"Smart decision. And it sounds like Glenn Pines is a good place to think things through."

This was not the conclusion she was after. She'd hoped Sam would convince her to let her guard down. At least a little. To encourage her to test the waters. That despite being afraid of getting hurt again, she should not become a nun. She should see what came of it.

Because that's what Alyssa wanted to do.

She pulled on her memory. "Didn't you date Michael soon after you learned Tom was having an affair?"

"It was a few months later. When I ended up in Crescent Beach for ten weeks due to my forced sabbatical from work." Sam's resentment was still prevalent in her tone even after all this time. "I resisted him at first. I didn't want to start something, knowing I was going back to Manhattan and he was staying in Crescent Beach. But he was hard to resist, so I figured I'd have a summer fling. It would put me in the right mindset for when I returned to Manhattan, divorced and needing to move on. It never occurred to me, but I was using Michael the same way you were using Cole. To get over a bad breakup."

"Except you and Michael worked out in the end."

"True. When I returned to the city, I couldn't get

through a day without thinking about him. I was miserable in the same city I thought I'd never leave. And now here I am. Living in Crescent Beach and married to an incredible man."

"He's the lucky one. You left your law partnership behind, sold your co-op, and moved to be with him. While I could try to change my attitude toward New York as a visitor, I don't see myself ever moving there."

"You're getting way ahead of yourself. Take one step at a time. You're not moving in with Gabe right now. You're getting to know him to see if you even want to continue this after you both leave Glenn Pines. Take a breath of that clean mountain air, clear your head, and live in the moment. Have fun with him, but not exclusively with him. And remember, there's no need to make a decision about a relationship by the end of the week. Return home, go back to work. See what you feel. If you miss each other terribly, then the two of you will figure it out."

The angst that had overtaken Alyssa before talking to Sam slowly seeped away, and a smile tugged at her lips. "That's great advice, Sam. I don't know what I'd do without you. Thanks for talking me off the ledge."

"Anytime. Let's all get together the week after you get back. I need my girlfriend time. And then you can catch us all up on the details of your week away."

"Sounds like a plan. I'll call you."

She drove back to Glenn Pines with a totally different mindset. She'd be calm, cool, and collected around Gabe. Not giving over too much of herself, but not being stingy either. And she'd stop putting pressure on herself to figure this all out by Monday.

Her schedule today included a class this morning and zip-lining this afternoon. The schedulers were going easy on her mid-week. A day to rejuvenate those aching muscles. Since Gabe wasn't registered for the Adventure Program, she probably wouldn't even run into him today. Just like she hadn't yesterday after their canoe lesson.

Disappointment sank in her gut, but it was for the best.

Sam's ultimate advice was to take it slow, stay open to possibilities, and not jump in with both feet, as Alyssa was prone to do.

Great advice, but not so easy to follow.

Chapter Eight

She's not going to show.

Gabe toyed with his now cold eggs before pushing the plate aside. He'd been sitting at his usual spot since seven ten, soon after the dining hall opened. It was now eight twenty-five, and the room had emptied.

Maybe his disappearing act last night had sent Alyssa in another direction. His fear that they were getting too close by sharing huge pieces of themselves had him rattled. Spending time with her was easy, comforting. Exciting. And he was dangerously enamored with her. His total opposite.

He needed some distance, time to think this through. But time away did not banish her from his mind. In fact, all he did was obsess about her.

He glanced at the clock on the wall. Alyssa had a class scheduled for this morning from nine to ten but was free after that until her zip-lining adventure at one. His plan had been to talk her into meeting him at ten fifteen for a class on Watercolor Landscapes where they could explore their artistic skills with paint. As a bonus, he would play with shading and light, much like he did with his camera, and Alyssa could move from medicine to art as a method to give her balance and enjoy nature through a different medium.

He'd even circled another class on the agenda for Alyssa's consideration in case she loathed the idea of painting a landscape—Building a Better You.

So much for his spectacular, well-thought-out idea. Without execution, it was a total failure. Disappointment crowded his mind and body as he cleared the table and headed out. He might have spooked her yesterday morning when he told her he needed her on the ropes bridge. Actually, he had spooked himself. But that didn't stop him from following her to the canoeing class in the afternoon where he learned she'd never travelled anywhere off the East Coast—an astonishing revelation. Further, her homebody nature was buoyed by countless family gatherings while his preference had been to avoid them whenever possible.

Uncovering his difficulties with his family was more intimate than he anticipated. Yet he trusted her by revealing his flaws. In return, she shared the painful ordeal she and her mother were going through in an effort to help him see the light where his family was concerned.

Their conversation, which made them closer in many respects, magnified their divide. As a result, he had stayed away last night to assure he wouldn't start something they couldn't finish. He wasn't the type to take advantage of her vulnerability, like that appalling doctor from the ER. Maybe she was intentionally staying away as well. Probably good for her mental health. She'd told him her purpose in coming to Glenn Pines was to give her needed time to think.

At ten of nine, he headed for a class on something about changing one's energy, whatever that meant, considering that might be the class she was signed up for.

His plodding steps took on a spring as he headed to the building housing the wellness lectures. Hope prodded his heart into a double beat. He slid into a seat in the back and studied the rows of participants. No Alyssa.

Since he was here for a week to rid himself of his peevishness, he might as well try to discover where to focus his energy—career wise as well as with his family relationships—by listening to the words of wisdom from the expert in the front of the room. Maybe it would help him in his quest to figure out what to do about Alyssa as well.

And just maybe he'd run into her after this educational session.

It didn't happen. Gabe struggled through Strengthen and Reset your Energy and chose The Healing Power of Food as a substitute for the painting class, since Alyssa might opt for something food related, given her penchant for eating. It was a disappointing class, Alyssa-wise, and only managed to set off hunger pangs. Not wishing to spend another sixty minutes scanning the dining hall for his elusive muse, he grabbed a sandwich and sat outside eating it.

"Hi, Gabe." Edie stood before him with a beaming smile. "Why are you eating out here?"

"A change of scenery…and it's a beautiful day." He didn't share that he was hoping to catch Alyssa in her trek between activities. Or heading in for lunch. But the telltale words did escape despite the casual way he dropped them. "Have you seen Alyssa today?"

"No. But we're both going zip-lining at one. Is that on your schedule?"

He had an open afternoon with nothing scheduled.

"No, but it sounds like fun."

"Why don't you join us?"

"Can't." He already knew zip-lining was full. He had checked. And with as much as he wanted to see Alyssa, he couldn't bring himself to weasel his way into the group under the guise of photographing the experience, knowing Edie would be watching every move he made toward her new friend. "I'll catch up with her later."

"Do you want me to give her a message?" Edie's sly eyes told him she was dying to pass on a seductive invitation.

Gabe chuckled at her transparency. "No, thanks." Any seductive invitation would come from his lips to Alyssa's ear.

"Okay, then. See you around." With that, she took off for the dining hall, leaving Gabe to contemplate his next step.

He should let her be today, since that's what she wanted. While he could stalk the zip liners and talk to her when it was over, if she didn't want to talk, then he shouldn't force it. He needed to let his obsession go for the time being and relax into the day.

With his new strategy, or non-strategy, in place, Gabe headed for Soul of Communication and Decision Making. Maybe that class could help him with planning his future.

The class was good. Surprisingly, it gave him food for thought. But enough was enough. He had sat in classrooms all day while his preference would have been to do something physical. He studied the offerings. West African Drumming stood out. The blurb promised he'd learn the basics of hand-drumming techniques and rhythms while making music together with the other participants. Physical, challenging, and cultural. Perfect.

The class met at four fifteen in a barn on the far end of the property—a message that this could be loud and annoying to those not participating. Most of the takers were men. Not surprising there.

And then he saw Alyssa.

Blood raced through his core, a much-too-eager response. He needed to bring it down several notches, act normal, even nonchalant, so as not to scare her off.

"Hey, stranger. I haven't seen you all day. How's it going?" That sounded casual, effortless.

"Good." Her smile lasered beams to his libido.

He inhaled to tamp it down. "What sessions did you take today?" He was interested in hearing to what lengths she'd gone to avoid him.

"I took a class in meditation as well as another attempt at yoga this morning."

She must have assumed, and correctly so, he'd never venture into either.

"This afternoon after zip-lining, I went to Enhancing Sleep, A Guide to Living an Empowered Life."

Why hadn't he thought to take that one? "Are you having trouble sleeping?" He sure was. Thoughts of her followed him from day to night.

Beautiful eyes slanted in his direction. "Yes. And it's all because of you." Her smile faded, and a charming vulnerability shone through. It lassoed his heart and squeezed his soul. He was so screwed.

"I was up half the night myself," he admitted. Her truth serum was infectious. "Thinking about my career and how I could change it." He didn't add the words "to work for you," but that's what he'd been thinking about. However, that unbridled truth was far too much to share.

"Let's get started, class." Their teacher addressed the participants. "My name is Barry. Everyone, stand before one of the drums."

Alyssa stuck with Gabe and took the drum next to his.

Barry continued. "You're each standing before a hand drum called a *djembe*. It's chalice shaped and covered with an animal skin. The body of the drum is carved from hardwood. Women don't usually play this type of drum, especially in West Africa." He looked at Alyssa. "But we won't tell anyone there."

The class laughed as expected, but Alyssa settled in front of her drum. She clearly wasn't going anywhere.

They learned different sounds using their hands on different parts of the drum, then added some rhythms. It started out slow but steady, with increasing beats as the students followed Barry's prompts. At one point, the students played the rhythm they'd been practicing while Barry went off on a riff, making their band sound almost professional.

While a lover of the arts, Gabe had never taken a music lesson. The freeing feeling of pounding on an animal skin while finding a pleasing rhythm and hearing unique sounds was an awesome experience. Totally different from his typical activities. And he couldn't wipe the smile from his face while sharing the encounter with Alyssa.

"Great job, everyone." Barry applauded them at the end of the class. "If you come back on Friday, we'll add to our masterpiece. There's a West African Dance class that will be joining us. It will bring the whole experience to life, so please come back."

"That was amazing." The flush on Alyssa's face undoubtedly showed joy. "I'm definitely coming again. What about you?"

"I agree. It was a blast. I'm game." It would at least guarantee he'd see Alyssa for one class on Friday if she kept to her scheme of avoiding him.

Activities were over for the day. This was the time that most went back to their cabins to rest, shower, and change before dinner. Did he dare push?

No, he shouldn't. "I'll probably see you in the dining hall."

"Oh. Okay." Neither joy nor disappointment displayed on her face at his lack of invitation.

She waved, turned, and left.

Poof.

****

Dressing for dinner took her more time than the past three nights. On the one hand, she had this thing going on in her head that she wanted to look attractive for Gabe. On the other hand, her conscience told her to dress down. No good would come from playing this mating game. She had missed him terribly last night—his fault—and that empty feeling continued today—her fault—until he had miraculously shown up in the African Drum class.

Alyssa perused her limited wardrobe and chose her nicest pair of jeans—black—and a red sweater that her friends said complemented her coloring. Despite the wise words from her conscience, and Sam, to play it cool, she fluffed her long, brown hair, then brushed any stray strands. Her usual ponytail was not making an appearance. A clear indication she chose to ignore all rational reason. And in total defiance, she applied some mascara, blush, and lip gloss.

As she looked in the mirror, she questioned whether she should have put on makeup. Maybe Gabe liked the fresh-faced look—the opposite of his models. She shrugged. She hadn't applied much, only a little enhancement.

Why are you doing this? Gabe could not give her what she wanted—a partner in life who would be there with her, side by side, having breakfast and dinner together, sharing time off from work. He'd be a worse choice than David, if that were at all possible. At least she and David had passed each other every day on their way to or from work, depending on what shifts they had at their respective jobs. And they had some time off that coincided. Gabe would be travelling more than he'd ever be home.

Yet she felt a connection with him. And the sparks that flew anytime she was near him couldn't be ignored. Although she should. Unfortunately, she wanted nothing more than for him to enfold her in his arms while he kissed her breath away. An image of them entwined and naked hijacked her purer version. Merely thinking about that scenario sent unadulterated desire to all her erogenous zones. She fanned herself, reveling in the heat of her fantasies.

But jumping into bed with Gabe was a non-starter. A decision that would never be made. She would fall for him. She already was. And he would leave to go to Paris, Rome, and who knew where else while she stayed in New Jersey and worked at the hospital. That picture was not even close to happy.

Besides, she'd come to Glenn Pines to work on herself, to learn from within what future would make her whole, make her happy. She hadn't come here to find love. Or more likely, to find hurt.

She grabbed her black zip-up hoodie for the walk over to the dining room and back. Almost thirty degrees cooler than the afternoon, the chill night air tended to seep into her bones. And she wouldn't have the warmth of Gabe by her side to ward it off. What a pity.

When she arrived at seven fifteen, the dining room was full. She searched for Gabe, who always sat in the same spot. But some other woman had taken the seat across from him, and they were deep in conversation.

"Alyssa, over here." Missy and Conrad waved to her and pointed to an empty seat at their table.

She motioned she would be right there after getting her food. While usually starving, she bypassed the main courses. Her dilemma over Gabe tied her stomach in knots. To further tighten the ball, she wouldn't be able to talk to him through dinner.

"How's the wrist, Missy?" she asked, sliding into the chair next to her with a bowl of soup and some bread.

"I'm getting used to the cast. Although Conrad and I had anticipated physical challenges this week, we're taking advantage of all the classes."

Conrad chimed in. "We're even learning how to cook healthier."

"I plan on taking more classes, myself." Alyssa tasted her soup. Delicious despite the anxiety wreaking havoc in her stomach. "I've been studying the roster, and there are dozens of interesting topics." If only they had How to Stay Away from Trouble.

"I see you've been spending time with Gabe. He's a cutie." Missy winked.

Alyssa smiled at her description but couldn't contain the sigh that followed. "That he is."

"So why the sigh?"

Missy, although her mother's age, reminded her of her girlfriends. Wanting to know her deepest thoughts.

"I like him. He's interesting, fun, intelligent. But I just got out of a relationship." She almost choked on her choice of words. "I definitely fall for the wrong guys."

Not only David, but Cole, too. She clearly didn't know how to read men at all.

Although she'd managed to stay away from Gabe for most of the day, when she finally did set eyes on him, her whole body reacted. In a good way. Sunshine and rainbows radiated around her, and she couldn't take the smile from her lips with a sledgehammer.

Not that she'd wanted to.

"You don't have to marry Gabe," said Conrad. "Take your time. Get to know him outside of this place."

"That's the bigger problem. He travels the world as a photographer. He's rarely at his apartment in New York City. I'm guessing, even if he was, with me working different shifts at the hospital, our schedules would never mesh. Besides, I live more than an hour away."

"That doesn't sound too difficult to manage if you want it badly enough." Missy gave her a questioning smile. "Are you sure you're not manufacturing problems in order to avoid the possibility of a relationship with Gabe?"

Maybe she was, and it was her right to do so, based on her fears, without any explanation necessary. So she changed the subject.

"How did you two meet? You're such a great couple." Alyssa could learn a thing or two from them.

Missy looked at Conrad and smiled. "We met at work. We were both new attorneys at a large law firm in Chicago. There was a policy against attorneys dating, but we figured if we lasted, one of us would get a different job. If we didn't, no one would be the wiser."

"Who left the firm?"

"Conrad did. When he proposed to me, he started looking for a new job. And of course, he found one right away." She took his hand in hers.

Conrad added, "I was lucky enough that she accepted my proposal. I didn't think it would be fair to ask her to leave the firm."

Alyssa's gaze wandered over to Gabe. What were they talking about? "Who is she?" She didn't mean for that to be spoken out loud.

Missy followed her gaze. "That's Dorthea. She's an artist. Paints landscapes. I think she lives in New York City, too."

Alyssa's gut tangled even more, and she pushed her bowl of soup away.

Missy must have noticed her inability to eat. "Don't worry about her, sweetie. There're probably talking shop."

A huge worry. They had something in common, both being creative people. Gabe was interested in more artistic photography, and she was an artist. They both lived in the city. What could be more perfect for them?

And why should she care? Minutes ago, hadn't she told Missy and Conrad it would never work out with her and Gabe? She'd said the same to herself. They both knew they were wrong for each other. Why wouldn't he explore a relationship with someone else here? She had no monopoly on him. They should both make other friends while here.

"I haven't seen you in the game room yet. Why don't you come after dinner?" suggested Conrad.

"I was there last night for a little while." Very little. When Gabe didn't show up, she'd left within a half hour.

"Then you know how much fun it is."

Alyssa didn't. She hadn't participated in any of the games last night, choosing to sulk instead.

"I'm the ping-pong champion so far," boasted Conrad. "Perhaps you'd like to try your hand against me." He puffed his chest out.

"You're on. I'll have you know we had a ping-pong table in our basement when we were growing up. I have four sisters, and I was the champ in our house."

"Maybe I spoke too soon." His smile belied his words. He clearly thought he'd beat her, hands down.

"Can I speak to you?" A whisper in her ear sent chills down her arm. Gabe.

She turned, and his face was just inches away. "Sure. Excuse me," she said to Missy and Conrad as she stood.

He took her by the elbow and whisked her out of the dining room.

"Where are we going? I thought you wanted to tell me something."

He didn't answer, keeping on his track. When they

reached the front of the building, he pulled her down a small, empty hallway. Taking both of her hands in his, he faced her and covered her mouth with his, insistent and hungry. Oh my. All angst disappeared as she found herself free-falling through space and time, without a second thought of where she'd land.

As if detached from her body, her arms travelled around his neck, bringing him closer, until she could feel the burn of his heat, his passion. Strong fingers threaded through her hair, sending an electric current from the top of her head to the tip of her toes. She clung to him, reveling in this captivating world he invited her into.

His mouth feathered kisses along her jaw, to her ear, where his wicked tongue played along her far-too-sensitive lobe. She nearly cried out with pleasure.

Then he whispered, "Come with me to my cabin."

She wanted to follow him anywhere, but reality came crashing back. "I accepted Conrad's challenge for a ping-pong game. I can't not show up."

"Yes, you can." He continued his assault with kisses between encouraging words. "He'll understand. Things happen. Plans change." He kissed her neck, driving her to distraction. "This is a fluid kind of place."

Her bones were certainly fluid, closer to jelly, and she wasn't at all sure she could stand on her own.

Her conscience chose now to continue the discussion that had started in her head before dinner. *Remember why you're here. To work on you. You can't do this. If you do, don't blame me when you fall in love and then get hurt.* This was the same record that had played when she started her affair with Cole. Yet she'd convinced herself if it was just sex, nothing more, she wouldn't fall. Then she had. Had she learned nothing?

"Where are you?" asked Gabe, looking into her eyes.

"Sorry." She backed away. "My mind is telling me this is a bad idea. Another one in my long line of bad decisions."

He drew her over to a couch, and they sat. "I knew you'd think that. But maybe it isn't. I'm so drawn to you, Alyssa. And I think you're drawn to me. It's not simply sexual chemistry. We've gotten to know each other better. We're good for each other."

"Maybe we are. Here. But our careers, our lives do not mesh. You travel extensively, and when you're not, you're in New York City. I have a stable job, working nights and weekends in a hospital in Princeton." She didn't add her commitment to seeing her mom through this very difficult time, but it was also an unyielding obstacle.

"What if I don't travel as much? What if I can figure out how to make this new idea work?"

"Maybe you can. And maybe you will. But we don't know that right now. I don't want to start something we can't continue. It's not good for me. I don't want to get hurt."

His green eyes turned almost gray in this light, but no matter the color, they searched her soul and hugged her heart.

"I don't want that for you. Or me." He caressed her face with his warm palm. "I'm very attracted to you, and I can't let that go. I want you in every way. Physically, mentally. Emotionally. I'm looking at this week as a bridge to the next chapter. You are, too.

We're helping each other cross that span. Who knows where we'll land. But I'm willing to find out. Aren't you?"

She swallowed, angst and hope vying for priority. "It sounds rational. So why do I feel like I'm jumping off that bridge and trying not to drown?" She focused on the pine floorboards, staying away from his searching eyes.

With a delicate touch, he lifted her chin, forcing her to look at him. "I can't promise forever. I can only promise this week with a plan to see each other when we leave here. Neither of us knows right now where we'll end up. You're thinking of changing jobs, maybe your specialty, and so am I." The intensity of his gaze drew her into his plan as if she had no will of her own. "We shouldn't make this harder than it has to be. Let's take it one day at a time."

Those were the same words as Sam's. As Conrad's. She nodded, wanting to follow him across that bridge. She touched the stubble on his jaw, his rugged handsomeness a mere runner-up to his empathic sensitivity.

He had silenced the incessant talking in her head for a few minutes, but it would come back with a vengeance.

"Let me sleep on it tonight. Then we can talk more tomorrow." Her voice sounded ragged, hoarse.

He nodded. "If that's what you need, then of course." He slid his warm hand over hers, then squeezed it before standing. "You better get to the game room and show Conrad who's the champion ping-pong player here." One side of his mouth curved up in a smile.

Then he walked out of the building.

Chapter Nine

Fitfully turning from side to side, Alyssa could stand it no longer. She threw off the twisted sheet and switched on the lamp. Her trusty notebook lay on the nightstand along with a pen, both calling to her. She fluffed her pillow, leaned against the maple headboard, and picked them up.

Pros and Cons of Having a Relationship with Gabe

Pros: interesting, driven, worldly, gorgeous, fun, intelligent, thought-provoking, sensitive, good listener, great kisser, smells good, makes me melt.

Cons: nomad, different lifestyle, lives in NYC.

She tried and tried for more cons but couldn't think of any. Even the second excuse could be combined with the first. Also those pesky first two cons might be alleviated if he balanced his career in fashion photography with art photography—assuming that would keep him closer to home. Then only part of his time would be controlled by advertising firms or magazine editorial departments.

Yet she knew that even with this change, their lives would rarely intersect. Despite all those pros overshadowing the cons, a relationship between them was doomed to fail. Instinctively it was a given. He was adventurous, and she was cautious, which could also be defined as unexciting and boring. Even so, she needed more lines filled in under the cons column if she were ever going to convince herself to stay away from the captivating photographer who was stealing her heart.

****

Gabe entered the dining hall the next morning the minute it opened. He scanned the room for Alyssa, but she wasn't there yet. After their conversation last night about taking their relationship further, she had to be as eager as he was to at least discuss it more after sleeping on it.

"Hi, Gabe." Edie broke into his thoughts. "You look happy this morning."

What an odd thing to say. Did he not usually look happy? Maybe not. "What are you up to today, Edie?"

"Kayaking this morning. Then a class in meditation this afternoon. I don't know if it will be helpful, but I hope so."

He waited for her to go on. And on. But she didn't. "That sounds good. Have you seen Alyssa?" No use trying to sound casual. It was already Thursday, and the days were slipping away all too fast.

"Not yet." A cunning smile crossed her mouth.

Was she hiding something? "Okay, well, have a good day."

"You, too." She studied him for another moment before heading off to the buffet line.

Gabe sat by the window with coffee, waiting for Alyssa before he ate.

"Good morning." Alyssa's upbeat voice got his attention. "Edie said you were looking for me."

Black yoga pants and a black tank top molded to her body. He should rethink his adversity to yoga. Watching her stretch and pose seemed a far better—and more sensual—activity than many of the other physically challenging pursuits.

He swallowed his carnal thoughts. “How’d you like to come with me on a hike, either this morning or this afternoon, depending on your schedule? Glenn Pines has a few different trails, and there’s one that includes a field of flowers. I’d love to photograph you there.”

Although he’d already been there, having a human to enhance his shots had many benefits, not the least of which was spending time with this human.

Alyssa’s face flushed, and she looked even prettier than usual. “I’m not a model. I’d be too self-conscious. You should get someone else to do it.”

His stomach fell at her rejection. “I don’t want a model. And once you get used to it, you won’t even know I’m taking your picture. I’m very good at setting my subjects at ease.”

“Oh, here we go again with the subjects.”

Her smirk lightened her words and gave him hope. Then she looked directly into his eyes, and he lost all train of thought. “So…is that a yes?”

“I was heading to yoga, but I wouldn’t mind getting my exercise outdoors.” A gorgeous blush covered her face.

Apparently he wasn’t the only one having lewd thoughts. Gabe let out a breath. That was close. “Let’s eat. I don’t want to lose you to famine on the way. I have the trail map so we know where we’re going.”

She smiled, but her usual exuberance was missing.

“Is everything okay?” He hoped his quest to photograph her hadn’t put her in a bad mood.

“Just a little tired. I had a lot on my mind last night.”

So had he, but he wasn't sure now was the time to broach the subject they'd tabled last night in case it went in a bad direction.

"Food and fresh air should revitalize you." Just being around her got his metabolism roaring.

"You're right. This place has a certain magic about it. In some ways I feel like I've been here for weeks, and other times it feels as if the days are flying by. I've done an incredible amount in four days, yet my muscles no longer throb. The sense of accomplishment with every new activity is uplifting."

"I know the feeling. Being out of your comfort zone, taking on challenges, and persevering through it is pretty heady. I even liked the classes, which initially sounded too touchy-feely for me."

Alyssa smirked. "I think the perfect one for you is Transitions. The blurb in the pamphlet says it's for those going through life changes, like divorce or a new job. The participants will learn how major life events can offer gateways for spiritual deepening and authentic transformation."

He couldn't contain his chuckle. "You sound like a commercial for this place. For some reason, I don't believe a one-hour session is going to do all that, but if you'd like to attend, I'll tag along."

"There's one at three thirty. If I make it back from mountain biking in one piece, I can meet you there."

"You got it." At least today she was including him in most of her endeavors. "Have you ever been mountain biking?"

"No." She shrugged. "But I've never done most of the activities here."

"It's pretty strenuous. Half the time you're riding

uphill."

"Great. I spoke too soon about my muscles no longer throbbing. I guess I'll be hobbling to the Transitions class."

"Let's get going so we make it back in time for lunch before you hit the mountain bike trail. You'll need that meal."

She rolled her eyes at him. "I want to stop in the reception area and pick up one of the books they have on plant life and birds. It may help us identify them along the way."

"Eager to learn, are you?"

"Of course. I want to get the most out of this week. It's probably the only vacation I'll take for a year."

He was in the same boat. He wasted many of his hours in foreign countries waiting for the right light or weather or direction from the higher-ups. And as soon as his work was done, he'd pack up and leave for the next job. When he did eke out a day or two for himself, he didn't always have the time or energy to study guidebooks, preferring the spontaneity of sightseeing.

After Alyssa took at least fifteen minutes perusing all the books on the shelf to assure they had the best one for their particular outing, Gabe led her to the trail he wanted to take.

"Have you thought more about changing jobs?" he asked. "Is that why you want to go to that seminar this afternoon?"

"I'm still considering my options. If I had cell service, I'd do some research while I'm here, but that's not going to happen. When I get home, I'll meet with our human resources director to see what's available in other areas of the hospital as a short-term fix. Then I'm going to work in earnest on my plan for the future."

"Have you ever thought about working for a nonprofit overseas for a month or more? That would take you away from your small town to a place you've never been before." Maybe she'd find her travel gene.

"Since I've never been anywhere, that's a sure bet." She laughed. "Talk about going out of my comfort zone. Interestingly, I did list that as a possibility, although it was last and under my column of hardest changes. I can't imagine living in a third-world country without running water or air conditioning, even if it is only for a month."

"I'm sure there are other options although the biggest need would be in areas of poverty. It would be tough initially, but once you got used to it, my guess is the rewards would far outweigh the lack of amenities."

"Oh, this from a world-renowned fashion photographer who doubtless stays at the Ritz or Four Seasons when spanning the globe."

"I only stay in those places if my employer books it and is paying. If not, I stay in hostels."

"Why would you do that?"

"I meet more interesting people. Besides, I don't always want to stay in the same hotels as the models, hair, and makeup people. They tend to hang out together at night and hit the clubs. I don't want to appear snobby by not joining them, so I don't put myself in that position."

"I can assure you, they think you're snobby by not staying in the same hotel. I know I would."

Leave it to Alyssa to highlight the flaw in his thinking.

He pointed his camera at her face and snapped.

"Hey. Some notice, please."

She put her hands on her hips and scowled. So he took another picture.

"Why do you do that? I'm going to have to delete all the photos I don't approve of."

The broad smile on her face belied her words, and he couldn't contain his laugh. She leapt at him in an effort to take his camera, but it was around his neck.

"Don't choke me," he sputtered as he deflected her efforts by picking her up and spinning her around. "It wouldn't look good to have a murder at Glenn Pines."

Her laughter echoed around him, and Gabe couldn't remember a time when he'd been this carefree and happy. They ended up on the ground, her beneath him on a soft patch of grass—their landing spot. He caught her gaze with his, and all mirth vanished as he was sucked into those brown depths, his lips mere inches from hers, her limbs tangled with his.

He lowered his head and captured her mouth, hungry for this connection. Passion flared in a nanosecond, and she kissed him back with equal thirst.

"Hey, you two. Get a room."

Gabe's head shot up. Eric's chuckle echoed through the group of hikers trailing behind him.

He sat up, pulling Alyssa with him, heat burning his face. "We were looking for a four-leaf clover," he called to the group.

"Good luck with that," retorted Eric, a silly grin on his face.

"Sorry," he whispered to Alyssa as he stood, then gave her his hand to help her up. "I didn't mean to give anyone the wrong impression. At least not until I know what impression we're giving to each other. Did you think about what I said last night?"

She avoided his eyes and moved away from him. "Of course. That's why I couldn't sleep." She attempted a smile, but it didn't work.

This could all be going in the wrong direction, but he had to know. "What decision did you reach?"

"That you're not the right person for me." Her milk-chocolate eyes held sadness, and he felt the kick to his heart.

"Oh." He swallowed, misery clogging his throat.

He should have had this conversation at breakfast so they weren't stuck out on a trail over a mile from their starting point.

She moved into his space and traced delicate fingers over his cheek, sending electricity to every cell within. Her floral scent competed with the grasses and shrubbery surrounding them, and he inhaled her sweetness.

"Despite that," she continued in a sultry whisper, "I want to spend more time with you while we're here. At the end of the week, we'll talk about what our future holds."

Had he heard her correctly? He studied her eyes, gleaming with a mixture of joy and caution. "You're willing to try it? Us?"

He required verbal confirmation in case he was misunderstanding her words, her cues.

"I'm willing to see what happens after we leave Glenn Pines." A shadowy sadness darkened her eyes, as if she already knew the outcome. But he was just given a life raft, and he intended to not only use it, but to pull Alyssa onto it with him.

He dared to breathe as he flitted kisses over her

mouth, her cheeks, her eyes. "We'll make this work," he promised before pulling her into him for a hug.

Doubt flashed through her irises for the merest of seconds. If only he could erase that uncertainty with heartfelt words, but he'd have to show her through his actions. It would take time, but hopefully, she'd give what he needed.

"So are you my boyfriend for the rest of the week?" A teasing smile accompanied a poke to his stomach.

"Absolutely. Which makes you my girlfriend." He took her hand and began walking toward the colorful field. "But right now you're my subject."

She gave him a friendly shove to underscore her disapproval of that word, then stepped back. "I have our map and guidebook." She opened it to the section on flowers in the area. "Let's look for these."

He peered over her shoulder, and the sweet scent of her silken skin inundated his senses. "Let's hang back a little. I don't want to run into Eric's group again. Find the section on birds in your book. We can see what's out here."

They walked slowly, with Alyssa reading aloud about different birds natural to this habitat. They spotted a black-capped chickadee, but a good photo was impossible since it flew away.

"No wonder Audubon killed his birds before drawing them," Gabe said wryly.

"What?" She looked at him wide-eyed.

"They wouldn't sit still, as you can imagine. A very difficult subject to draw since they refused to pose. So he shot whatever bird he wanted to draw. Then he had a captive subject."

"That's extremely cruel."

"He had a purpose. He studied birds in their natural habitat—the way they soared, the way they captured their prey. He didn't want to show birds in a stiff profile view. He painted them in life and death struggles—complete with blood and gore." He pointed to a red-tailed hawk soaring not far away. "His challenge was to create the illusion of life from the dead specimen before him. The detail of their feathers, markings, even their eyes were important to him. So after he shot whatever particular bird he was painting, he would pin and wire it up in a natural position."

"You know an awful lot about this for not being a painter of wildlife."

"I like to read about how other artists—whether painters, sculptors, or photographers—got to be good. It's helpful to me in my work."

"I hope you don't start pinning and wiring your subjects."

He chuckled as he looked through his viewfinder. "It's not necessary with live models. They're good at posing in the same position for long periods of time."

When they reached the field of flowers, Alyssa's smile spread from ear to ear. "Wow. This is incredible."

She entered the field and inspected different blooms, smelling them, touching them with delicate fingers, and she might have even been talking to them, for her lips moved. Gabe knelt and snapped away, seeing exactly what he wanted—pure joy at experiencing one of nature's miracles, without her posing or feeling intimidated by the camera. He switched to his telephoto lens to capture the beauty of her eyes, her face, along with the intricacy of each flower.

"Put your camera down and come here. You have to see how beautiful these are."

He followed her demand, leaving his camera and backpack behind. She knelt next to some pink flowers, their blooms huge.

"These are Michaelmas daisies." She picked up her book and read. "They come in shades of pink, purple, blue, and white and start popping open in late August and continue until the frost."

He crouched down beside her, listening to her melodic voice float over the field, and he ached to kiss her again. But she was enthralled with the beauty around her, and he didn't want to interfere, for he'd be able to replay this video in his mind for years to come.

"You're taking too many pictures. You should try to enjoy what you're seeing instead of looking at everything through a lens."

He took a strand of hair that escaped from her ponytail and placed it behind her ear, his fingers grazing her smooth, silky cheek in the process. "You're right. You're much more beautiful up close and personal."

She pulled back. "To avoid a repeat of our last embarrassing session, we should focus on the purpose of our hike today." Her eyes sparkled as she looked to him for agreement.

"As you wish." He tamped down the raw desire that inundated his every nerve.

They stood and looked at the trail map, picking up a path through the woods. Gabe stuck to Alyssa's request that he observe with the naked eye and kept his camera and lenses stowed in his backpack as they explored. He found himself enjoying this leisurely time more than he thought possible. His habit of automatically reaching for his camera was a little hard to break—a career hazard he'd never even noticed before.

Alyssa read aloud from her book, pointing out different trees and plant life as they moved along. Her brain was like a sponge, taking in all the information she read and recycling it when they came upon the same foliage an hour later.

"We should head back," she said, glancing at her watch. "It will take us a while to reach the dining hall from here."

"You must have a tapeworm in your stomach. I've never met a woman who could eat so much."

She elbowed him. "Of course not. Your model friends don't eat at all. Maybe a piece of lettuce here and there."

"My model friends," he echoed, shaking his head. "I told you I don't hang out with them between shoots."

"Except for the ones you dated."

She had him there. "Dated is the operative word. A relationship has been totally absent."

"So you what—went out to dinner, had a piece of lettuce—then took her to bed?"

He chuckled, shaking his head to negate her impression. Her joking fueled his craving for her beyond reason. He ached to pull her into his arms and gaze into her mocha eyes. Even more, he wanted to take her to bed—now that she brought it up.

He wrangled with his libido, cautioning himself to ignore the erotic images flowing through his brain. But he couldn't turn off the flood once she'd opened the spigot. Perhaps a teasing remark would splash a dash of cold water on the conversation. "I can do the same for you. Lettuce. Bed. It works."

The laughter disappeared, and Alyssa faced him. "I…I don't know what to say to that."

He wanted to kick himself for being so cavalier about what should have been a sincere discussion. He tossed his teasing demeanor. "The preferred answer would be I'd like that, too." He smoothed the furrow in her brow with his fingers and gazed into her now sober but still mesmerizing eyes. "No pressure." He smiled, even though a lead weight dropped in his stomach. "I didn't mean to make all my past encounters sound so careless or casual. And I certainly don't want you to think that if you agreed to be with me, it would be the same."

He struggled to find the right words to explain his newly enlightened outlook. "While I want nothing more than to make love to you, I would also like to be in a relationship, to share adventures or just alone time with you. Which was never something I thought about before. My career was my world. But things have been shifting within me lately. I've been thinking about how nice it would be to come home to the person I adore instead of an empty apartment." He would love that person to be Alyssa, but saying those words out loud would make him too vulnerable.

"You want what everyone wants. I'd like that, too. My problem is that I make bad choices. Your problem is that you're never in the same place long enough to establish a real connection."

"Is that why you believe I'm not the right person for you?"

A deep sadness settled onto her beautiful face. "Without a doubt."

He took her hands in his, willing their connection thus far to soften that barrier until he could make it crumble. He needed to find the solution to tame his crazy life. Only then would he be able to convince her he was worth a shot.

"We should head back." He held on to her hand as they started walking. "We need to get you fed."

****

The afternoon class on Transitions was packed by the time Alyssa arrived after her mountain bike session. She spotted Gabe on the other side of the room, but every seat near him was taken. He caught her eye and held up his hands with a shrug, indicating he wasn't able to save her a space. She inched over a few legs and feet to grab a seat on the opposite side of the room and two rows back. At least she had the advantage of being behind so she could sneak a glance over at him without being caught.

Alyssa took copious notes in her notebook during the hour-long class. It gave her something to do besides commit Gabe's features to memory and obsess over their incompatible lives. Plus she'd have good advice to follow when she read through these notes at home—since she wasn't paying one bit of attention to the lecturer in front of the room.

Memories of high school flooded her brain, especially senior year. She had set her sights on Mark Flynn, despite having hated him in elementary school when he stole her favorite green and purple scarf and cut it into pieces. But by the time they were seventeen, he'd made her stomach swoon with butterflies. Eerily like the way she was feeling now when she glanced over at Gabe, some fifteen years later.

Focus, Alyssa.

But focus was absent. Just yesterday morning Sam had told her to take things slowly, get to know Gabe, but not spend all her time with him. So what did she do today?

At least she hadn't gone back to his cabin last night, opting instead to wrestle with the sheets while fantasizing about what they could have been doing. Her mind was filled with him. Even now—especially now—that she could ogle from afar. She shook her head to dislodge his tantalizing aura.

Putting pen back to paper, she rationalized that she looked as if she were paying attention in case the man occupying her thoughts happened to glimpse over at her. Hopefully, he wouldn't ask her any questions about the subject matter after class, because she didn't have a clue.

Nor did she have a clue as to how this was going to work with him.

Chapter Ten

Take one step at a time. You're not moving in with Gabe right now. You're getting to know him to decide if you even want to see him after you both leave Glenn Pines. Take a breath of that clean mountain air, clear your head, and live in the moment. Have fun with him, but not exclusively with him.

Sam's words reverberated in her head as Alyssa walked to the dining hall for dinner. Her morning with Gabe had been magical. Which could shift into tonight if she followed her own heart and not Sam's advice. At least Sam did maintain that she didn't need her permission, and Alyssa could do whatever she wanted. It was up to her. She had the power to move forward with him or let this little dalliance fade into a sweet memory from her time at Glenn Pines.

She stood in line and placed a small piece of salmon on her plate along with a few green beans, then went in search of her could-be lover.

"Hi." She sat across from him, feeling odd, off-balance.

"Is that all you're eating?" he teased. "Did you fill up on junk food before you arrived?"

That set her at ease. "No. I'm…nervous."

His face gentled, and he reached for her hand. "About us?"

She swallowed her angst and shrugged. "It sounds

ridiculous. But I've been having this battle in my head, and there's no clear winner."

Gabe nodded. "I know you've come off two bad relationships and you're afraid of the possibility of another. I understand that. But the more I get to know you, the more enchanted I am. My gut tells me how right we are for each other. It's only been a few days, yet I know we're meant to be. I'm loving what I've been experiencing with you. I don't want to leave here regretting that we ignored our attraction because of fear."

She put her fork down, then looked into his eyes. "I don't want that either."

"Let's eat. Then get out of here. We'll go back to my cabin. Hang out. Talk. I can show you my photographs from today."

She arched her brow. "That sounds like the line *I'll show you my etchings*."

"Does it work?" His smile found its mark.

"It works."

Once they finished dinner, they skirted the perimeter of the dining room to avoid friendly conversations with new acquaintances. Once outside, Gabe guided her to the right of the activity center where a semicircle of cabins stood. Hers was in the opposite direction, far, far away.

They entered his residence for the week, similar to hers in that it had a bed, dresser, couch, and bathroom. His was much tidier with far fewer clothes strewn about. No surprise there.

They sat comfortably on his couch, and he shared his photos with her, explaining not only the location or some artsy tutorial about the way the light hit the subject, but why he thought the photo relevant. Some had a person or group, some just trees, flowers, or the lake. Some were of her. They were all beautiful in their composition, and Alyssa was drawn into the story Gabe seemed to be telling with his photos.

"Why don't you write about this place? Put words to the photos. Then send it to a travel magazine. You have such a gift. I know if I saw these and read the thoughts that go along with them, I'd want to come here."

His chuckle was smothered, inhibited. "That's not what I do."

She shrugged. "So what? You've spent all your time here snapping away. Even though it's not your job, you love it. You get satisfaction out of it. Why not share your gift with those who don't travel much? Like me." She smiled at the thought of reading about this place, or some other more remote location, through Gabe's photos and words. "It can't be hard to write about what you've experienced. I'm listening to you, and I'm enthralled. Even though I've experienced it myself. It's different hearing it from you who saw it through the eye of a lens."

He stared at the clay-brown rug. "That's an interesting thought, but I'm not a writer. I never took a class in journalism or creative writing."

"I don't think you need any specific type of education to write what you felt when you took your photos. Or what you feel when you look at them after the fact. That's the subjective part. The objective part is labeling whatever it is."

"It never occurred to me to do anything with the photos I've taken while travelling." He stared at an image on his LCD display. "I never had time. But you may have a great idea there."

"Glad I could be helpful. It's one more option to consider if you decide to pull back from your high-fashion photography."

"It's so different, though."

"That may be the beauty of it. Doing something totally opposite of what you've been doing. It will give you a break, possibly make you less cranky on photo shoots, and you may be able to turn it into another revenue stream." She leaned over and put her chin in her palm, her thinking pose. "It might also encourage you to take time for yourself between shoots to explore those little towns you love so much. While it's not the fine art photography you talked about the other night, it may be a whole lot more interesting. You could talk to the people in town while you're photographing them. Find out who they are, what they do."

"Are you trying to change my career?" His smile hugged all her cells.

She smiled back. "Now wouldn't that be some feat. But the answer is no. Only throwing out another idea to consider."

He took her hands in his and forced her to face him. "It would be a whole lot more fun if you did it with me."

"I don't travel, remember?"

He leaned in, placing his forehead against hers. "That can be remedied. But right now I'd rather discuss how beautiful you are. In the dim light of this rustic room, you're the only thing I see. You're everything I need." He inhaled. "And more."

His gaze branded her skin and stole her breath as

his fleeting kiss pulled her into a dreamlike aura, a halo of stars surrounding him, guiding her to his light.

She could no longer fight the ember of desire. His words ignited a spark deep within, and that one little kiss detonated an explosion, turning her emotions into a forest fire.

Alyssa brushed her lips over his, softly teasing, until she took more and more, drinking him in, breathing his musky scent, imprinting her soul on his.

Strong arms pulled her closer, but her busy hands kept them inches apart as she quickly unfastened each annoying button on his flannel shirt before splaying it open, desperate to feel his skin, his heat. She placed her palms on his bare chest, and untamed want moved through her with hasty efficiency. He drew her sweater over her head, and her hair spilled around her bare shoulders. He stood and pulled her up with him, then shrugged out of his shirt, allowing it to fall on the floor next to her sweater. His firm hands on her waist inched over the swell of her hips before undoing the clasp, then the zipper of her pants. Her stomach muscles jumped as teasing fingers fluttered over her now bare abdomen.

"Beautiful," he whispered, dragging black denim down her legs.

He looked up at her with eyes blazing fire as she stood in only her black lace bra and bikini underwear. And instead of feeling vulnerable, she felt desired.

He quickly discarded the rest of his clothing before drawing her to his bed. Lying beside her, he brushed his fingers along the swell of her breast before pulling the lacy cup down and laving her aching nipple. She moaned and arched her back, giving him more as his hand cupped and fondled the delicate, exposed skin.

She ran her hand through his soft hair, pulling him up to her mouth for one of his earth-shattering kisses. His shaft pressed against her belly, and she maneuvered beneath him so he could rock against the thin wisp of her bikini panties, sending waves of euphoria through her being.

He unclasped her bra and dragged her panties off before reaching over to the nightstand, opening the drawer, and pulling out a condom.

The command to hurry was on her lips, but she held it in. He ripped open the foil and sheathed himself, kneeling before her in splendid glory.

Hot palms massaged the inside of her thighs, pushing them wider with each pass, teasing her as his thumb brushed over her opening. A cry of impatience escaped, and he answered with his penetrating fingers.

A growl emanated from his throat. "You are so ready," he breathed, maybe panted.

He inched into her slowly, and she welcomed the exquisite sensation.

His magnetic eyes connected with hers, and he kept that bond as he thrust in and out, never disconnecting from her soul. The emotion was so powerful, so intense, she knew without a doubt she was falling in love with this man. With that realization, waves of orgasmic pleasure built and built until they crashed through her like an avalanche. Her inner walls spasmed in explosive enchantment, taking Gabe right along with her.

So much for protecting herself.

****

She breathed softly in sleep, spooned against him, her long brunette hair lying over his shoulder. When Gabe booked this week at Glenn Pines, his goal had been to spend time on his own, photographing, contemplating his life, making small talk at lunch and dinner. That's it.

Then he'd met Alyssa, the nymph in his arms.

Now all he wanted to do was spend every waking and sleeping hour with her. In trying to come to his senses, he'd invited Dorthea to sit with him at dinner last night. They had a lot in common, both artists and city dwellers who spent most of their time on their craft.

But she didn't shine like Alyssa. During dinner, his gaze strayed all too often to the object of his craving as he watched her talk animatedly with Missy and Conrad, all the while longing to be part of their conversation instead of his.

Tonight, he couldn't drag her out of the dining room fast enough. Sure, he wanted to jump into bed with her. Who wouldn't? But he loved her depth. She challenged him, made him laugh, helped him with his fear of heights, and encouraged him to put his camera down.

She also tried to get him to think outside the box where his career was concerned. While he'd only considered one option in his quest to travel less, she pushed him to think of others—even if they were far-fetched—like sending his sightseeing photos to a travel magazine and writing about his experiences. Even though he'd probably never do it, she had an inspirational effect on him.

In listening to the options she'd listed for herself, he realized that even though most of them weren't in her comfort zone, she would at least consider them. It opened up the world to her—despite her fear of stepping out into that world.

She was refreshingly unguarded with her thoughts and feelings. Guileless. He loved that she didn't play games, that she didn't hide her past mistakes.

She also *felt* more than any human being he'd met thus far. She was so afraid to take this step with him. But he cared about her concerns, what she wanted. She was infinitely more than he bargained for.

Could he really be falling for her this quickly? They'd met four days ago. This was insane.

He brushed his hand over her smooth shoulder and dragged his fingers through silky tresses. So beautiful.

And possibly even life-changing.

****

Alyssa smiled down at him, lifting her head from his chest. "Now that's a nice way to wake up this morning."

"I couldn't agree more." Gabe ran his hands down her arms, connected with her fingers, and brought them to his lips. "Much better than sun salutations in the exercise room."

"We definitely burned more calories." She unfolded her legs and stretched beside him. "I have my whole day planned. Would you like to join me?" She slipped out of bed and headed for the shower, calling over her shoulder. "Feel free to join me in here as well."

That wouldn't take any convincing at all. "I'm right behind you."

While standing under the slow trickle of water, she took his face in her hands, as if to get his attention. "I'm hungry."

"Well there's a surprise."

"I couldn't eat last night. I was too worried about the night to come. I hadn't yet decided whether I would go to bed with you."

"I'm glad you made the right decision."

"The other night you were sitting with a beautiful artist from New York City. Are you interested in her?"

He took her chin in his fingers and looked directly into her eyes. "Absolutely not. She doesn't come close to you." He swallowed the words he shouldn't say as they bubbled up in his throat. "I had dinner with her because you'd been absent most of the day. You even skipped breakfast, which is very unlike you, given your tapeworm. I was giving you the room you wanted." He smiled. "There is no one else here, or anywhere, that has my attention. I'm crazy about you, Alyssa." At least he didn't say the L word.

"Good. Because I'm feeling the same way about you. So here's the day's plan. Breakfast. Tennis. Team Challenge at the obstacle course. Lunch. Connection to Vitality and Happiness. Then some African Drumming."

"Is that all? Haven't you missed a half hour in there somewhere?"

"Nope. It's all accounted for. And we better get going so we can eat and get to the tennis courts on time." She squeezed the water from her hair and grabbed a towel.

"When do I get you to myself?"

"Tonight. After the game room. There's a dance, and I love to dance."

"You're killing me. I didn't come here to be social. And I don't dance." He turned off the water and found only a small towel left to dry himself with. "Hey. You stole my towel."

"I know. I guess if we're going to stay together the next three nights, we're going to have to bring our own towels to each other's room."

Perfect answer. She was planning ahead. With that now a given, of course he could go to the game room and watch her dance.

Breakfast and tennis were a breeze, but now they were heading to the team challenge with fifteen others.

"Is it really necessary to do this challenge?" Gabe was definitely less of a team player than most, and now he was going to have to coordinate with other team members to do whatever it was they had to do. He might even have to cede control.

Alyssa gave him a playful push as they walked through the woods toward their destination. "That's what this place is all about. Taking us out of our comfort zones to see what we're capable of."

He grabbed her hand and kissed her knuckles. He did have fun playing doubles tennis, a game he hadn't played in years. Like the many things he had given up in his life for his career—fun activities had been the first to go. When had he become so mono-focused?

After a few practice rounds, he got his swing back—a little rustier but acceptable.

"Hey, guys, wait up." A familiar voice called from behind, and he turned.

"Edie. How's it going?"

"Good." She rushed to catch up. "You two seem cozy." A satisfied smile crossed her lips.

Gabe released Alyssa's hand as if to deny their connection, but Alyssa laughed. "Gabe doesn't want you to know."

"That's not true," he defended. And to prove his point, he took Alyssa's face in his hands and kissed her on the mouth.

The rest of the group, who'd been witnessing the exchange, started clapping, and heat blazed in his cheeks.

Alyssa arched her brow, surely wondering what was going on with him. He didn't know himself. It must be all those happiness seminars hovering over him.

Edie effervesced over his out-of-character exhibition. "I knew it. I knew you two would get together. I saw it in both of your eyes the first time you met. There was this really strong connection. I could feel it while being around you." She beamed as if she were the one who'd made it happen. "And then I saw you both disappear after dinner last night. Conrad said he was supposed to have a game of ping-pong with you, Alyssa, but he doubted you'd be back."

Alyssa jumped in and took Edie aside for an almost-private conversation, although Gabe was close enough to hear.

"Edie, remember what I said the other day? Talk a little slower. Take breaks. Listen to others."

Edie blushed. "I know. I have been trying. It works sometimes. I have to think about it, though."

"So think about it now." Alyssa smiled, taking the bite out of her comments.

Gabe loved that Alyssa tried to help Edie with her social skills. Another point in her favor, as if he required more.

Edie nodded. "Will do. Thanks."

Alyssa put her arm around Edie's shoulders as if to prove she was her friend despite the life lesson.

"Okay, group." Cody, the course director, took charge. "Everyone listen up. The first thing we're going to do is the blindfold trust walk. All of the activities this morning involve teamwork, trust, and communication. We have fifteen people today. For this exercise, break into five groups of three. One of you will put on a blindfold, and the other two will direct that person whether to walk left, right, pick up their foot, or whatever so he or she doesn't trip, fall, or step on any of the obstacles. We're going to be over at that field to the left. As you can see, there's nothing dangerous—some branches, logs, rocks, that sort of thing. Each group will be in a different area. Each of you will take a turn with the blindfold for about ten minutes. Then we'll meet back here to debrief."

Cody handed out the blindfolds and sent the groups to their designated spot.

Gabe took the blindfold and put it on Alyssa first. He wanted to see how the challenge worked before he donned the eye mask. Edie quickly joined their unit, and she spun Alyssa around to disorient her, as instructed.

When Edie tried to take over the instructions to Alyssa, Alyssa reminded her, "Edie, this is a team. I need to hear from Gabe, too."

"Do you mind if I take a few photos?" he asked. "I thought I might write up a piece about my experiences here this week and do a photo documentary to go with it."

"How nice of you to ask this time." Alyssa smiled sweetly, looking adorable with the blindfold on, her ponytail swinging as she turned in his direction. "And you're taking my advice. What is happening to Gabe?"

He chuckled. Edie wasn't the only one learning social skills from their resident nurse. Then he moved into her space and whispered in her ear. "Keep the blindfold for tonight. We can play our own trust game."

Her smile faltered. "Oooohhhh. That sounds interesting."

He kissed the tender spot on her neck—her lilac scent and fantasies of the night to come rocketing straight to his groin.

"No touching," yelled Cody from the sidelines.

"Busted." Gabe moved away from Alyssa, his hands up to show Cody he wasn't violating the rule. With his hands, anyway.

Gabe and Edie took their turns, and when the entire group met up, most agreed they were tentative at first in trusting the others, but after a few minutes that hesitance diminished.

"Next, we're going to do the Giant's Finger challenge. Break up into three groups. Try to mix it up a bit. Alyssa and Gabe, you need to be on two different teams."

Really? Were they in high school? Gabe shook his head but followed instructions.

Cody continued with the rules. "There are three ten-foot poles over there. We call them the Giant's Fingers. Here are three rings." He gave one to Edie, one to Alyssa, and one to Gabe as if to assure they would be on different teams. "With your group, you need to get the ring on the giant's finger without touching the finger. You can't use any implements either. Only your brains and your bodies. Good luck."

Each team walked to their respective *finger* and discussed how they were going to accomplish their task.

"The only way I can see this happening," said Gabe, "is if two women get on the shoulders of two men and the person on the ground hands one of the women the ring. Then the two women can take turns tossing it until one of them gets it over the finger."

They all agreed, choosing who would take each position. Although it sounded easy enough, the ring was heavy and very hard to toss over the finger. Eagle eyes Cody was making sure no one touched the pole, and if they did, they had to get down and start all over.

A cheer rose up from Alyssa's team as their ring slid down the Giant's Finger. How had they done it so quickly? He'd been too busy working with his team to watch the others, sure his team would come out on top.

They moved on to two other activities before their session came to an end. Everyone enjoyed the challenges, proven by the laughter and banter still happening amongst the groups.

Cody brought them all together. "Tomorrow's challenge is a little more physical with the Team Wall, the Human Ladder, and the Two-line Bridge. Hope to see you there."

Alyssa came over to Gabe, beaming. "How'd you like it?"

"Surprisingly, it was good."

"Did you get any photos?"

"A few. I was too busy trying to help our team win. But maybe I can get more tomorrow."

"You're going to sign up?" She looked surprised.

"Aren't you?"

"It's part of my schedule."

"Why are you stunned that I'd come back?"

"You don't like to collaborate, and these games are all about that."

Her words hit home, and he came close to denying them. But he couldn't. She was right. He was a solitary guy, not only in his work, but also in his pleasure pursuits. He'd come here to spend time alone—hiking, kayaking, photographing. He'd initially joined the hike last Sunday to take photos of people enjoying nature, not necessarily to commune with them. The kayak races and some of the other challenges were a great way to exercise.

And then he got to know Alyssa. She'd kept him coming back for more.

"How did you win the Giant's Finger challenge?"

Her breezy laugh filtered through him and took up residence in his being.

"We took the first few minutes to throw out ideas—to hear from all the team members. Then we combined two of the ideas. While we were talking, the other two teams were already trying to toss the ring over the finger. We had a similar plan as your team. Two women got on the shoulders of two of the men, and the one person on the ground handed the ring up. But the two women on top of the men worked together, not individually, to get the ring over the finger since the ring was so heavy. It only took one try." She glowed at their victory.

He should have known Alyssa would have encouraged hearing different options. That was the way to win. These games were all about accomplishing the goal through teamwork.

"The second day here we talked about how you collaborate at the hospital, and I was a little skeptical. I always believed that someone had to be in charge. But seeing your method in action is a powerful lesson."

"Well, thank you, Sutton." Her eyes glistened with pleasure over his compliment.

"You're welcome, Beckman." He snaked his arm around her waist and pulled her into him, planting a kiss on her forehead.

The no-touching rules no longer applied.

Chapter Eleven

"We finally made it to the game room together," Alyssa enthused as she took in the crowd of over sixty people already there, and more were headed from the dining room because it was dance night.

Music played from the speakers, not too loud yet, but with a good beat. A DJ hovered over his equipment, listening intently through earphones. Alyssa loved to dance, and her body moved to a Michael Jackson hit. Gabe stood beside her, perusing the same scene, his camera conspicuously missing. People played pool, ping-pong, and pinball, but most were waiting for someone else to hit the dance floor before venturing out.

"I'm going for a walk or something." Gabe's discomfort rose to his surface, whether at the crowds milling about or the thought of having to dance, Alyssa didn't know.

"Please stay." She entwined her fingers with his. "Dance with me."

A smirk crossed his face. "The only place I want to dance with you is between the sheets."

"Is that so?" A thrill ran through her, but she wasn't ready to give in to those carnal pleasures yet.

Just then the lights dimmed, and the sound increased by several decibels. "Uptown Funk" streamed through the room, and the crowd easily moved from the sidelines to the dance floor.

“Come on.” Alyssa dragged Gabe out to join the masses.

The pulsing thump moved through her core, and she was in her element—finally an activity she knew something about. “I Gotta Feeling” followed, and she sang along with the Black Eyed Peas, knowing every word that went with every beat.

Gabe’s initial hesitance disappeared after a few minutes of following her moves. She couldn’t contain her smile as he started to get more into it, his innate rhythm shining through. Why had he always been so opposed to dancing?

After a while, he asked for a break, and they moved over toward the game tables.

Conrad’s booming voice called to her. “Alyssa. I do believe you owe me a game. What happened to you last night?”

She nodded toward Gabe. “He kidnapped me. Sorry.”

Conrad winked. “I don’t blame him.”

He handed her a paddle, and they got down to serious business as Missy cheered for Conrad and Gabe for her. She pulled it out at the end and whooped in celebration.

“I still have it,” she preened. “I can’t wait to tell my sisters.”

Just then “Billie Jean” began playing, one of her favorite songs. Alyssa started dancing in place, moving her hips, waving her arms, and singing. Music took her to her happy place, and having Gabe with her tripled her joy.

Gabe laughed. “You’d think she had a few too

many," he said to Missy and Conrad. "But there's nothing to drink here, so that can't be it."

"She's just an exuberant person," Missy noted. "A great quality." Her wink was meant for Gabe.

Gabe drew Alyssa toward the dance floor. "I can't let you dance alone, but I'd feel better amongst a crowd than on the sidelines."

"Whatever it takes."

"You must have magic powers that keep me in your orbit." His grin buoyed her spirits.

The next song was a slow one. "Did you bribe the DJ?" she teasingly accused.

"I should have."

He pulled her into his arms, and hot strength tamed by tenderness stirred through her.

"This is nice," she whispered, her voice husky with desire.

He bent his head and kissed her mouth. "I'll say. I'm never going to complain about dancing again. It's excellent foreplay." Green eyes sparkled as she gazed into them.

She fleetingly thought that it was Friday night already, and a gloom so deep strangled her heart, threatening her high. She pushed it away and found his lips with hers, drinking him in, begging for some divine intervention to make this work out.

He slid his mouth to her ear, sending delicious shivers through her blood.

"I want to ravage you."

She almost lost her footing—and her breath. They stopped dancing as he held her close—an island in the middle of the crowded floor.

"Please do," she rasped.

With her consent ever so vocal, he guided her from their island to his oasis.

****

He was doomed.

Gabe stared at the ceiling as dawn broke, casting dim light where the shade didn't quite cover the window. His arm had fallen asleep under Alyssa's head, but he didn't want to awaken her, for they hadn't gotten to sleep until well after two.

He smiled to himself as the video of him dancing with Alyssa to some Rhianna song played in his head. He never danced. Not at high school proms, not at college frat parties, not at friends' weddings. But all Alyssa had to do was take his hand, and he was a goner. Interestingly, it was fun, too. He assumed he'd feel awkward, uncoordinated, but as long as he took his cues from the dancing queen, it came easily.

Better yet was slow dancing. He must have been crazy all those years past to not even try it. What could be better than holding a beautiful woman close while swaying to the rhythm of a love song?

Of course he wouldn't have felt the same with merely any woman. It had to be Alyssa.

He studied her face. Dark, thick lashes framed closed lids. Soft, flawless skin covered smooth cheeks. Delicate, feathered eyebrows arched over her eyelids, and full lips rested together in repose. She looked beautiful in sleep but even more so when she smiled at him, her mocha eyes flashing, her mouth inching up into a wide grin, her perfect white teeth gleaming. Maybe they weren't absolutely perfect. Her bottom front tooth was slightly crooked, overlapping a hair, making her even more stunning.

The angel in his arms challenged him, changed him. She took his camera out of his hands on several occasions and stowed it in his backpack, telling him to experience life in real time. Her admonition always came with a smile and sometimes a kiss. She was teaching him how to have fun, whether on the obstacle course, at a touchy-feely class, or in the game room.

If he hadn't met Alyssa, he would have kept to himself and taken endless numbers of photos. He would have never taken the seminar on Transitions.

Alyssa stirred, then opened her eyes. "You're awake." A slow smile inched over her lips. "What time is it?"

"Six fifty."

She jumped up, her feet hitting the floor in record time. "Sun Salutations is at seven." She rummaged through the drawer he gave her and found yoga pants and a top.

"We can lie here and look out the window," suggested Gabe, already feeling the chill from lying in bed alone. "Eventually the sun will come up over the trees."

"Yeah, at ten. That's too late." She turned toward him, her hair tangled and sexy. "What are your plans today?"

"If I can't convince you to stay in bed, which clearly I haven't, I guess I'll go to Sun Salutations with you. Not sure I'll be able to do any of those poses." He shook his head as he quickly dressed. "Sometime today I want to work on a story to go with a few of the photos I took. Your suggestion got into my head. My friend Adam, who has the travel magazine, may be interested in publishing it."

Her flashing smile said it all. “I’m glad you’ll be sharing at least one of your experiences. Maybe it will lead to others.”

“In full disclosure, I have an ownership interest in Adam’s magazine. I invested most of my savings in *American Traveler* about six months ago. In order to replace those savings, I’ve taken on more international assignments than usual. Which probably added to my stress. And crankiness.” He studied her face, searching for any negative thoughts about this revelation. He hadn’t been sure that sharing it now was the best idea he ever had since she was thinking more positively about continuing to see him after this week. But keeping a secret was never a good way to start a relationship.

“If you have an interest in a travel magazine, why haven’t you published your photos in it in the past?” Her brow furrowed. Adorable.

“It’s not what I do. Besides, I’m a silent partner. I have nothing to do with what goes into the magazine.”

“Oh.”

Not wanting her to think too much about the issue, or go down the road of asking how long it would take before he recouped his savings, he looped back to their schedule. “There’s an astrology class at one that I might look into. Would you like to try it?”

“Sure. What about the obstacle challenge? We told Cody we’d be back today, and it’s part of my schedule.”

“I’m in if you’re going.” When had he become such a follower? “But I’m taking my camera if we do.” He had to assert some independent thought. “I’ll get a few photos for my story. Can I interest you in a rowboat ride later?"

"Absolutely. When can we squeeze that in?"

"How about four?"

"Perfect." She kissed him on their way out the door, but he held her back, stealing more.

"I'm so glad I met you," he murmured against her lips.

The serious intenseness in her eyes as she stroked his jaw was the only response he needed.

Walking down the path toward the exercise studio shouldn't have elicited a kick to his gut, but it did. They'd both be leaving in two days. How could he feel this strongly about Alyssa after only knowing her for such a short time? This couldn't be real.

Yet his heart ached at the thought of their parting ways. They needed to come up with a plan for the future. Although every moment today was accounted for.

For the two hours following their astrology class, Gabe holed himself in his cabin to work on his story. He'd left Alyssa to explore the grounds with a promise to meet her at the lake at four. He'd already shuffled through hundreds of photos and tagged the ones he thought would go with the words he wanted to write about Glenn Pines. At least he could use his laptop to compose a document, although he wouldn't be able to download the photos onto his computer with no internet service.

Making it personal would surely draw more readers while describing the many challenging activities would give the full flavor.

I had a week off with nothing planned, a rare occurrence in my job as a high-fashion photographer.

Being October in New York, it wasn't cold enough to dream of an island vacation, and I had been travelling for the last two months throughout Europe and Asia on photo shoots, so the lure of a foreign land was definitely absent.

Since it was autumn, the leaves were spectacular in the northeast. Why not go to a retreat-type place where I could hike, kayak, and take photos of something other than very thin models in couture fashion? Maybe I could even think about my future.

He typed fast and furiously for the next hour and a half, intermittently studying photos of Alyssa amid the flowers, sitting on a log, staring off into the trees, paddling the canoe in front of him. But his favorites were from the first day before he even knew her. When Missy had fallen and injured her arm. Alyssa was bent over her, taking charge, compassion on her face, confidence in her hands as she tested Missy's injuries. Her long ponytail hung over one shoulder, but strands had escaped and framed her face. Her beautiful brown eyes looked into Missy's, and Missy smiled back at her, even though she had to be in pain. Alyssa's manner did that.

He went back to his laptop and told his story, bringing in the various people he met, describing the classes he'd taken, the challenges he encountered, but always coming back to Alyssa. He was writing a love story when his intent was to write a travelogue. Worse yet, he feared his love story was not going to have a happy ending. He'd have to work on that. His time at Glenn Pines wasn't over. He had the rest of today and all day tomorrow. He'd end his piece with hope.

Because that's all he could do.

****

Alyssa nearly sprinted to the boat launch at three fifty-five. She hadn't seen Gabe in the last two hours. How could she be this eager to meet him when she'd spent almost the entire day with him already?

Gabe stood at the boat launch looking ever so gorgeous—like a sports enthusiast. He wore a long-sleeved zip-up over his toned and tanned body with lightweight pants that could morph into shorts if it got too hot. *American Traveler* should put him on the cover. That would increase sales. His unruly hair blew in the wind, and aviators covered his eyes. She ran up to him and threw her arms around his neck, giving him a powerful kiss.

"Wow. I'm going to make sure to put more than one break in our day tomorrow if this is the welcome I get."

"No breaks tomorrow. It's our last day together." She kicked the depressing thought into the lake and smiled at Gabe.

"I suggested rowboating because we can be face-to-face, and you don't have to do a thing."

"I don't have to row?" How did she not know this? "I'm liking the idea more and more."

"I'd like to take some photos while we're out there. If that's okay with you."

She snaked her arms around his neck and swooped in for another kiss. Not just any kiss. She definitely made it worth his while as evidenced by a low moan coming from his throat.

"We don't have to go boating," he offered, gazing straight into her eyes and trapping her there. "Your cabin isn't far from here."

"Very tempting. How about if we go there after our boat ride? I want to hear about your story."

"You're on." His smile stroked every inch of her heart, and if women today swooned, she would have.

He helped her into the boat, then removed his top, wearing a tight T-shirt beneath. He began rowing out toward the center of the lake, and her focus strayed to his biceps flexing with each pull. Maybe she should have taken him up on his suggestion to forgo their outing.

Shifting her attention from his physique, she shared her investigation from the last two hours. "There's a computer in a little room off the reception area. I was able to connect to the internet and did some research on Doctors Without Borders."

His brow furrowed at her admission, but he remained silent.

"I told you it's in my column of options that is the least likely. You had suggested a nonprofit in a foreign country, and after being here for a week and doing so many things I never thought I'd do, I decided to at least look into something way out of my comfort zone. I probably won't do it." She shrugged, but the sense of satisfaction she reaped from only perusing the website was worth it. "If I'm ever going to fly out of my cocoon, now's the time. Well…not right away, but once my mom gets through her chemo and she's doing better. I'm single, I'm in a transition period, and it could be the thing that allows me to see a little piece of the world."

Gabe's jaw tightened. "Go on."

"I doubt I would ever pull the trigger and do something like that. As I told you, I've never been off the East Coast. When I think of travelling, which is rare, I picture going to London or Venice or Barcelona. Third world countries have never been anywhere near a thought. But I do want to challenge myself. I simply don't know in which direction I'll go."

"Maybe you should start closer to home. You said you might consider a job at a hospital out of state. How about New York City?"

She chuckled. "That is also on my list. And of course, I've been there many times before. School trips to the museums. Shopping with my girlfriends. My friend Samantha lived there until recently. She's a lawyer. Was at a big firm on Park Avenue. But she met someone in Crescent Beach, at the Jersey shore. She moved in with him last year and married in May."

"Does she still practice law?"

"Yes. In Red Bank. A nice small town near Crescent Beach."

"Another defector." He didn't smile when he said that.

"Is everything okay? You seem off. Not your usual controlling self." She smiled, attempting to get a rise out of him.

"I am off. As well as trying to take control. I've been thinking of ideas to keep you close. Which is why I'm suggesting that you apply to hospitals in the city. There are several. I'm sure you'd get a job right away with your credentials. And it would be something new, different. Maybe all you need is a change of scenery."

Her stomach fluttered. He wanted them to be together after this week. She wanted that, too. But at what cost? "I never thought about living in the city. It's too big. And intimidating." Alyssa was not a big-city person, choosing instead to stay in the town where she grew up. Maybe boring to some, but predicable, which met her needs. “I suppose I could consider it. After my mom is better. Along with everything else. It wouldn’t really help us much, though. You’re rarely there.”

“I’m considering other options for myself as well.” He rolled his neck, as if tense. “You said along with everything else. What else are you thinking about?”

“Transferring to the oncology department at my hospital, Nassau General, and eventually getting my certification. It requires working in the field for one thousand hours and taking a course, then a test. From there, I could either stay at the hospital or work at a cancer care center. I’ve been thinking about this change more and more, especially now that my mom has cancer.”

They rowed in silence for a while, then he locked the oars, and they came to a standstill. He took his camera from his backpack and captured a blue heron flying close to the lake. She didn’t pay much attention to the focus of his lens, for she was distracted over their conversation.

He wanted her to be close. That was a good thing. But she didn’t hear him offering to move to her town. He could get to an airport from there as easily as from New York City. She gazed out over the lake toward the trees, her brain tilted in confusion. She’d come to Glenn Pines to figure out her life in an organized, rational manner. Meeting Gabe had thrown all her reasonable options up in the air before they crashed down into one big messy pile.

“What are you thinking?” he asked, clicking away in her direction.

"We both came here to contemplate a change. For me, I was also hoping to learn to be more independent, to stand on my own." She didn't say "without a man," but that had been her goal. "Having met you, I'm struggling to keep my life on an even keel. Instead things are getting more complicated." She inhaled and gazed out at the shimmering lake. "You came here to take a break and talk yourself into falling in line. At some point you realized you may want to take a different path. We should probably make our decisions, our transitions, independent of each other. Then, once we figure ourselves out, we can see if we fit into each other's lives."

Stating their issues out loud highlighted both of their quandaries and depressed her even more. Especially her conclusion—despite the sense it made.

Gabe put his camera down and focused on her. "I agree we came here for our own reasons. But you changed me, Alyssa. Not this place. You opened my eyes to the reality that I have options. I don't have to fall in line. As soon as I save enough money to replace my investment in *American Traveler*, I can pull back from the high-fashion photography that takes me overseas, and focus more on the photography I want to do. You helped me see that as well as other things. I would never have gone to a meditation class or a Spiritual Connection to Happiness class or been part of a team trying to get a ring over a giant's finger. And I certainly would never have danced."

She smiled, remembering his reluctance at first. "I'm really happy that I influenced you to not only take advantage of the offerings here, but to consider your career options." She bit her lip to erase the smile, because what she had to say now was excruciating. "I can't make decisions affecting my life because of a man. I've done it before, and I made very bad decisions. I certainly can't move to New York City because you're there. Or more likely, not there. It's not a place where I feel comfortable. I need to find what will make me happy."

Tears stung the backs of her eyes. All it would take was one look at him before they'd be streaming down her face. She blinked and focused on the trees.

"Look at me, Alyssa."

His words were so tender, so full of the same pain she was feeling, she could no longer hold back. Tears slipped down her cheeks as she turned to him.

"I'm falling in love with you." He held her captive with his gaze, and his words melted through her like warm chocolate syrup.

She didn't trust herself to respond. How could this be happening so fast? "I…I…"

"Shhhh." He held his finger to his lips. "There's no need to say anything."

Her heart nearly broke at his sensitivity. She was falling in love with him, too, but fear of making another mistake kept those words trapped in her throat.

"We have tonight and tomorrow together. Don't shut the door on us yet. Let's keep talking. We could make this work."

His optimism curled around her and steeped her heart in wine. Maybe they could succeed. But they probably wouldn't.

Chapter Twelve

With a pact to spend the rest of their time together, whether with others or alone, they ate dinner with Missy, Conrad, and Edie but declined a trip to the game room.

"The two lovebirds are ditching us," said Conrad, a teasing glint in his eyes.

"They should," confirmed Missy. "They might not be able to see each other too often once they leave here."

Truer words had never been spoken, and Alyssa felt the weight of those words on her soul.

She and Gabe left and picked up several blankets from his room before stopping at hers so she could add a few layers of warmth over her blouse. Then they headed to the lake—and the stars—a show just for them.

"I'm starting to think of this lake as ours." She helped him spread a blanket on the ground and watched as he rolled up two towels for pillows. "Who did you bribe to get extra towels?"

He chuckled. "I took them from your cabin. It's not easy getting extra linens around here."

She sat between his legs, his strong chest her support, his warm arms enfolding her in his bubble. "I never want this night to end," she whispered, gazing up at the vast expanse dotted with millions of twinkling stars.

"I'm right with you." He tightened his embrace and kissed the top of her head.

They sat in silence for a while, thinking their own thoughts, until Gabe spoke his out loud. "When I look at the sky like this and think about the universe, I wonder if there are two people like us sitting under the stars on some other planet, in some other galaxy, enjoying the same view."

"I choose to think we live on the only inhabitable planet. It's too weird to think of others out there. But looking at the night sky does put us in our place. We're so insignificant. A mere pinpoint."

He kissed her temple, then moved down to her cheek. "You're not insignificant to me. You're the only person I need in my universe."

He captured her lips, and she swirled into his world, kissing him back with unrestrained passion boiling deep in her core. She loved him and wanted him to feel her love. Because she couldn't say it. Not when they were leaving each other.

He eased her down to lie beneath him. She opened her eyes and was greeted by a sparkling backdrop, immense and beautiful and wondrous.

"I have the best view," she rasped. "Your eyes and a million stars."

She immersed herself in his deep green orbs, and the stars melted into the background. After inching her hands over his shoulders, she feathered her fingers through soft, brown hair before lifting her head to get lost in another kiss. Her lower body pulsed against his, stirring hot embers into flames. She wanted him, needed him. Desperately.

She tugged his jacket down his arms, then helped him remove some of her layers—the cold no longer an issue. He eased each button out of its hole on her blouse until the cool air whispered over her shoulders, her torso. His warm hands were everywhere, heating her skin like a branding iron. The clasp of her bra released, and he pulled the fabric away, replacing it with his hands, his tongue, his mouth. Flashing sensations zinged through her blood, and she wanted urgently to be one with him. Here. In their place.

She yanked his hoodie over his head, then his T-shirt. "Why do you have so many clothes on?" She laughed.

"I clearly wasn't thinking ahead. And I'm usually pretty good at that."

He unbuttoned his jeans, and she pulled the zipper down.

"All it takes is a little teamwork." She couldn't take her eyes from the bulge in his boxers. "Could you lose the clothes a little faster?"

"Your wish is my command." He stood and undressed, a completely naked god under a canopy of stars.

Then he knelt beside her and helped her attain her own nakedness before lying next to her and gazing into her eyes.

"Kiss me." Her words were husky, needy.

"You're very demanding tonight. I like it." He covered her mouth in a languid kiss, his tongue dancing with hers, his hands roaming over exposed skin.

She placed her palms on either side of his face and searched his eyes as if she could read clear down to his soul. "Come inside of me."

He sprang into action, searching in his jeans pocket for a condom. She laughed as frustration at choosing the wrong pocket came out in a curse.

Within seconds, he nudged her legs apart with his knees and rubbed the tip of his rod at her juncture. She arched toward him, feeling his hardness, his length, overpower her. Desire built until she could no longer exist without him inside her. She guided him, reveling at their oneness amid the beauty of the universe.

Everything around them magnified to the tenth degree. Black night, dazzling pinpoints of light, cool breeze, rustling trees, hooting owls, lapping water—until it all converged into Gabe, the only being she saw, the only touch she felt, the only breath she breathed.

He stroked her walls as they clenched around him, the intensity building until she peaked, and wave after wave of orgasmic pleasure crashed through her body and soul. Her head fell back, and the stars surrounded her as he joined her in the most fantastical sexual coupling she'd ever had. A once in a lifetime experience she would remember until the day she died.

Alyssa clung to him as her muscles relaxed, her breathing slowed. Gabe drew the second blanket around them as they snuggled for seconds, minutes, hours. Time was irrelevant, and all she wanted was for it to stand still.

"I hope Eric doesn't lead a group of night hikers by." His warm chuckle reverberated through her.

"Maybe they already passed. I wouldn't have heard a pack of wolves if they tore through." She caressed his face, tracing the angles of his cheekbones, the strong line of his jaw.

"I love that we've found our own world here." He

hugged her closer, tangling his legs with hers.

Her throat constricted. "I wish we didn't have to leave."

He smoothed her hair behind her ear. "I've been thinking about what we both want to do in the future. After the next few weeks at the fashion shows, I'm going to tell my agent to focus more on studio jobs in the city. I might be able to substitute some of the income I'll lose from travelling less if I can figure out a plan to add fine art photography to my résumé. While I'm doing that, you can be working toward your certification if that's the direction you're going in."

Her heart expanded at his will to make this work. "I know your career is based in New York—" She faltered. "—but I don't think I could ever live there. I need you to know that. I'm really close to my family and don't want to be too far away from them, especially my mom. I love living in that area. I'm not opposed to looking for work at a hospital a little farther north—maybe New Brunswick. Would you ever consider moving to New Jersey and commuting to New York?" She held her breath and bit her lip.

The grimace on his face advised her that moving to New Jersey might be akin to cutting off his arm. "I could consider it." His weak smile had to be a Herculean effort, and she suspected the possibility never entered his mind. Sadness wended its way through her bones.

But if they wanted to continue their relationship, they would both have to compromise. People living in different cities made relationships work all the time—some much farther away than the sixty-five miles that separated them.

"Let's go back to my cabin. It's getting cold." Gabe untangled their clothes and handed Alyssa hers. "I want to show you what I worked on today."

When they arrived at their destination, he consulted a piece of paper. "I've numbered the photos I'd like to use for the piece I'm submitting to *American Traveler*. I wrote a draft of the article that goes with them, but I'm not ready to share that yet. I loved the writing process. Using a different part of my brain." He went through the photos methodically, showing Alyssa his choices. "This one is my favorite."

She was in a field of blooms, crouched down, studying a fringed gentian with the most vibrant blue hue. The side view of her face held a quiet, introspective smile. Anyone seeing this photo would think she was alone, taking in the beauty of nature. In fact, she was in a way. Although Gabe was standing on the edge of the field, she hadn't even noticed he was taking her photo.

"Did you use a special lens for this? I look really close, and I know you weren't near me."

"I used a telephoto lens. I wanted to capture your feelings while you looked at the flowers. I have quite a few."

He advanced through the photos, and she was amazed at the sheer number of pictures he had taken of her.

"Here's another of my favorites. From today."

She was sitting in the rowboat, looking off toward the trees, a sadness shadowing her eyes. She remembered exactly what she'd been thinking. That they should work on their separate goals independently before seeing if they could make it work together.

"You make me look beautiful," she whispered, her voice breaking.

He kissed the side of her head. "The camera doesn't lie."

****

Gabe awoke alone. "Alyssa?" The cabin was infinitesimal, so he could see the entire space except for the bathroom.

No answer.

He tossed the sheets aside and stood. A note was tucked under a book on the dresser.

I couldn't sleep. Going to the reception area to see if I can sneak into the computer room. See you in the morning. Alyssa

It was quarter to seven on Sunday—their last full day here—so he quickly donned his workout shorts and T-shirt. *Guess I'm taking yoga again.* He shook his head. He had no other reason to even consider it, except that she'd be there.

He arrived with four minutes to spare before class, and his eyes trained in on Alyssa stretching. "What happened last night?" he whispered in the quiet studio.

She smiled, but her eyes looked tired. "I kept tossing and turning, and I didn't want to disturb you."

"Were you able to get to the computer?"

"I did. I started looking at the hiring pages on websites of hospitals in New York City. I just don't think I can take that leap." She bit her lip.

He smoothed her brow with his fingers. "No worries." His heart expanded threefold with her openness to consider that option despite her negative views of the Big Apple. He grudgingly moved behind her to his spot since more people were coming into the studio. "I can't believe I'm going to take another yoga class."

"I think you secretly love it. It's such a good morning stretch, and it's very calming."

He did not secretly love it, but he was in love with her, so he muddled through, unable to do half the poses properly. If taking yoga kept him near Alyssa, it was a small price to pay. And he had to keep her near to erase all skepticism.

When class was finally over, he asked, "What are we doing today?"

"Horseback riding is scheduled for this morning." She blanched. "I've never done it before."

"You'll do fine. I'll coach you." He kept things light and teasing so they'd get the most out of their last day together.

"Of course you will." Her smile belied her sarcasm. "This afternoon there's a class on the Art of Mindfulness. It's supposed to teach us how to move away from our habitual patterns to experience a more meaningful, vibrant life."

"Have you been memorizing the brochure again?" He pulled her into him for a hug.

"I love how they put things. Another class I want to take is the Healing Power of Food. That's later today."

"Do they let us taste some samples?"

"I don't think it's one of their cooking classes. But we can do one of those, if you'd prefer."

"I'd prefer to do something outside. The weather is perfect. But I'll let you call it."

If he could solely focus on the present and not get melancholy over leaving tomorrow morning, they could have a great time today. Unfortunately, even with all the mindfulness classes he'd taken this week, reality kept sneaking in and kicking him in the gut.

They headed to the horse paddock and found they were the only two riding along with their guide, Luke. Gabe took his camera out of his bag and started shooting. The horses were beautiful, and Alyssa looked amazing sitting astride Cinnamon, an odd name for an equine, but who was he to say.

The foliage was brilliantly colorful, especially out here, away from the pine woods. The reds and golds of the maple leaves shone magnificently in the sun, and Gabe managed some up-close and personal shots of just leaves—so intricately veined.

But he also snuck in a few of Alyssa while Luke showed her how to handle her horse. For the next two hours, they rode the trails, at times walking, trotting, or cantering. But the most fun was when they finally got to gallop.

Alyssa's hair flew behind her like tawny silk, and her face glowed with exertion but also joy. He couldn't let this picture go, so he stopped in the middle of the paddock, clicking away as Alyssa circled with Cinnamon, having a ball.

"Let me take some of you," she called on one of her passes.

"You'd have to stop to do that." He dismounted his horse.

She pulled on the reins, looking like an expert horsewoman, and trotted over to him. She swung her leg over the saddle and would have jumped, but Gabe reached up and encircled her waist, bringing her down gently against him. He nuzzled her neck and held her close, breathing in her lilac scent. To memorize it.

Turning in his arms, she gave him a quick kiss, then took the camera from him. “Get on Pepper and gallop around. I’ll take your picture.”

He showed her a few buttons on the camera, then followed her instructions. The cool breeze blew through him as he circled the paddock, exhilaration pumping through his blood. He didn’t even pay attention to whether she was snapping away.

“Slow down and head over here. I want to get a close-up.”

“Are you directing me?” He smirked.

“Yes, I am.”

He complied, finding it impossible to wipe the smile from his mouth.

“So much for a cool cowboy shot,” she teased.

“I need a proper hat and boots for that. These jeans and hiking shoes hardly accomplish the right look.”

“You look mighty fine to me,” she drawled.

He swooped down and took the camera. “Get back on your horse. Luke is waiting for us.” He watched as she stepped into a stirrup. “Do you need help?”

“Of course not. I can do *almost* anything on my own.” She chuckled.

“Don’t put thoughts in my head that you’re not going to carry through on.”

Tossing her long mane over her shoulder, she loosened Cinnamon’s reins and kicked his flanks, spurring him to gallop past Gabe. In her wake, she called back to him. “What makes you think I’m not going to carry through?”

He couldn’t catch up fast enough.

Chapter Thirteen

"What are you doing?" Alyssa demanded when Gabe pulled the ping-pong paddle from her hand and gave it to Conrad. "I just won that game."

"I know you did. And I'm very proud of you. I'll have an award ceremony for you later."

She laughed as Gabe tugged her out of the game room and toward the sofa in the reception area where they sank into well-worn cushions.

"I thought I'd never get you away from that table." He kissed the side of her head.

A roaring fire flamed in the stone fireplace, and its warmth as well as Gabe's melted into her being.

"It's not easy to leave when everyone wants to play the champ." She polished her nails against her sweater, then glanced at the flashing amusement in his eyes. "But this is much better." She laid her head on his shoulder, reveling in the peace and calmness after the blaring racket of the game room.

"Being the best has its pitfalls." His eyes crinkled at the corners.

"I'm going to miss seeing you every day. Every night." Seriousness replaced levity, and she snuggled farther into his side. "It's only been seven days since we met. I can't believe how sad I am that it's coming to an end."

"It doesn't have to come to an end, Alyssa. Let's

make a plan, right here, right now. So it's real and not only talk about getting together. Meet me in Rome in three and a half weeks."

"What?" Her heartbeat kicked against her ribs.

"You heard me. Come to Italy."

"Just like that?"

"Just like that. You've never been to Europe. You accomplished so many challenges this week, and you're looking ahead. You said yourself you've been thinking about going to a foreign country."

Excitement at the thought flew through her with only the tiniest nag about pulling off another vacation in less than a month, so close on the heels of this one—plus her anxiety of venturing too far from home. If she could manipulate her schedule to get five days off in a row, she could surely push aside any lingering apprehension and get on a plane—especially if Gabe would be at the other end of her flight. And the thought that she might spend some time with him in one of the world's most fascinating capitals left her breathless.

She spun through her schedule. "I work three days on and four days off, since they're twelve-hour shifts. I usually work overtime, too, but I can get off the list for a week." Her stomach jumped at the possibility. "I could probably trade with one of the other nurses for an additional day. I know it's not the ideal amount of time, but it's something." How fabulous would it be to see that incredible city with the man she was in love with?

"Let's look at a calendar." He dug out a yearly planner—in paper—from his backpack holding his ever-present camera. "I need this for those times when there's no cell service."

"All your important items are in that backpack,

aren't they?" So amusing that he didn't seem to need much.

"If you mean my camera and lenses, then yes. If I throw in a change of clothes and a toothbrush, I'm good to go."

"I assure you I cannot pack that lightly. Even coming here, I brought way too many outfits, not knowing exactly what I'd need or want."

He chuckled. "I know. I saw your room. But if you come to Rome for four or five days, all you'll need is a carryon. I'll tell you exactly what to pack so you won't be bogged down."

"Three and a half weeks from now goes into Thanksgiving weekend. Didn't you say you were going home for the holiday?"

He hit his head with his palm. "I did. And my mom will never speak to me again if I cancel, but this is more important. I'll tell her the shoot ran over."

"I thought you were going to try to change where your family's concerned. Stop putting work before them."

Remorse shadowed his face. "But it's not work this time. It's you."

A pang of guilt ricocheted through Alyssa, but spending five days in Rome with Gabe won out. She'd also be missing Thanksgiving with her family. If she told them the truth, they'd think she was certifiable, falling in love so quickly after what she'd been through.

"How much will it cost? Other than the money I've put aside to buy out the house, I don't have much in savings."

"I'll already have a room. And I have points you could use since I fly so much. We can both work on the follow-up story to the one I'm writing now for *American Traveler*, so it will be a business trip. With plenty of pleasure added in."

His enthusiasm was contagious, and she started to believe in the real possibility of making this trip happen. But it didn't guarantee they'd be able to carry their relationship forward in their day-to-day world.

"Now that that's settled, let's go back to my cabin." Gabe stood and held out his hand to her. "I want to make our last night together at Glenn Pines memorable."

****

They walked back to his cabin in silence, but Gabe couldn't switch off the thoughts running through his head. This had been an incredible week from start to finish, and he didn't want it to end. How had he managed to meet this caring, unworldly, but oh-so-interesting woman at a rustic resort in the Poconos?

He always assumed he'd end up with an artist type, maybe even another photographer who'd understand the demands of his crazy schedule because she'd have a crazy schedule, too. He never dreamed of falling for an ER nurse. Someone who'd never been anywhere outside of the northeastern part of the United States.

They were vastly different. She had a predictable workweek—albeit a schedule that included nights and overtime—working at the same place day in and day out. He moved from state to state or country to country, depending on the job, with no regard for weekdays or weekends.

If he changed direction and only did studio work for the magazines and ad agencies while moving into fine art photography, the first question was would he survive? Would he find the right balance to make him happy as well as successful?

If he could make this work, he'd be more in charge of his schedule, and he could stay put. How wonderful it would be if Alyssa was the person he came home to. But every time he pictured them living together, it was in the city, not in the suburbs of New Jersey. He loved the energy of New York, the culture, the diversity. Not that he'd had much time to experience it in the past few years, but he'd looked forward to when he would. In addition, his livelihood was focused in the city. What if he couldn't convince her to join him there after her mother recovered?

When they arrived at his cabin, he switched off the lamp and pulled Alyssa onto the bed, lying beside her, inhaling her sweet scent as he inched closer and tightened his arms around the woman he didn't want to live without.

"What time is it?" Her voice was low, sexy.

"After eleven."

Time to shut down his thoughts and reawaken his libido, a very easy accomplishment with her in his arms. She burrowed into him, and that's all it took. Finding her mouth with his, he tempted her with the promise of ecstasy, and she followed him willingly.

Her hand strayed over his chest, pulling his shirt up before wandering over his sensitized skin. She inched her leg between his, rubbing against his shaft with her thigh. *Oh yes.*

Gabe slid his hand under her sweater, seeking the clasp to her bra, and once successful pulled the encumbrances over her head so she was at least half nude. He teased her nipples, gently tugging at them until they were peaked and straining against his fingers. A sigh escaped her lips, encouraging him to continue.

She moved on top of him, his erection pushing against the zipper of his jeans, pushing against the vee between her legs. Grinding against him, she leaned forward, and he took her breast into his mouth, greedy for more sighs, more moans.

Reaching between them, he unbuttoned her pants and slid the zipper down before inching them over her hips. "I need your help," he whispered, desperate to get them both naked.

His goddess stood and slithered out of the rest of her clothing as he yanked his off even faster, then grabbed a condom. All he could see was her shadow as she moved from the side of the bed back to her position on top of him. He was so ready.

She teased him by pressing her opening to the tip of his manhood and moved her hips in a slow circle. He held his breath, savoring every ounce of pleasure while at the same time begging for her hot, wet heat to surround and engulf him.

Sinking onto his shaft, she exhaled, digging slender fingers into his shoulders, moving above him in a rhythm of exquisite pleasure.

He held on to her hips, and tiny gasps told him she was close, so he released her and let her guide the pace as she threw her head back, the tips of her long hair brushing his thighs. Her breath caught, and she called out his name as she came, so erotic, so arousing. He exploded within seconds, followed by a dizzying freefall into time and space that he would not soon forget.

She collapsed on top of him, her breathing ragged

against his chest, her soft hair fanned out over his arm—a spirited angel he never wanted to release. He stroked her back, her cheek and brought her hand to his lips and kissed it.

The words "I love you" were precariously close to the tip of his tongue, but they stuck in his throat. Not because he feared putting himself out there again—he'd already said it once—but because he and Alyssa had a long road ahead of them, and serious words would only make it harder for both of them—until they figured this out.

She lay tangled with him the rest of the night. He dozed off and on until dawn peeked through the shade. In a few hours, they would both be on their way home, miles and lives separating them—but with the glimmer of Rome sparking their anticipation.

****

Alyssa heaved her heavy suitcase into the trunk of her car, glancing across the parking lot for Gabe.

Edie appeared instead. "Bye, Alyssa. I'm so happy I met you. I want to thank you for pointing out one of my flaws. I'm still working on it, but I'm getting better."

Alyssa hugged Edie. "It was good to meet you as well. Good luck finding a job."

"Thanks. I made a list of a few places that will be a good fit. I'm going to reach out to my contacts as soon as I get home. I'm not stressing about it as much as when I first arrived. The classes here have been extremely helpful."

"I agree," said Missy, joining them as Conrad wheeled both his and his wife's suitcases over the gravel parking lot. "I would have missed those classes if I hadn't fractured my wrist." She turned to Alyssa. "Thank you for being there for me when this happened. Your calming manner and professional expertise really helped. It was wonderful getting to know you. I especially enjoyed watching you put Conrad in his place at the ping-pong table."

Alyssa looked at both women as a surprising sadness overtook her. She'd probably never see them again. "Maybe we should meet here sometime in the future. We can catch up with each other while wrapping some spiritual and physical wellness around us."

They exchanged email addresses and agreed to a reunion at a date to be determined.

"What are you ladies talking about?" Conrad approached with a smile on his face.

"Our wonderful week here where we made special friends," responded Missy.

"If I'm not mistaken, I think Alyssa has a lot more than a special friend in Gabe." He gave her a wink and a smile.

"Did I hear my name?" Gabe joined the group, his ever-present backpack and a small duffle dangling from his hand.

"You're the winner." Conrad chuckled. "You and Alyssa make a great couple. I see in the two of you a lot of what Missy and I experienced when we first met."

"At least you were at the same law firm in the same city." Alyssa's spirit drooped.

Even though they had a tentative plan to meet in Rome in a few weeks if everything in their worlds aligned, would they really pull it off? And what would come next?

Alyssa hugged Conrad, Missy, and Edie and stood

next to Gabe as they watched them drive off. Alyssa intended to delay her departure until the very last minute, although the melancholy was building much too quickly to be able to enjoy the last of their time together.

"Well." She shrugged. "I guess this is it."

"For now." Gabe lifted her chin with his finger. "Look at me. We are not saying goodbye."

She smiled through unshed tears and nodded, unable to speak.

His eyes shone in the light of the sun like tourmaline crystals.

She stroked his cheek as she connected with his heart. His soul. "This has been an amazing week that I'll never forget." A mere eight days earlier she had questioned the saneness of this trip, praying it wasn't another one of her mistakes. In the end, it had taken her from angry and confused to strong and confident.

He leaned down and kissed her gently on the lips. "I'll never forget it either. You've opened my eyes to possibilities I never contemplated. All while getting to know the most amazing woman I've ever met." He kissed her again. "I'll call you before I get on the plane tomorrow. And I'll email and text you from Paris."

She nodded. "Three and a half weeks seems like a lifetime before I see you again."

"Please don't let the time eat away at your resolve. Make it happen, Alyssa."

"I will," she whispered. "Until then."

Chapter Fourteen

Alyssa rushed into her favorite local restaurant on Friday night at eight to meet her best friends. "Thanks for meeting me for dinner. I got off work at seven and had to dash home to change." She gave each of them a hug before sitting down. "I miss my girls." Tonight was the first time since she'd left Glenn Pines that her spirit lifted.

"We missed you, too," admitted Nicki, tossing her long, blonde hair over her shoulder. "And we know you don't like to travel more than twenty minutes from Lawrenceville, so we decided to indulge you this time."

"That's not true." She laughed. "Well, maybe. I'm working on it."

Nicki's smirk said it all. "I can't wait to hear all about your vacation."

Sam, the only one of them who knew something about her adventure, smiled slyly.

"Do tell," said Denise with a grin. "I can't believe you chose a cabin in the woods over the Jersey shore. So unlike you."

"Going anywhere by myself was so unlike me." Alyssa scanned the menu, although she knew it by heart. "It was the best thing I could have done."

After they ordered drinks, Alyssa launched into the trials and tribulations of the adventure package at Glenn Pines, her ill-preparedness, the challenges she conquered, and the amazing people she met. Although she painted Gabe as a minor character for now, he would be the subject of a much longer conversation once she raised her dilemma.

Her friends were nearly falling off their chairs with laughter as she took them through mountain hikes, kayak races, ropes challenges, and more.

"I feel extremely strong and competent now." She raised her arm, bent at the elbow to show off her muscle.

Throughout her telling, she glanced at Sam periodically, but Sam didn't interrupt her story to direct it toward Gabe. Although Alyssa knew it was coming. Not quite ready to go there, she turned to Sam. "After six months, how is married life? Have you come down off your cloud yet?"

"I hope I never do. It's been great. Michael is the most supportive, wonderful man in the world. My new law firm is doing even better than expected, and I don't regret for one second that I moved out of Manhattan to Crescent Beach. You know how worried I was about leaving the city."

New York City was Sam's love. The electricity, the culture, the millions of people energized her, although Alyssa would never understand the attraction. Ever since she was in high school, Sam had wanted to live and work there. And she had accomplished her goal of not only working and thriving at one of the biggest and best law firms in the city, she had become a partner. And then she gave it all up—for Michael. Their love story was epic.

Nicki chimed in. "Anytime you need a city fix—any of you—come and visit me and Dex. Philadelphia's not New York, but it's a great city, too."

Nicki was a power player at Snow Leopard Music, the vice president in charge of marketing. Her life plan had never included a long-term relationship. Until Dex had come along and upended her world—and her heart.

"We don't want to disturb the newlyweds." Denise pouted. "Besides, you're always too busy. Scheduling a visit with you in Philadelphia is like trying to get front row seats to the latest Broadway mega-hit." She shrugged. "It would never work out anyway. My kids take up every bit of air, space, and time."

While Alyssa loved Denise's kids and would ask questions later about them, she wanted info from Nicki first. "How are you and Dex doing? I still can't believe you eloped."

"I know it was a surprise. For me, too. But given how I messed things up when we were supposed to get married last April, I didn't want to give myself time to ruin it again. We had gotten back to a good place, and it seemed like the best thing to do. A simple ceremony on the first day of autumn. A new season. A new life. It just worked."

"We haven't seen you since your big day," Sam acknowledged. "Do you have any photos to share, other than the one you sent us?"

"A few." Nicki dug her phone out of her purse, found the requested pictures, and passed her cell over.

"Tell us more," demanded Sam.

A delighted smile lifted Nicki's lips. "We went to city hall. I wore a white lace dress, and Dex wore a dark suit. It was quick and to the point. Then onto our honeymoon in Bermuda. I know it's not what most brides want, but it was perfect."

"Who were your witnesses?" Sam again, who had clearly decided the cross-examination must continue.

"Two people who worked there."

"Nice." Denise's sarcasm escaped, but Nicki ignored her.

"It was nice. The two of us pledging our love and commitment to each other."

"Wouldn't it have been nicer to pledge that love and commitment amongst friends?" Denise's apparent disappointment in not being invited to the wedding hadn't ebbed in the past six weeks.

Nicki bit her lip. "It would have been wonderful to have you all there. But after having planned a wedding that didn't go off, I didn't want to go through that again. I'm sorry I disappointed you, Denise. All of you." She looked at each one of them, a request for forgiveness pleading in her eyes.

Nicki was right to do things the way she wanted to do them. Especially given the angst that accompanied her first engagement to Dex. They all had to understand where Nicki was coming from when she made the decision. Alyssa reached over and grabbed Nicki's hand. "I'm glad you're happy."

Nicki smiled through glassy eyes. "Thanks, Alyssa."

Sam was next. She gave Nicki a hug and congratulated her. Then all eyes turned to Denise.

"You know how I love traditions and how family means everything to me. You're part of my family. All of you. I want to be there for your disappointments, but I also want to share in your joys." She reached over to Nicki and took her hand. "I'm upset because I missed a wonderful milestone in your journey." A tear slid from

Denise's eye.

Nicki squeezed Denise's hand. "I'm sorry." She pulled back and included them all in her apology. "Dex and I were thinking of having a party to celebrate our wedding next spring. We'll wear what we did when we married, at least for a while, so we can all take pictures. How's that?"

Denise nodded, appearing slightly appeased. "Can you repeat your vows?"

"Now you're pushing it." Nicki's laugh rang around the room. "I'll talk to Dex and see what he wants to do. No promises on that one." She slipped her phone back into her purse. "It's been getting harder and harder for the four of us to get together. I can't believe the stars aligned tonight." She glanced at Alyssa. "Now that we're here, we want to hear about Gabe, the guy you brushed over in your tales."

Alyssa speared Sam with her gaze. She was the only person she had shared her plight with during that early morning call, which now seemed like a lifetime ago instead of only a week ago.

"Did you tell them anything?"

Sam shrugged. "Just enough to make tonight happen."

Of course. As Nicki said, their busy schedules made it next to impossible for all of them to be free at the same time. Unless an emergency was posed.

"Thank you." She peered at each one of them. "I need my friends right now, and this in-person session is the best way to discuss it. I feel like every time I see the three of you, I have a problem. You were incredible in dealing with the fallout from my broken engagement to David. And then the breakup with Cole."

"We're your friends, Alyssa," said Denise. "We've been together since ninth grade—longer than any of our love relationships. And we'll always be there for each other."

Nicki motioned the waitress over to order a second round of drinks. *Great idea.*

Alyssa told the three of them—although Sam had already heard an abridged version—a little about Gabe, the world-travelling photographer who'd somehow connected with her, and she with him, during their time at Glenn Pines. The more Alyssa shared, the more the weight of her quandary strangled her heart.

"You sound depressed," noted Nicki. "Did you and Gabe part ways?"

"No. I mean we did when we left Glenn Pines, since we live in two different states, but…"

Their second round of drinks arrived, and Alyssa grabbed her beer to quench her dry, aching throat. But liquid courage wasn't the answer. "Don't let me have any more of these."

Sam arched an eyebrow. "Got it. Continue, please."

"Since I talked to Sam on the phone Wednesday morning from Glenn Pines, things developed more with Gabe." Why was she sugarcoating this by using words like *things developed*? She had shared all of her sexual escapades in the past, including the details of her affair with Cole. "What I mean is…we ended up in bed."

Sam's facial expression didn't change. She had her divorce lawyer mask on. Nicki's broad smile told her she would have high-fived her if they were still in their early twenties.

Denise apparently required more information before having an opinion. "Was that a good thing or a bad thing?"

Alyssa's grin broke free. "It was amazing. Gabe is so sensitive and sensual. Maybe that comes from being an artist."

Sam's mouth opened, but she held back any comment.

"I know, I know. I should have followed your advice, Sam, and taken it slow. But he was very persuasive. And we all know I leap before I think. Thus my ill-fated engagement to David. And the affair with Cole." She sipped her beer.

"Okay. So you went to bed with Gabe while you were away. That doesn't sound disastrous." Nicki was always of the mind to have fun, have sex, and leave one's heart out of it. Until she'd met Dex, of course.

Tears welled up in Alyssa's eyes, but she held them back. "I think I'm in love with him."

Quiet enveloped. Sam lowered her lids and took her time responding, obviously not wanting to say the wrong thing. No wonder she was such a great lawyer.

"Is he in love with you?"

"Yes. Well…I think so. He said he was falling in love with me. I guess that's not exactly the same as being in love. But it's close, right? We were inseparable the second half of the week. I met him the first day, which didn't go so well, but the second day, after a little mishap, it all went zing. How does that happen? Am I some sort of magnet for the wrong men?"

"Why is he wrong for you?" asked Denise, the mellow and reasonable one most of the time—always asking the next question to get at the heart of the matter. Rarely judging. Having three kids, two under five and an adopted teen with leukemia—now thankfully in remission—must have given her those superpowers.

Alyssa exhaled some of the angst that came with this answer. “As I told you, he’s a high-fashion photographer who travels all the time. He was at Glenn Pines for a much-needed break from his whirlwind life. The good thing is that by the time he left, he had started to think about transitioning his career so he’d be travelling less.”

Denise nodded, taking it all in. “Did you figure out your next move career wise?”

Good question. “Yes. As a matter of fact, Gabe was a great sounding board. My short-term goal is to transfer out of the ER to get away from Cole. I’ve applied to the oncology unit at Nassau General. My long-term plan is to work toward a certification to become an Oncology Certified Nurse. Maybe even add a Chemo Biotherapy Certification.”

“That sounds like a great plan.” Denise beamed as if one of her offspring finally made a good decision. Then she sobered. “Did you choose oncology because of your mom?”

“Yes. I know I’m being really helpful to her while she’s going through treatment. I can do that for others as well.”

“I’m sure you’re a great support to your mom. And you’d be fabulous in that job,” continued Denise. “You’re so empathetic. You were there for me after Bobby was diagnosed with leukemia. I would have fallen totally apart without your help and guidance.”

“You give me too much credit. I was more than happy to help you get through that awful time.”

The waitress came by for their order, and they all quickly chose one of two specials so they could get back to their conversation.

"Then your vacation was a success," added Denise, jumping right back in.

"For my career plan, yes. For my love life, no. Gabe lives in New York City. You know how much I hate the city. Maybe hate is a strong word. I'm not the New York City type. Unfortunately, his world is there. He's sought after by some of the biggest names in fashion as well as magazines. And even though he told me as much, I couldn't resist looking him up when I got home." She chuckled. "The resort had basically no internet connection. The whole week was device free. Kind of nice."

Nicki cringed. "I can't imagine a whole week without email. My clients would think I deserted them."

Sam sipped her iced tea. "I'm liking this retreat idea more and more. But go on. What else did you find out about Gabe?"

Alyssa sighed. "In addition to *StyleSelect*, he's done work for all the top women's magazines. He was one of the photographers for the *Sports Illustrated* swimsuit issue last year."

Nicki's eyes widened.

"He's also done ads for almost every well-known designer in Europe." Alyssa's stomach knotted. "I should be happy that he's so respected in his industry. But if he decides to stay on that train, it means our lives will never sync."

Sam took over. "You said Gabe was at Glenn Pines to take a break and figure out his future. What is he looking to do?"

"He still plans to do high-fashion photography, just not travel as much. He wants to do more studio work.

He'd like to add fine art photography to his résumé. But he's worried he may not be as financially successful as he is now. I haven't figured out whether he's in some sort of competition with his father, who he is not close to but who's a world-renowned nature photographer."

"And Gabe's a sought-after fashion photographer. He'd be the winner in my eyes," said Nicki.

"Maybe so, but there's something going on behind the scenes. He refused to learn photography from his father, because he doesn't want to be anything like him. He chose a different path."

"I guess he has some internal issues to deal with. I should know. I'm the queen of internal issues."

Nicki and Dex had broken up several times because of her past. At first she'd refused to share her innermost secrets, and then when she did, she let her stubborn resolve from years earlier rule her life. Thankfully, Dex had knocked down her walls.

Nicki's words bounced heavily on her shoulders, although she already knew Gabe faced some heady complications. "Only time will tell if he follows through on his new plan and whether he succeeds." She inhaled, deciding now was the moment to drop her more surprising revelation on them and get their opinions. "Gabe invited me to meet him in Rome in a few weeks."

"Wow. That's a romantic invitation." Sam's tone didn't quite convey the excitement she hoped to hear. "Are you going?"

"I want to. For a few reasons. I've never been outside of the United States, and I'd love to go to Europe—to Italy. Sharing that experience with Gabe raises it to a whole other level. But the most important reason is that I miss him so much my heart aches. I need to see him, spend more time with him. It could be anywhere. Lawrenceville, New York, Kalamazoo. But the invitation on the table is Rome." She took a shaky breath. "What do you think?" Her gaze moved over each of her friends.

"Why not?" Of course Nicki would say that.

"My fear is that this trip won't change anything, and I'll be in more serious trouble than I am now. Our worlds are too different."

Denise gentled her voice. "You're in love with him."

She nodded as a tear slid down her cheek evidencing the deep sadness that settled on her soul. She swiped it away.

"Then go," said Denise. "See what happens. Talk more about the future while you're there. Spending additional time together, wherever it is, can only help bring the two of you closer. And if in the end you decide he's not the right one for you, at least you'll have the memories of experiencing Rome together."

Alyssa heaved a sigh. "Thanks. I needed to hear that. But what happens after Rome if I decide I can't live without him?"

Sam picked up the thread. "If the two of you work out, is there any chance he'll move to New Jersey? A lot of people commute to the city from here. And he'd be close enough to two major airports if he did need to travel."

Alyssa shook her head, her stomach in knots over this whole thing. "When I raised the issue, he grimaced. He said he'd never considered it before. I didn't get the impression he'd give much weight to it even after I raised it. I'm probably being naïve in hoping he'll compromise. Maybe a charming suburban town somewhere between Lawrenceville and New York. He grew up in Morristown. It's nice there." Although not what she was used to. And too far away to help out her mom if she was needed. She looked to Sam for her take.

Sam seemed to choose her words carefully. "It's not like you have to stay in the town you grew up in. You can move anywhere, given your career."

"True." Alyssa waited for her "but."

"That decision is not one that needs to be made now or when you get back from Rome. If the time comes that you want to live closer to each other or move in together, you have a bigger decision to make. You'll need to figure out what is best for you, with or without a man in your life. If you and Gabe break up, will you be happy living and working in a different town? If the answer is yes, then do it. If you are only moving because of Gabe, then you need to think about it a little more, all while giving the relationship more time."

Alyssa squirmed in her seat, but the discomfort she felt had nothing to do with the chair. She'd said the same thing to herself, but hearing it from Sam hammered it home. "When you left New York to move to Crescent Beach to be with Michael, what swayed you?"

"It took me a while to make the decision. I had left Crescent Beach in the beginning of August to go back to the city. Our apartment looked as if no one lived there, since Tom was off in San Diego with his girlfriend. From the moment I walked in, I knew it was a good time to sell. We were getting divorced and would have to split the proceeds. Why wait? I went back to work, and whenever I could, I looked for a new apartment. But my heart wasn't in it."

"Did you see Michael often after you moved back to the city?"

"No. I knew I was going to his Labor Day party a month later, but we never got together during August. We were both incredibly busy." Sam peered into her now-empty glass as if to see her past. "I got the partnership at my firm, which is what I had always wanted—what I had worked so hard for. My workaholic ways were what had ultimately destroyed my marriage to Tom. But when I heard the news that they were making me a partner, instead of being ecstatically happy, I felt numb. Not what I was supposed to feel."

"That's telling."

Sam nodded. "Things changed that summer once I met Michael. He had left the city the year before, and he loved his small-town life. He worked at a two-person law firm, was the town prosecutor, and was getting involved with the town council." Sam laughed. "What self-respecting New York City lawyer does that? But he was happy with his move, and I couldn't see him making the decision to move back to the city. At the same time, I wasn't excited about finding a new residence, nor was I into my job—the job I once lived for. So I reassessed my priorities.

"I had enjoyed living in Crescent Beach over the summer, and I knew I loved Michael. But I didn't want to make a decision because of a man. What if it didn't work out?"

Alyssa nodded vigorously. "That's exactly how I feel. I'm my own person. I can't move to New York or anywhere else because of Gabe."

"Right. And once I decided the city held none of the excitement I craved anymore, it was easy to make the decision. For me. Because I wanted a change. That's the process you need to go through. At least in my opinion."

Alyssa obviously had a lot more thinking to do. "I had hoped that my week at Glenn Pines would have cleared my head and helped steer me in a new direction. Instead, things got even murkier than they were before."

"Isn't it amazing how a guy can do that to you?" Denise put her arm around Alyssa's shoulders and hugged her. "You'll figure it out. And you'll make the right decision. Just don't do anything hastily. Think it through. And enjoy every moment in Rome."

Alyssa's spirit soared at the thrill of spending time in Rome with Gabe. "Thanks. To all of you. Talking this through really helps."

Their food arrived, and Sam dug into her salad with roast chicken. "I'm starving. Missed lunch today since I had to be in court."

"Why didn't you get a burger or something more substantial?" asked Alyssa.

"I'm trying to eat healthier."

Alyssa raised her brow. "Is there something you're not telling us? Why did you order iced tea instead of your usual white wine?"

Sam's cheeks reddened as she stuffed a forkful of lettuce into her mouth.

"Silence means I'm right. Are you pregnant, Sam?"

Alyssa's voice rose with excitement.

Sam's smile burst wide open. "You are a mind reader. Yes. Yes, I'm pregnant. I was going to tell you all tonight, but I was waiting for the right moment."

Alyssa bounded from her seat and came around the table, dragging Sam from her chair before enveloping her with the biggest hug she could, squeezing her tight. "Congratulations. I am so happy for you and Michael."

Denise and Nicki followed suit, the decibel level in the restaurant rising with their excitement.

Sam glowed with her happy news. "Thanks. You're the first people to know, other than Michael, of course."

"Are you taking your prenatal vitamins?" asked Alyssa.

"I forgot I'm here with Nurse Beckman. Yes, I'm taking my vitamins."

"When are you due?" Denise was the pro on this subject.

"Mid-May. Close to our anniversary."

"That didn't take much time to happen," continued Denise. "I didn't know you wanted to get pregnant right away."

"I can't say that was the goal. We simply decided not to use any form of birth control. We both knew it could take a while, and we aren't getting any younger."

Alyssa heard her own clock ticking as if Sam had held it up to her ear. "You're right. We're thirty-three. I guess I had better find a husband or sign up with a sperm bank if I'm planning on having kids before it's too late."

"You still have time," counseled Nicki. "A lot of women have babies into their forties now."

"True. But so many things can go wrong when you're of advanced maternal age."

Sam pouted. "I hate that medical term."

"Well, you're not there yet. In any event, you should eat more than a salad for dinner."

Sam's guilt surfaced on her face. "You're right. But I hate the thought of getting fat."

Alyssa laughed. "You will not be getting fat. You're pregnant. Besides, you've never had an issue with weight. In high school you were so skinny. I remember you couldn't find jeans tight enough—they always sagged under your butt."

"Nice memory." Sam rolled her eyes. "I certainly don't have that problem anymore." She speared a cherry tomato and sucked it into her mouth.

The rest of the evening was spent in nonstop talking, laughing, joking, and true friendship.

On her ride home, Alyssa teetered between the thrill of anticipation in seeing Gabe for five glorious days in Italy and the discouraging outlook over their future together.

Happy anticipation won out. Five days with Gabe was five days of joy. The added benefit would be making some real decisions about their future together while tossing coins into the Trevi Fountain and wishing not only to return to Rome, but for love everlasting.

Chapter Fifteen

Gabe collapsed into the desk chair in his hotel room at nine p.m. The day had been long and strenuous for all involved in the shoot of four different fashion shows during Paris' Fashion Week. He'd gotten some great shots and knew the editor who'd hired him for this job would love them.

The following days would be repeats of the previous days, only different designers. The anxiety and energy behind the scenes seeped into his blood, and he'd had a hard time staying focused on the job when everyone around him was crazed. As usual, the clothes were *avant-garde*, the models' hair and makeup unconventional, and the set designs edgy.

He used to love that about the shows, in awe of the artistry, the creativity of the designers, and everything involved in helping them carry out their imagery. Now he looked at all this hoopla as an egotistical waste of time and money, catering to the celebrities and millionaires of the world, who had nothing better to do than fly to Paris for a fashion show.

Why was he so cynical? Was he getting old? He was only in his early thirties. The electricity in the air and the flirtatious words exchanged as he photographed the models wasn't as thrilling as in the past. This year he ignored the coy come-ons as well as the outright invitations, surely giving him the reputation as a curmudgeon.

He turned on his laptop and prepared to spend the next hour or so responding to emails that he couldn't get to during the day. An email from the advertising agency for the shoot in Rome was marked *urgent*. His stomach dropped. *Please don't change the dates on me—unless you cancel. I can live with a cancellation.* He opened the email.

Hi Gabe.

I'm sorry to do this to you, but our shoot originally scheduled for November 22-24 has been rescheduled for November 25-27. Here's hoping you can get some sightseeing in while waiting for us to arrive. Sorry for the change of plans, but it couldn't be helped.

Best, Rob Amato

Director of Advertising

He sat back, closed his eyes, and exhaled the utter distress strangling his entire being. Alyssa was due on the twenty-fifth. He should have known something like this would happen. There was always a fifty-fifty chance. He'd just talked to her last night, and her excitement was through the roof. Now he'd have to ruin it all.

Gabe stared out the window toward the City of Lights without seeing anything but Alyssa amid a field of flowers, smiling at their beauty. His gut clenched. The one thing keeping him enthusiastic about the shoot in Rome was seeing her at the end of it. That result had just been obliterated.

Disappointment, so raw and painful, clawed at his insides. He couldn't remember a time when he'd felt this devastated. And he now had to break the news to her.

He picked up his cell and called.

She answered immediately. “Gabe! You must really miss me to call two days in a row. Unless you’re bored.”

Her teasing laugh spiraled to his heart. “Definitely not bored, but I do miss you.”

“We only have six days until we see each other. I started packing.” Happiness flowed through her voice.

He had to interrupt. To cut through her cheeriness and rip off the Band-Aid. “Stop packing.” His voice was raspy, rough.

“What?” She chuckled. “Don’t worry. I won’t bring more than I can fit in a carry-on.”

Her naïve amusement stabbed at his soul. She thought he was kidding. Words caught in his throat.

“Gabe, is everything—?” She paused, and his spirit wept.

“No.” He exhaled, but the dread remained. “I’m so sorry to have to tell you this, but the shoot got moved to November twenty-fifth—the day you’re supposed to arrive.”

Silence met him before her choked voice managed a response. “How long is it?”

“Through the twenty-seventh, unless we don’t get what we need and it goes longer.”

Her words were nearly a whisper. “That’s over Thanksgiving. Do you work on holidays?”

She was grasping for a lifeline to save this trip, but none appeared.

“It’s not a holiday in Europe.”

“Oh. Right.”

Stillness and an ocean fell between them.

“I’d quit the job if I could so we could be together.

But it's too close to the date. Besides, I'm under contract." A lump in his throat threatened to cut off all oxygen. "I don't know what to say, Alyssa, other than I'm so very sorry."

"I don't know what else to say, either." Emotion clogged her voice. Then radio silence.

He had the same problem. Nothing would change this. He couldn't offer to move their trip later by a few days since he had to be in LA the next week. Besides, he knew it would be impossible for her to rearrange her schedule again. There were no fixes, no making this better.

"I have to go. Goodbye, Gabe."

"Alyssa—wait."

But she was gone.

Damn. That was not the way he wanted to end this conversation. Of course she was blindsided, crushed, upset. He was, too. And although getting the words out had been tough, he had desperately wanted to talk it through. Come up with another plan.

But apparently she didn't want to. He'd send an email for now. Give her time to get over her disappointment. He started and stopped, not knowing the exact words that would ease her disillusionment—and not sure any words would.

Dear Alyssa, I probably should never have invited you to Rome, knowing that shoots get rescheduled all the time. But I was so hopeful. Unfortunately, my work has a way of interfering with my best-laid plans. I am so sorry this happened. I know you were looking forward to seeing Rome, and I was beyond excited to show you that fabulous city. But even more, I couldn't wait to see you.

I'll miss Thanksgiving this year (as usual), but I'll be visiting my parents that weekend after the shoot. After our talks at Glenn Pines, it appears I have some bridges to mend, and I'm ready to start. I'll be heading to LA the first of December for a week, but I'll be in New York for most of the month after that. I really want to see you, Alyssa. Please, let me know your schedule.

Gabe.

He reread the email. No words could make this better. She'd been afraid to start something with him for fear his travel schedule wouldn't mesh with her needs. And the first opportunity he had to prove they could make it work was an utter failure. All he could do was hope she'd give him another chance.

He hit Send.

Now that their vacation wasn't happening, he'd have to come up with a different angle for the article and photos he'd promised Adam for *American Traveler*.

During Alyssa's visit, he had planned to do a follow-up story to his Glenn Pines piece. But the story could no longer be about the man who met the woman of his dreams at an adventure resort, and a few weeks later they reconnected in Rome. Now it was man and woman were supposed to meet in Rome, but career got in the way, and man trudged through the sights on his own, taking photos and daydreaming about how romantic a vacation it could have been.

If only…

****

Gabe's news sent Alyssa into a funk like no other. She had fallen in love with him, despite her refusal to say those words out loud. Self-preservation, of course, for she believed if she said them aloud, it would only lead her to feel the pain even sharper when things didn't work out. Which, in the back of her mind, was a foregone conclusion.

Another mistake to add to her list.

Although he'd seemed disappointed, too, this adjustment was all in a day's work for him. It happened all the time. He should have known, he said. To add insult to injury, when he returned home, he was going to visit his family the weekend following Thanksgiving. Not her.

She heaved a sigh that made it to the other side of the room, hoping to keep from yelling out her pain to the four walls. Her feelings for him were too strong. She needed them to fade.

But first, she would respond to his email so it didn't hang over her.

Dear Gabe,

Thank you for your email. I need time to think things through. I'll reach out—when would she reach out? In a few weeks after she had time to get over her disappointment? Or never?—*when I can. Things are crazy at work since I transferred departments. And the holidays are always a busy time with my family.* Would that give him the correct impression that she didn't want to hear from him and that she'd give him a shout if or when she wanted to reconnect? *I hope you have a nice weekend with your parents after Thanksgiving and a productive shoot in LA.* That was certainly warm and cold at the same time, but that's all she had.

She sent it off and followed her plan to get through the next week as well as the Thanksgiving weekend. She worked her shifts plus overtime, had dinner with her parents and four sisters, along with their entourages on Thanksgiving after work, and met her friend Nicki at a Princeton boutique on Saturday—not Alyssa's favorite thing to do, but an adequate distraction.

"You're in a bad mood," Nicki commented after they'd been together for all of five minutes.

"That's because instead of seeing the sights in Rome with Gabe right now, I'm stuck in an overpriced boutique in Princeton where I'm never going to buy anything."

"I'm sorry, Alyssa." Nicki's lips turned down, and her eyes held the same sadness Alyssa felt. "That's why I came to Princeton today. To try to cheer you up."

"Not sure that's possible, but I appreciate the effort." Alyssa's surliness couldn't be contained.

"Have you talked to him since he cancelled?"

"No. He followed up with an email, and he's called a few times while I was at work. I keep my cell phone in my locker during my shifts. I haven't called him back, although I did respond to his email. My communication was clear that I'll reach out if and when I'm ready." She sighed. "I knew this relationship wouldn't work. He tried to convince me otherwise—thus the invitation to Rome. And all he managed to do was reinforce my belief that it was doomed from the start."

"You should talk to him. He obviously cares about you if he keeps calling."

Alyssa bit her lip. "I'm not ready. I'm sure he just feels guilty." A heavy sigh escaped. "I need to decide whether I want to try again with him or cut off all ties."

Nicki pierced her with one of her steely looks. Then she softened. "You're upset. He cancelled the trip you were looking forward to. But I'm sure he's upset, too."

She shrugged. "His apology email seemed so matter-of-fact. He said he shouldn't have invited me to Rome in the first place because his shoots get rescheduled all the time. His work always interferes with his plans. If he knew that, then he's right, he shouldn't have invited me. Better yet, he shouldn't have agreed to the shoot being rescheduled. He should have told the ad exec it was impossible. He had plans."

Nicki stood before the mirror in a gorgeous, sapphire-blue, off-the-shoulder gown, perfectly accentuating the blue of her eyes. The long blonde hair didn't hurt either.

"I don't know, Alyssa. I'm sure it's built into his contract that he has to perform even if it gets rescheduled."

"Whose side are you on?"

Nicki turned to her, surprise in her eyes. "Yours, of course. I'm simply pointing out that he probably couldn't say no to the rescheduling."

Alyssa relented. He'd said as much. "He also said he was going to his parents when his shoot was finished. That would be now. Today and tomorrow. If he was that upset about cancelling, and he knew how distraught I was, why didn't he come to see me this weekend?"

Anger flashed in Nicki's eyes. "You're right. Why didn't he?"

"So you agree I should just end it?"

Nicki's searing gaze made Alyssa squirm. "What aren't you telling me? If you're asking me whether you should end your relationship, then there's something he said that has you wondering."

"He said he'd be in New York City for most of December, he'd really like to see me, and he asked for my schedule."

"He's leaving it up to you, knowing how much he hurt you."

"What he should be doing is begging my forgiveness by showing up on my doorstep with flowers and a promise to stop travelling as much. And while he's at it, he can add that he's moving to Lawrenceville to be with me."

A chuckle escaped. "Oh, if we could only get what we want."

"Until Gabe decides whether he's going to travel less and substitute other work for his travels, a relationship between us doesn't have a chance."

"Are you going to do anything to tilt the balance in your direction?"

"No. When I went to Glenn Pines, my intention was to work on myself. That's what I'm going to do. Gabe can work on his career goals or not. That's up to him. But I'm not going to wait around hoping he'll change."

"Good. You made a decision that works for you. I'm proud of you."

Nicki moved Alyssa away from the mirror and held up her mane in a loose do. "Should I wear my hair up or down if I get this gown?"

Alyssa shrugged. "It looks great either way. Where are you going? Why do you need a gown?"

"Dex and I are going to The Philadelphia Art Museum's gala. His accounting firm is a sponsor of the event." Nicki turned her head from side to side, inspecting the result. "I think it looks better up. With crystal dangling earrings."

Nicki released her hair and started unzipping the gown. "Maybe I should try on some others to make sure. Could you go out and get that red halter gown we were eyeing before?"

Alyssa complied and brought in the requested gown. "I'm really happy that you and Dex love each other enough to have gotten married." She gave a wobbly smile. "I hope I can find that someday."

"You will, Alyssa. I never thought I'd find 'the one.' I wasn't looking and had convinced myself I didn't need a life partner. I was content to date who I wanted, when I wanted. No strings. Then Dex appeared in my life. If Gabe's the right guy for you, he'll reappear with a plan in place to make you take notice. In the meantime, you have a plan of your own. Whatever is meant to be will happen. Just like it did for Dex and me."

Alyssa wasn't so sure.

****

"It's nice to have you around for a few days, although we were hoping you would have been here for Thanksgiving." Gabe's father sat in his special armchair in the family room, reading the newspaper Saturday afternoon after Thanksgiving.

"I promised Mom I'd show up as soon as I could."

Gabe had arrived soon after two for the weekend. After having had a late lunch with his parents—including a running monologue with his mom—he sat on the sofa across from his dad, but not engaging. His laptop held his interest as he worked through emails.

"Oh no," he murmured as he read an email from

his friend Adam.

His father looked up. “What’s wrong?”

“My friend who owns *American Traveler* needs another cash infusion.”

“What does that have to do with you?”

“I’m a silent partner. I invested in his magazine last year when he first started it. If I don’t want to lose my investment, we’re both going to have to come up with more funds.”

His father’s eyebrow rose. “Why invest in such a risky business?”

Did he really want to get in a discussion with his dad about his personal investments? Why not? He had to engage with him sooner or later this weekend if he had any hope of having the more difficult discussion about why he carried around such anger toward the man.

“At the time, I thought it might be a business I’d want to work in when I got tired of doing what I’m doing. It wasn’t something for the near future, but possibly when I decided to settle down.” He looked straight at his father. “I never wanted to be an absent husband or father like you were.” *Whoa!* He wasn’t planning to go there right now. It just fell out of his mouth.

His father closed the newspaper, eyes downcast. “Ouch.” He crossed his legs and repositioned his glasses. “I know I wasn’t here for you and your brother a lot of the time. My career took me away.”

“Your career took precedence. It was more important to you than we were.” Gabe kept his voice even, trying with enormous effort not to roil the deep-seated anger in his gut.

"I know it seems that way. But we needed the money—for this house, you and your brother's private school education…and college."

"So you think living in this house and sending us to an expensive private school made up for you not being at any of our games or awards ceremonies or graduations? Or hanging out with us once in a while?"

His father swallowed, his Adam's apple rising and falling in his throat. "No. I don't think money made up for not being around. I missed almost every important milestone in your lives, and as I get older, I realize it and regret it. Maybe it's too late, but I wish we could spend more time together now. We missed you on Thanksgiving…and all the holidays when you're travelling and can't make it back to celebrate as a family. I'm the last one who has any right to say anything about it, but I know your mother and brother would love to have you here. Probably more than they want me." Deep lines in his face showed hurt even though he'd brought it on himself. "You were always here with them when I wasn't. They're hoping you'll see the light sooner than I did."

Surprise filtered through Gabe. He didn't expect his father to acknowledge any wrongdoing. And he didn't know his mom and brother placed him in the same category as his dad—absent when it mattered.

He exhaled, shaking his head, as if to deny the obvious. "Instead of learning what not to do, I seem to be following in your footsteps. Footsteps I swore I wouldn't follow."

"Is *American Traveler* the answer?"

"I wasn't really thinking about that as a solution to my current issue. I was considering taking on less travel assignments and moving into fine art. But now that I either have to sign on for a loan or come up with more cash, I don't see how I can refuse foreign projects. The pay is almost double that of studio work."

His heart sank with the realization. His plan to show Alyssa she could trust him when he started travelling less in the not-too-distant future was disintegrating fast.

He let out a huge sigh.

"Those photos you took in Pennsylvania that you sent your mom last week were incredibly good. You caught the emotion on that woman's face in such a beautiful light."

Surprised at his father's compliment, he dared to discuss his artistry further. "I could do so much more with fine art photography. I've been playing around with it for the past year while I've been on my shoots for *StyleSelect*, although the editor there doesn't appreciate my talent."

"I've seen the photos in *StyleSelect* and some of the ads you've done. But I'd like to see what you've kept in your computer files."

Surprise turned to astonishment over his father's words. Maybe shock was more like it. He couldn't remember a time when his father had shown an interest in his work. But then again, Gabe rarely engaged with him about his career choice. He assumed he'd been written off as merely a photographer for hire instead of a real artist.

They moved to the dining room table and sat side by side as Gabe shared the photos he had taken over the years, explaining his thought process and what he was going for.

"Your work is very good."

His father paused, and Gabe sensed a "but" was coming.

"The photos from this past year are spectacular."

Gabe nearly lost his breath. A compliment from the master.

His father's brow furrowed, seemingly lost in thought. "I have a gallery show coming up in a few weeks at Kingston Gallery in SoHo. I know it's soon, but I'd be willing to give up some space if you'd like to show some of your work."

"You're kidding, right?" Why would he offer him space which would take away from his own showing? The concept was so far out in left field that Gabe couldn't wrap his mind around it.

"I'm serious if you are about where you'd like to take your photography."

Maybe his dad was mellowing in his old age. Or maybe his generosity had to do with his guilt over being an absent father—and the fact that Gabe had just called him out on it. A contributing factor might be that Gabe was finally talking to his dad and ready to move past the hurt. Alyssa's words had opened him up to the possibility at Glenn Pines, and he'd mused about it while in Europe when he tried to take his mind off her. Whatever the reason, they had bridged a gulley and were now on the same side—although still dozens of feet apart.

"Don't you have to check with the gallery owner about adding some of my work?"

"I will if you agree to do it. Bill won't object, though. I know him well."

"Then I agree." His insides were doing flips and

cartwheels as he tried to focus on the logistics of it all. "How many pieces do you think you'd have room for?"

"Depends on the size of your work."

For the entire rest of the weekend, Gabe worked with his father, plotting out the space, along with determining the size that certain photos should be. They went back and forth over which photos to show, but in the end, they were both satisfied. Actually, Gabe was ecstatic. Not only to be showing his work at a well-known and respected gallery in New York City, but because his father was being present for him.

On Sunday evening after dinner and before returning to the work that still had to be done before the show, Gabe asked, "How's your job going?"

"Good. I'm slowing down a bit. Letting the younger guys and gals take the more prestigious shoots. I'm past that. Had my time."

"I bet Mom's happy. Does she have you doing all kinds of chores around here that you've been putting off for years?" Gabe chuckled.

"Of course. But we have a few trips planned for next year. It will be nice to finally experience some travelling together."

"Dad, I have a question. When you and Mom met, you were both from different states. How'd you work it out?"

His father arched a brow but stuck to answering the question. "We met in college at Cornell. Fell in love. Her plan, though, was to return to her small town near Boston. I was going to New York City. I convinced her to look for a job near the city since she didn't want to teach in the city. She was more of a suburbs type of woman. So we compromised. She applied for teaching jobs in northern New Jersey where my commute wouldn't be too bad. Once she had one, we looked at apartments in the area and ended up living in Morristown. It worked out. Especially once we married and had you and your brother."

Compromise. Alyssa had raised the issue of both of them moving to a new place that suited each of their goals. He said he'd think about it, but every time he did, his thoughts brought him back to Manhattan. She'd have so much more opportunity there. And of course that's where his world revolved.

"How did you and Mom manage to stay together with your career as a photographer and your base in New York?"

"It was tough at first. Even though we lived in a place we both chose, your mom was the stable one. She was working at the elementary school as a second grade teacher, and I was flying off to Borneo, Indonesia, the Philippines, Greece. You name it. Wherever the magazine sent me."

"How much time were you gone in a month?" To Gabe, it had seemed like always.

"In the beginning, a lot. I had to pay my dues. Your mother understood, and during the summer months, she came with me if it was a place she wanted to see. But once we had you and your brother, she couldn't do that anymore. Or at least we didn't think it would be a good idea traipsing around Egypt or Turkey or Malaysia with two young boys.

"After many years, I was able to pick and choose my locations, and things got better. But I know those years while you and your brother were growing up weren't easy on your mother. I was lucky she stuck with me."

No, it didn't sound like it was easy for her. It actually sounded like a recipe for disaster that only the strong could survive.

His father zeroed in on the reason for his interest in his parents' relationship. "Is something going on, Gabe? Have you met someone special?"

Gabe couldn't contain his smile. "I did. And yes, she's special."

"Who is this woman who has you asking your old man for advice?"

"Her name's Alyssa. She's a nurse from central Jersey. I met her at Glenn Pines."

"Is she the beauty in some of the photos you showed me this weekend?"

"That's her. She's very photogenic. The softness and angles of her features really show. She looks completely different in various light. The camera loves her."

His father studied him. "What about you? Do you love her?"

He sighed. "I do. But I've only spent a week with her. Then I left for Paris, and she went back home. She was supposed to meet me in Rome for a long weekend—this weekend." His face heated at the admission he was going to blow off Thanksgiving with his family for a woman as opposed to work. "Until my shoot got rescheduled and ruined everything. Don't tell Mom."

His dad chuckled. "Your secret's safe, although she'd be thrilled to learn there's a woman in your life. Why aren't you seeing her this weekend?"

"I hadn't been here to see you and Mom in a while.

I wanted to touch base." He omitted that he'd planned to have the confrontation he had with his dad. "I was hoping to see Dylan, too. We need to get back to a better place since the mess I caused over his wedding weekend. Besides, I don't think Alyssa wants to see me right now after I cancelled our trip because of work."

"I'm sure she understands that work comes first."

"Of course. But a travelling photographer is not who she wants to settle down with. She wants a relationship with a real partner—someone she sees on a daily basis and shares her life with. A nomad doesn't fit the bill. That's why I've been seriously considering a change of focus in my career. I want to prove to her that I can be the man she wants in her life. It's also partly why I wanted to spend this weekend here. Alyssa is very close with her family. She sees her four sisters and parents all the time. She didn't understand how I could let months go by without seeing my family. How I could allow work to interfere with spending time together on holidays. She started to open my eyes to the importance of it all."

"I'm liking this Alyssa more and more. It sounds like she's worth the changes you want to make."

"I can't just want to make them. I have to do it. Having cancelled our vacation together, I've set our relationship back by miles. And now that I have to come up with an additional seventy thousand dollars for *American Traveler*, I don't know when I'm going to be able to change my focus."

"Are you going to see her tomorrow?"

"Can't. I'm heading to LA for a week. I told her to let me know her schedule after that if she wants to get together."

"When you get back, we're going to have to be at the gallery as much as possible to help organize the showing. In the meantime, send me your mailing list. My invites went out already. I'll edit the invitation to include you for your guests."

"I appreciate it." He dragged his hand through his hair and shook his head. How was he ever going to win Alyssa over when he was adding more to his plate instead of taking something away? "I never wanted to be like you, Dad. Leaving family behind for work. I think that's why I've avoided relationships in the past."

"I can understand your opposition to being away as much as I was. And you're right. I put my career ahead of my family. As I told you yesterday, I'm not proud of it. I owe your mother a lot. I'm hoping to make up for lost time—at least with her. I know I can never make it up to you and your brother." A sad weariness settled in his gray eyes.

"Is that why you're offering me space at the gallery?" His stomach bunched, hoping against hope it wasn't the reason. This whole weekend he'd been flying high thinking his father respected his work.

"No. I'm offering it because I'd be proud to share gallery space with my very talented son. But if it helps mend our relationship, I'd call it a double win."

The concern disappeared. Forgiveness had to come sometime. His father was extending much more than an olive branch—maybe the entire grove.

"Thanks, Dad." Further words were stuck behind the clog in his throat.

"I'm looking forward to sharing the stage with you, son. Perhaps this will be the start of our Act Two."

With any luck, the audience would be applauding.

Chapter Sixteen

Exhilarated from her run in the park—a side effect from her stint at Glenn Pines—Alyssa flipped through the mail on Thursday afternoon, expecting nothing but bills and catalogues. She stopped at the high-quality calligraphed envelope that signified a formal invitation and ripped it open.

The Kingston Art Gallery in SoHo, New York City
invites you to a special showing and cocktail party
for Phil and Gabe Sutton
Father and Son—Photographers and Artists
Saturday, December 19th at 7 p.m.
RSVP

She traced the raised letters of Gabe's name with her fingers, aching to touch his hand, his shoulder, his face. Fluttering moths crashed through her stomach at the thought.

How could she not have known Gabe was having an art gallery showing? With his dad no less? Of course she hadn't returned any of his calls or otherwise communicated. Maybe this meant he was repairing their strained relationship.

After meeting up with Nicki, she had strengthened her resolve to disengage from him, having convinced herself to keep her distance as they both worked to sort out their lives. Although Gabe had called several more times, she was unavailable—whether at work or keeping her phone on silent to avoid the temptation of answering. He must have gotten the message since his calls dwindled.

Ignoring him killed her, but she had to protect herself. He was off in LA anyway, so it wasn't like they could get together. And now, once he did arrive back in New York, he'd be too busy putting together a gallery show.

Alyssa fired up her laptop and searched for the gallery. It had been in existence for over fifteen years and had glowing reviews. *Congratulations, Mr. Sutton.*

Her initial reaction was to throw the invitation away, but something kept her from being so dramatic. She looked back at the envelope. It was only addressed to her. No guest. So if she did decide to go, which she wouldn't, she'd have no fortification from one of her girlfriends. Maybe this was why he'd been calling. To invite her as his date for the night. If so, wouldn't he have said something about it when he'd left messages? Or at least he could have written a personal note on the invitation. No, she wasn't his date. She'd be one of many invitees making up his network of friends, colleagues, and acquaintances. He'd be too busy talking lighting, shadow, and composition with the guests to spend much time with her.

Should she go?

Three weeks had passed since he'd cancelled their rendezvous in Rome. She'd mellowed somewhat. Yet this wasn't a personal plea from Gabe, presented while on her doorstep with flowers and the words "I can't live without you." But, as Nicki pointed out, the ball was in her court. He'd left an open invitation in his email to share her schedule for December so they could get together. He'd called at least eight times since. Perhaps this was his way of opening the line of communication again—the line that thus far she had refused to acknowledge.

Maybe, maybe not. It surely wasn't an easy commute—a drive to the train station, an hour and a half ride into the city if she ended up on a local, then a subway or cab ride to SoHo. And right around Christmas when the city would be packed with tourists.

Alyssa headed for her closet. Nurses uniforms, jeans, sweaters, and a few casual dresses. Nothing to wear to an upscale art gallery party in SoHo. That should have been enough to answer her question.

But no. She took the next step and found her cell phone.

"Hi, Denise. I'm guessing you have a slew of little black dresses. Any chance I could borrow one for a cocktail party in New York City?"

"Of course. When do you need it?"

"A week from Saturday. If I go. I don't know. I thought I should have an option if I decide."

"What's the occasion? It's not like you to go to the city."

Alyssa heaved out a breath. "I know. Some of Gabe's photos are being shown at a gallery there. Kingston Gallery in SoHo. I got an invitation in the mail today, and I'm considering it."

"That's fabulous, Alyssa. You have to go. It's so hard to get a showing."

"You know the gallery?" A million such places must populate New York.

"I do know it. Your Gabe must be a very good photographer to have landed an exhibition there."

Alyssa chuckled at Denise's choice of words. "He is hardly my Gabe. I haven't seen him since I left Glenn Pines five and a half weeks ago."

"Here's your chance. You've been ignoring him long enough, and it hasn't helped you get over him. When can you come over? We'll play dress-up."

Denise's excitement was catchy, and she could use a sounding board, in person.

"Tonight's the only night I have off. Are you around?" Denise lived a mere twenty minutes away.

"I am. Does eight o'clock work? By then the little ones will be in bed, so they won't be hanging on you. Bobby lives in his room doing whatever seventeen-year-old boys do. And Ben won't be home until late tonight. He has a meeting in the city. This will be fun."

Alyssa looked at the oven clock. "Perfect." She had a few hours to clean, make something for dinner, and take a shower.

"I'll see you then."

When Alyssa arrived, Denise was ready for her. She brought her into the guest room where she had at least ten dresses lying on the bed.

"I have sleeveless, spaghetti straps, strapless, three-quarter sleeves, long sleeves. And if you don't like any of these, I have dresses in different colors. I only pulled the black." Denise worried her lip as she looked to Alyssa for input.

"This is better than going to Nordstrom's." Alyssa picked up the top dress from the pile. "I really don't know what will look good. I might as well start trying them on."

"I have shoes, too," added Denise. "But let's figure out what style dress you like before adding accessories.

You must look sophisticated and chic."

"Yeah. That's me," she scoffed. "Why do you have so many?" She pulled off her yoga pants and T-shirt, her typical wardrobe if she wasn't going anywhere.

"When I worked in New York, before kids, Ben and I went to quite a number of fundraisers. Since we moved to Princeton, we go to a lot less, but we still support a few of the nonprofits by attending galas. It's a night out, and I love to get dressed up. Since some of the same people were at the various events, I ended up buying a new dress for each fundraiser. I'm thrilled you may be able to wear one."

Alyssa slipped on a black, crepe halter dress with black beading around the neckline and hem. "This is pretty." She spun in front of a full-length mirror. "But it will be cold out. Do you think I should wear something with long sleeves?"

"I have a little jacket that goes with this. Here you go." Denise helped her into it.

"This is beautiful. I love it."

Denise smiled. "You can't stop at the first one. Try them all on. Then you'll be sure the one you pick is the best."

Alyssa played model for the next hour, with Denise pulling out shoes, jewelry, shawls, and jackets to add, depending on the dress. The end result was a long-sleeve, black-velvet sheath with a plunging V-neck and a slit up to mid-thigh. Very conservative except for the vee. And slit.

"That looks amazing on you, Alyssa. You should keep it."

"No way. If I have a future need of a little black dress, I'm coming back for something different."

Denise boxed up some jewelry and a pair of elegant pumps for her as well.

"I can't thank you enough, Denise. This is saving me a fortune. I don't have anything like this in my closet."

"Knock him dead, sweetie. Make it hard for him to breathe when he sees you."

If only.

****

The angst built to a crescendo as Alyssa took a cab from Penn Station to SoHo. She should have called Gabe to ask where to stay overnight. Then she would have known whether she'd be staying at his place. Now she was working with no plan, no hotel room, a small overnight bag, and the possibility she'd end up turning around to go home after the opening.

Alyssa was more than a little hurt Gabe hadn't called since receiving her response to the invitation. Although she RSVP'd to the gallery, surely he knew who was coming from his guest list. Even if he was frantically working to get his photos displayed perfectly, why treat her as merely another invitee?

This wasn't the first time she'd second guessed whether she should go at all. But here she was in New York City heading to the Kingston Gallery. As predicted, the streets were mobbed, and it wasn't easy to get a cab. The taxi line outside Penn Station had stretched more than half a block. However, now she was minutes away from walking into the gallery and seeing Gabe for the first time in seven weeks.

She wiped her clammy hands on her coat before putting her leather gloves back on. As she looked out the cab window, she fretted she was overdressed. She'd never been to an opening night at a gallery, but Denise wouldn't have steered her wrong.

Inhaling to beat down the nerves clawing at her stomach, she paid the driver and got out. She stood in front of the Kingston Gallery, taking in the scene. A fully decorated Christmas tree occupied a place of honor right inside the door, and dozens of twinkling lights outlined the plate glass windows. Gazing through one of those windows, she let go of some of her anxiety. The guests wore cocktail attire with men in suits and women in elegant dresses. One bullet dodged.

The front door opened, and the man holding it ushered her in. "Please sign in over there." He pointed. "The coat room is behind that wall, and refreshments are being passed."

"Thank you." Alyssa's voice croaked as if she'd swallowed a toad. Nice.

She gave her name to a woman sitting behind a table, who checked her off. As she headed for the coat room, she scanned the photos before her. This side of the room contained Gabe's father's nature photographs—bold and beautiful—the colors of the landscapes jumping from their frames. She spun around to glimpse the far side of the gallery. Gabe's arty high-fashion photography, with stick-thin models wearing tons of makeup and edgy outfits in exotic locales.

And then her skin pricked and her blood heated. There was Gabe. Dressed in a black tuxedo. Her breath caught in her throat. She'd never seen this Gabe. Sophisticated, urban, classy. She swallowed.

She wanted to run to him, but her brain told her to take it easy, play it safe. While she stood there watching him, a tall blonde beauty in a red gown snaked her arm around his shoulder and whispered in his ear. He smiled at her and pulled her close as he spoke to two other people.

Spears stabbed at her heart while fear-induced tingles tightened her scalp. *Nooooo!* She wanted to scream. She closed her eyes to erase the image, hoping that when she opened them, Gabe would be alone.

That wasn't the case.

She retraced her steps and walked out of the gallery into the cold, wintry night. A blast of wind feathered her hair over her face. She gathered it in one hand, no longer caring about her carefully coifed look, and walked fast in no particular direction—just away. Tears blurred her eyes, and she could barely see where she was going. Although what did it matter? She didn't know this area and had no goal in mind.

Alyssa walked briskly for a few blocks, dodging crowds and cursing their rudeness as they crashed into her, rushing to destinations unknown. When she crossed at a light, her feet began to hurt. She couldn't go at this pace for very long in the high heels she'd borrowed from Denise. In the next block she saw a W Hotel. Pulling her coat closer around her, she dashed across the street and entered the warmth of the lobby.

After waiting in line for at least fifteen minutes, she requested a room, having come to the decision to stay the night instead of turning around and going back home within an hour of arriving.

"I'm sorry, ma'am, but we're booked tonight."

She narrowed her eyes at the person who had the nerve to deliver this news. "Are you sure?"

He had the gall to laugh. "I'm very sure. It's the Saturday before Christmas, and almost every hotel in the city is full."

At least he said almost. "What hotel might I find a room in?"

"I really couldn't say."

Not helpful in the least. "Great. Well, thanks."

Alyssa turned to go but saw a bar tucked in the corner of the lobby. She'd be better off sitting there to determine her next step. No use walking aimlessly in stiletto heels while the wind whipped around her.

She found an empty stool and ordered a merlot. Taking out her cell phone to Google hotels in the area for availability, she noticed she had four missed calls. All from Gabe. Also a text.

Her heartbeat quickened as she read the words.

—Where are you? I can't wait to see you.—

She also had a voicemail from him. She listened. "Alyssa." His voice surrounded her, heating her blood. "I saw your name checked off at the desk. I've been looking for you. Did you leave? Please call me."

She took a sip of her wine and begged for calm and collectiveness to overtake her. Maybe she'd jumped to the wrong conclusion. People in the arts world were more expressive, more openly affectionate, no?

She decided to text him.

—I'm at the W Hotel bar a few blocks away. You looked busy when I arrived.—

What else should she say? She started typing *I'll be back in a little while*, then erased it. Unable to come up with more words, she hit Send.

Now she had a few minutes to think of her next step.

****

The profile of her beautiful face gave him pause,

and Gabe watched her from afar, drinking in the woman who invaded his dreams, day and night. Alyssa's shapely legs were crossed, and the black dress she wore slit to mid-thigh. He swallowed, but his throat was dry, tight.

His gaze roamed from her glorious mane of chestnut hair, thick and wavy, to the plunging neckline of her dress, to the sparkly bangle that graced her wrist, to the high heels amping up the entire look. He had never seen Alyssa dressed to kill, but oh, could she pull it off.

He strode over to her, took the glass of wine from her hand, placed it on the bar, then pulled her into his arms, desperately needing the intimate connection.

"You look amazing," he whispered as he inhaled her familiar lilac scent.

He closed his eyes and treasured the moment, implanting it in his brain for future reference. He took a step back, all the better to see her.

Cocoa brown eyes searched his, and she finally spoke. "You left your own show? That can't be good."

He chuckled. "When I knew you were a few short blocks away, nothing could stop me from seeing you in person. Holding you." He exhaled, taking her hands in his. "What you do to me."

Her full lips parted slightly as she studied his face. "When I arrived at the gallery, you were with a woman. Blonde hair, tall."

"That was Beth. She's the manager of the gallery. When she takes on a show, she's all in. You'd think we were best friends by the way she acts."

"She looked like more than a best friend." Hurt tinged her voice.

He shook his head vigorously. “No. She’s not. It didn’t even occur to me that our demeanor might give you the wrong impression when you showed up. There’s nothing to it.”

He took her face between his hands and did what he’d wanted to do since the moment he walked in. Crushing his lips to hers, he stole a kiss, then gentled his mouth over hers, teasing until she let him in. He didn’t care that they were in the middle of a lobby bar, although he’d like nothing better than to get a room.

He broke their connection with supreme effort. “Let’s go to my place.”

Surprise shone in her eyes. “You can’t leave your show.”

He chuckled. “You’re right. But I’d like to now that you’re here.” His gaze penetrated hers. “I missed you so much. It’s hard to put into words. Why didn’t you return any of my calls over the past month?”

She inhaled. “I thought it would hurt less if we didn’t talk to or see each other while we’re figuring out our lives.” Pain shadowed her eyes. He hated that his actions did that to her.

“I know you were struggling with the idea of a relationship with me when we were at Glenn Pines. And Lord knows I blew any chance of convincing you we could make this work when the thing you most feared came true. But, Alyssa, we have to find a way. I’m not trying to exert undue pressure on you. I don’t want to make this harder. But I can’t stop thinking about you.”

Since he called her that night from Paris to break the news of his rescheduled shoot, he’d put himself in her shoes and tried to understand her refusal to communicate further, despite his messages. She didn't want a relationship hinging on his travel schedule.

Yet he hoped that giving her time would make her miss him as much as he missed her. That whatever she felt for him would soften her heart as opposed to building a fortress to keep his force field away. During the weeks of radio silence, he gave her a door to consider, and she'd opened it.

He dared to ask about tonight. "I was cautiously thrilled that you accepted the invitation to come to the opening. What changed your mind about seeing me?"

"I wasn't sure I would come and went back and forth even after I responded to the invitation. It wasn't until this afternoon that I made the final decision."

He exhaled and thanked his lucky stars the ultimate result brought her back to him—at least for tonight. "I'm ecstatic that you're here." He leaned in and seized another kiss.

His heart buzzed and his soul soared. He'd missed her with every cell and atom of his being, and the happiness she spun within should have been illegal.

The storm he'd battled the last two weeks over whether she'd show had finally abated, and he could breathe again.

On the way back to the gallery, he held her tight, sharing his warmth and exhilaration. When they entered, even more people crowded the rooms than when he'd left. Out of the corner of his eye, he saw Beth make a beeline for him.

"Where have you been?" Her gray eyes speared him with displeasure before transferring a withering look toward Alyssa.

"This is my friend, Alyssa Beckman. She came for

the show from out of town. I had to meet her at her hotel."

Alyssa's cheeks flamed at his little white lie meant to get Beth off his case, but Beth didn't back down.

Her tone was disciplinary. "I understand you may want to take care of your muse. But do you know how many contacts you missed? Everyone was asking for you. At first, I said you stepped out for a few minutes, but when you didn't come back, I was at a loss."

Gabe mustered a bit of contriteness. "I'm sorry, Beth. I was only gone for a half hour. I'll be here the rest of the night. I promise."

Beth glanced at Alyssa, gave her the once-over, then huffed and strode off to places unknown.

"Hey, Gabe. You're on fire." His agent clapped him on the back.

"Hi, Scott. What are you still doing here? I thought you were leaving an hour ago."

"Is that any way to talk to your amazing agent? Beth asked me to stay when she couldn't find you. To answer questions about your work from potential buyers. You're welcome." He glanced at Alyssa, and a smile covered his lips. "And who is this?"

"This is Alyssa Beckman. Alyssa, my agent, Scott Preston."

They shook hands, and Scott's smile turned into an "oh" as he studied her face.

Within seconds, he segued into business mode. "I booked you for a Calvin Klein ad in Rio, a Donna Karan job in Miami, and an Armani spread in Florence. I'll send you the dates and details. I'm working on a few others for you. You'll be raking it in, my man."

Gabe flashed him a stern look as a hint for Scott to

shut up, but he kept talking. Before Scott could add to his list of international jobs, he cut him off. "I really appreciate all your help. You know that. But when I told you a few weeks ago I wanted to curtail my travelling, I was serious. Have you noticed that side of the gallery?" His arm swept out, gesturing to the left. "I want to start focusing on fine art photography."

Scott's mouth opened, and his face registered shock. "I know that's what you said. I figured you'd do that in your downtime. When you don't have a high-fashion shoot. You are in demand, my man."

Scott quickly glanced at Alyssa, presumably to see if she had a horse in this race. Or maybe to determine if she was the one behind Gabe's reluctance to take the jobs Scott set up for him. Alyssa kept her face neutral, but her body tensed.

Gabe had to get Alyssa away from Scott and this damning conversation. "We'll talk about this next week. I want to show Alyssa something."

The bliss of seeing her and picking up on their hopeful future didn't stand a chance of continuing if he was booked all over creation for who knew how long. While he reveled in his stellar reputation, being at the top of his game only assured more high-fashion contracts—most of which required international travel.

He took her elbow and steered her toward his side of the gallery. Above his photos stenciled onto the wall were the words *The Two Faces of Gabriel Sutton.* They moved around a free-standing divider, and Alyssa stopped in her tracks, her gaze falling on a huge photo of her in the field of flowers, surrounded by other smaller photos of her from Glenn Pines.

She held her hand up to her mouth. "They look like

paintings, not mere photos taken while away for a week. I saw these through the window on your camera, but they didn't look like this."

"What do you think?" Until this moment, he'd been excited about this exhibition. But having his muse register shock and a myriad of other mystery emotions put him off balance.

"I…I don't know what to think. They're…" Her face flushed—surely embarrassed. "I wish they were of someone else." She took in the other photos of her. "Now I know why Beth referred to me as your muse and Scott studied my face a little too long. They were comparing me to these."

Gabe's smile slipped from his mouth, and he took her hands in his. "I was hoping you'd love them as much as I do. But you're scaring me. Do you?" He searched her eyes for the answer she was struggling to give with words.

"I'm not a model. Look at those women." She angled her head to his other works. "Perfect hair, perfect makeup, perfect skin, perfect clothes. I have on jeans and a sweater. My hair is in a ponytail."

He lifted her chin with his fingers and sought to connect with her eyes. "You are much more beautiful than those women. You're natural, and your glow comes from within. Anyone who looks at these photos can see the joy in your eyes, the wonder on your lips. All because you're surrounded by the simple beauty of nature. Your emotion makes the viewer feel. And it makes people smile. They want to be there, out in that field."

He hoped his words would slither through her veins and touch her in places she'd never been touched.

She needed to see the magic of these photos—so intimate, so powerful.

She turned to him, tears in her eyes. *Uh-oh.* Was she that unhappy about being the subject of his art? But then she reached up and stroked his cheek.

"Thank you for capturing all that."

He was a goner. He cradled her face in his hands and leaned in for a kiss.

"Well, well, well." A booming voice broke through their connection. "Is this the mesmerizing Alyssa?" His dad held his hand out to her. "I'm Gabe's father, Phil Sutton."

She took his hand. "I'm very happy to meet you. I heard a lot of good things about your work."

"And I heard many wonderful things about you from Gabe. I understand it's thanks to you that Gabe has been making more of an effort to see his family."

Alyssa glanced at Gabe, who nodded.

"It's true. I told Dad how close you are to your sisters and parents and how you encouraged me to get past my anger. Talk it out."

Her beaming smile was all he craved right now. The emotions of the last few minutes had him tied up like a contortionist.

"Excuse me, Gabe." Beth took his elbow. "A gentleman over here would like to talk to you about your work."

"Go," said Alyssa. "I'll wander around. I want to see your father's photography as well as your other photos."

"I'll make sure Alyssa feels welcome," his dad offered.

Gabe kissed her on the cheek and left with Beth as

his father started giving Alyssa a tutorial on his work.

For the next hour, he answered questions from his guests, the more interesting inquiries having to do with his high-fashion photos.

"What is the significance of the pineapple hat on that woman's head?" or "Does that model have no bones, draped like that over a table?" or "Is that dress made of hundreds of real flowers, or are they silk?" All interesting queries and when it came to his craft, he could talk for hours.

Every once in a while he would catch Alyssa's eye as she wandered around, and he'd miss the issue posed, all focus on the woman who owned his heart and soul. When he was able to get away from the guests for a while, he sought Alyssa out, introducing her to acquaintances and making her feel as welcome as possible in his world.

The gallery finally closed at eleven, and although he should probably stay and check on sales, he had other plans.

"Are you ready to go?" He slipped her coat over her shoulders.

"I am. My feet are screaming."

"Sorry. There's never any seating at these opening nights, and the concrete floor is not forgiving."

"I'm glad I was able to share this with you." Her smile faltered. "You're an amazing photographer, and I'm sure you'll be even more sought after than you already are."

Her touching words held the hint of regret, as if the success of this evening would make their worlds even harder to mesh. He had to get her out of here.

He carried her overnight bag and ushered her out

the door. “I don’t want to get bogged down in a conversation with Beth right now. Let’s ditch this joint.”

They stood in the street while he hailed a cab, keeping his other arm encircled firmly around her waist. Then he kissed her forehead. “You made my night.”

But could he convince her to make his life?

Chapter Seventeen

Gabe unlocked the door to his Central Park West co-op on the twelfth floor of a pre-war building. Alyssa hadn't said much on the cab ride over, and during the silence he worried about the conversation he'd had with Scott in front of her. More travel with no end in sight was the way she'd see it. But he shut down those concerns, as well as Alyssa's silence, by fantasizing about the night ahead.

She did speak now, though, as she entered his co-op. "This is…huge." She stood just beyond the threshold, taking in the living room with its crown molding, nine-and-a-half-foot ceilings, and oversized windows that framed Central Park.

Yes, it was large, especially for New York City standards. Previous to this, he'd lived in an efficiency that was about seven hundred square feet. He could see the entire apartment from the front door. But once he started making real money, he'd invested in real estate through this three-thousand-square-foot space with three bedrooms, two and a half bathrooms, and assorted amenities in the building that he rarely used.

He gave her a quick tour of the kitchen, dining room with no furniture, library, and empty guest rooms before entering the master suite. His king-sized bed took up the center of the room, and one dresser graced the wall. Instead of setting up a desk in the library, he had placed an old oak table with a chair in the corner of the room overlooking the park, his laptop open. Dozens of photos were strewn on the table and floor around it.

He mentally thumped his head. Hadn't he anticipated bringing Alyssa back tonight if she showed up?

"Sorry about the mess. I should have cleaned up."

"The only mess is where you work. There's no furniture anywhere else except for a couch in the living room." Her astonished expression struck a chord.

"You're right. I guess I never got around to it."

She glanced at the walls. "You have thousands of photos, yet not one of them is framed and on the wall. Are you sure you live here?"

Embarrassment flooded his senses. "I'm rarely around."

This uncomfortable acknowledgement only highlighted the reason she was fighting a relationship with him. After easing her coat over her shoulders, he hung it in his half-empty closet. Most of his clothing fit in drawers and didn't require a hanger.

"You look absolutely beautiful tonight, Alyssa. I've never seen you in a dress, heels." He couldn't stop his gaze from roaming over her gorgeous curves.

He moved into her space and touched her cheek, then dragged his fingers over her jaw, down her neck, and to the exposed skin framed by black velvet. Her shiver told him everything he needed to know. He gathered her into his arms and kissed her with all the pent-up passion he'd stored for weeks.

"With as beautiful as you look in this thing"—he caressed her face with tender hands, his eyes seeking to unlock her soul, before he gently turned her around—"I need to get it off you." He moved her hair to the side, kissed her nape, then tugged the long zipper all the way down her sexy back.

"Please be careful. This dress isn't mine."

"How can that be? It fits you to perfection."

"It belongs to my friend, Denise."

"Ahhhh. The woman with three kids who lives in Princeton."

She chuckled. "So you did listen to me when I talked about my friends."

Her soft laugh spread warmth and joy to his core.

"She used to work in the city and had a need for dozens of little black dresses."

Gabe ran his fingers down Alyssa's spine, reveling in her reaction. "I bet she misses New York." He kissed her smooth back, then eased out of his tuxedo jacket.

She spun around to face him without responding to his comment. "Let me help you."

Her eyes twinkled as she worked the studs through each hole of his shirt. He tamped down his burning need to touch her as she dealt with his shirt cuffs, but impatient fingers itched to get back to adoring her body.

"It's been hell without you." He captured her mouth once again, hot and eager. He wanted nothing more than to get lost in the aura of Alyssa.

Moving her toward his bed, he carefully removed her dress and laid it over his desk chair before tossing his pants and the rest of his clothing on the floor. Red lace underwear filled his view. *Very sexy, Ms. Beckman.*

He fingered the lace over the swell of her breast. "Did you borrow these, too?"

"Of course not."

Her musical laugh spun though him, and he felt lighter and happier than he had in weeks.

“I bought them for our vacation in Rome.” A cloud passed through her eyes, but she didn’t dwell on the subject. “I was really surprised that you and your dad were doing an exhibition together.”

“A lot has happened over the past few weeks since I returned from Rome. Some good things, some bad. We’ll catch up, I promise. I just can’t do it now, with you standing here in lacy underwear that is begging to be removed.”

She pushed him back on the bed and crawled on top of him, her long brown hair tickling his torso as she sprinkled kisses over his shoulders and chest. He couldn’t stop his hands from wandering over soft skin, toned muscles, and feminine curves. How had he gotten through the last month and a half without her?

Alyssa sat up, straddling him, and brushed her fingertips over sensitized skin where her mouth had just been. He had before him a beautiful goddess, silhouetted by the streetlights filtering through his shades. Needy hands reached up to fondle her breasts, and she arched into them, a moan escaping full lips.

He unhooked the clasp in front and parted the lace before slowly dragging satin straps down her arms. Molding his palms to her full mounds, he watched her face transform from tension to pleasure, and she rocked against his hard length.

Moving against her with only her lacy panties as a barrier had him panting for more, but he didn’t want this night to end—this coupling with the woman he’d been dreaming about since he left Glenn Pines. He took her hips in his hands and held her still, warding off the waves of pleasure she'd just given.

Her eyes, the color of melted chocolate, questioned his action.

"I don't want to rush this."

He raised her off him and laid her down, taking one hand and kissing each finger with his tongue, then moving slowly to her wrist, her elbow, her shoulder, her neck, before kissing his way to her other fingertips. She squirmed and writhed beneath him, sometimes more than others, as he explored and learned her passion points.

She giggled when he got to the inside of her left elbow, as well as her right shoulder. She moaned when he laved her neck, right below her ear. And she shivered when he blew on her wrist. Learning Alyssa's body was intriguing and oh so erotic.

"Please come inside of me," she begged as he sucked her index finger into his mouth.

His gaze wandered from her head to her toes, taking in the glorious scene. "I have a long way to go before that."

"You can't," she squeaked, reaching out to caress him.

He backed away. "I can. And I will. I want you to be the most turned on you've ever been in your life. I want to slip into your soul."

Her eyes locked on his, and in them blazed need, passion, desire. And maybe even love. Did she see the same in his?

He bent over her and took her breast into his mouth, teasing her nipple with his tongue and teeth, stroking the other with his thumb. Delicate fingers sifted through his hair, holding his head to her, as she silently, then not so silently begged for more. And he would give it. Anything and everything she wanted.

They had tonight. He didn't know what tomorrow would bring, and he didn't want to think about it.

He moved lower over her torso to her hips, which danced under him. He continued his assault down one leg to her ankle, her instep, her toes.

She tried to pull away, now laughing. "Stop, please. My feet are ticklish."

He held her foot in a strong grip, not allowing her to escape. "Now I know how to torture you." She kicked to break free, but he wasn't allowing it.

Instead of tickling her, he massaged her foot, using strength instead of light touches. Her whole body relaxed, and she sighed.

Furtively moving up the other leg, he stopped at her juncture, and her whole body tensed. He smoothed his palm over her abdomen, going from side to side, a little lower with each pass.

"Breathe," he whispered.

Following his instruction, she inhaled, and he pulled the edge of her lacy thong aside before slipping his finger into her hot, wet core. She was more than ready for him, and her guttural moan sent every blood cell to his shaft. If he didn't do this soon, he was going to die of pain.

He stretched out next to her and pulled her back on top of him where she'd been earlier—before he'd taken full advantage of learning every nook and nerve ending that was Alyssa.

Fluttery hands danced over his chest, and she leaned forward to imprison his mouth with hers, invading it with her tongue. He sucked her in, a primal clash of lips, teeth, tongues, and oxygen.

Her willing body rubbed against him, and he feared he'd detonate if he didn't enter her soon. She took control, removing her panties first, then rolling a condom over him before guiding his rigid manhood into her hot, welcoming center.

She inched down over him, slowly. With aching anticipation, he felt every flex of her inner walls embrace him until he was fully sheathed in her heat. Starting at a slow pace, she worked him until he couldn't see, couldn't hear, and couldn't feel anything but the intense pleasure being drawn from him with every thrust.

With effort, he came back to the surface, wanting, needing to bring Alyssa to ecstasy before joining her. She was now riding him, fast and hard, and her walls clenched around him, spasming as she threw her head back and called his name.

He joined her, rocking beneath, until every last atom of his being was fused with hers.

****

Alyssa awoke, tangled in sheets and limbs belonging to the man she adored. A flashback to Gabe's cabin at Glenn Pines placed a smile on her lips, and she kissed his forehead, the closest body part to her mouth.

Gabe stirred and pulled her closer in his embrace. "Good morning." His voice was thick with sleep, but she knew that voice intimately.

"I was thinking," he continued, but nothing more came out.

She nudged him. "Did you fall back asleep while thinking?"

His lips twitched and inched up. "I wish I never

had to sleep while you're with me. Then we wouldn't lose any time together."

"Is that what you were thinking?" She looked at him, but his eyes were closed.

"No. I was thinking we should go back to Glenn Pines. For the long weekend leading into New Year's."

A thrill cascaded through her veins. Glenn Pines brought out such positive, amazing feelings. And all because of the gorgeous, talented, and passionate man beside her.

"I would absolutely love to do that. But only if there is no chance of it being cancelled. Are you home for the holidays?"

Just asking the question affected her mood, and her happiness slipped a notch. It underscored their different lives, their opposing schedules.

"I am. I'll be in Colorado for a few days that week. I'm leaving Christmas night, a Friday, and I'll be back on Tuesday. We can plan on meeting at Glenn Pines on Wednesday and stay until Sunday. Do you think you can get away?"

Alyssa had been working nonstop since she'd gotten back from Glenn Pines. Partly to keep her from falling apart over Gabe, and partly to be indispensable in her new job on the oncology unit, where she was learning a whole new area, including a different vocabulary.

"I think I can swing it." Thoughts of five days with Gabe, skiing, sledding, snowshoeing, doing yoga, taking classes, or simply staying in bed, was the greatest gift she could imagine.

"I hate to move right now, but I stupidly made breakfast plans with my friend Adam, the publisher of

American Traveler. But at least you'll be able to see that I do have at least one friend." He chuckled.

Tossing the sheet off them, he then pushed Alyssa out of bed and toward the bathroom. "We have to get going. We're meeting at ten."

They showered, dressed, then headed to Carmel's Cafe, a trendy breakfast spot on the Upper West Side within walking distance from his place.

"Can you stay tonight?"

Alyssa's heart plummeted. "I can't. I have to be at work by seven. The night shift."

She calculated the number of hours they would have left today before she had to leave. No use dwelling on that. It only made her depressed.

"No worries," said Gabe as he pulled her close and kissed her cheek.

Yet worries were the only thing that inundated her brain.

****

She sat by the window on the packed train, passing through small cities between Newark and Princeton, travelling ever so slowly to make stops in places she'd never been, even though not all that far away—Elizabeth, Linden, Rahway, Menlo Park, Metuchen, Edison. She knew very little about cities in her own state and even less about cities around the world. Frankly, she couldn't wait to get back home, to her comfort zone.

The throngs of people populating every nook and cranny of New York City during the holidays made her teeth hurt. But she knew it wasn't only the holidays. Normal weekdays and weekends were just as bad. Millions of people dashing here and there, oblivious to the person trotting beside them. Some people, like Sam, found it electric. Alyssa found it daunting.

What did Gabe think? Sure, he lived there. Had his career there. But did he love it, hate it? Accept it?

She absently fingered the leather gloves in her lap, thinking back to the gallery show. Gabe's photos were phenomenal. *The Two Faces of Gabriel Sutton.* His artistry jumped off the walls—each work a masterpiece. No wonder he was sought after by some of the most famous designers in the world.

But he'd seemed more enthusiastic about his Glenn Pines photos, pointing out the nuances of light, shadow, composition, and color. And the facial expressions of his so-called favorite subject. At first, embarrassment had coiled through her at the comparison she knew would occur between his models and her by people strolling through the gallery. But when she saw the works through Gabe's eyes, she could almost forget it was her in those photos.

She sighed deeply and closed her eyes. She was in love with Gabe. No question, no idea of falling. She was there. And it hurt.

Love wasn't supposed to feel like this. She should be flying, somersaulting, shouting to the heavens. Instead, a lead weight lay on her heart, deflating it.

In going to New York, she'd had the slightest hope they'd be able to talk about a future together and work toward a plan. That hope had been dashed in the few minutes it took for his agent to lay out Gabe's schedule for the next however many months, with the promise of more.

And then the meeting with Adam this morning sealed their fate. Gabe needed to add on a few more months to his crazy schedule to earn what was required for his half of the cash infusion. After that, he pledged to work with Scott to make his life a little more manageable. He clung to the days they planned to meet at Glenn Pines, claiming they'd figure things out between them during their holiday together. But hadn't he already promised to do that at the end of their week at Glenn Pines in October? Yet he was no closer to changing his life now than he had been then. Maybe even farther, given the cash-flow problems at *American Traveler*. The money he and Adam needed now was a short-term fix. In a few months, if circulation didn't pick up, they'd be in the same boat.

When she was near him, she breathed the same air, and he demonstrated his affection in more ways than one—keeping her close at the gallery, introducing her to everyone in his orbit as his muse, giving her credit for his new lease with his family. But most importantly, taking her home and making love to her with exquisite passion. Unfortunately, that was for one eighteen-hour period. Now she was out of sight, out of mind, and Gabe would spin through his world with ease and competency.

He thrived in New York City, the hub of his existence. Ad agencies, marketing firms, galleries, studios. Managers, agents, buyers. And from there he spread his tentacles across the country and across the world.

His life was exciting, challenging, adventurous. Hers was predictable, conventional, boring.

Before she could even anticipate a further discussion with Gabe about melding their worlds, she had to be truthful with herself about what she wanted her future to look like. How far was she willing to go to compromise?

"Next stop, Princeton." The conductor strode through the aisle as he called out the destination. And right outside Princeton was Lawrenceville.

Was this the home she'd never leave or a springboard from which to jump?

Chapter Eighteen

The shift that night at the hospital was quiet.

"Alyssa, can I talk to you?" Cole's familiar voice caught her up short.

"Is something wrong, Dr. Peterson?"

She still worked with him on occasion when she pulled overtime in the ER, but she kept her distance personally and mentally.

"No." He caught her arm and turned her to look at him, something she managed to avoid as often as possible. "I need to tell you something. In private."

She shouldn't go. She thought of refusing. But he was her superior in the ER, and frankly, curiosity had her teetering.

He slipped his hand into the crook of her elbow and ushered her down the hall. She panicked and glanced to see if anyone else was witnessing their exchange. While rumors had run rampant during their affair, things had died down at its demise, and she didn't want any gossip to start up again. Especially for no reason.

"Let go," she hissed. "I'm coming."

Following him to the room where he rested between emergencies—also known as the Garden of Eden—Alyssa inhaled in an effort to slow her racing heart. She should not follow Cole anywhere. Especially here. He was trouble.

He entered the room, turned on the light, and closed the door behind her.

She swallowed. "What's going on?"

"I want to apologize for the way things ended between us."

She held up her hand. "No reason to apologize. You're married. I was fully aware of that fact. We made a mistake. End of story." She placed her hand on the knob to leave.

"Please hear me out."

She leaned her head back and closed her eyes. If this was something he had to do to move on and feel better about himself, then so be it.

Her sigh echoed around the room. "Go ahead."

Cole nodded. "Things were so hot between us. Incredibly good."

She couldn't argue with that. But the operative word was *were*.

"When my wife started asking questions, I freaked. I wasn't ready to break up my marriage over something I wasn't sure would last."

"You already told me the first part." She hadn't known he questioned whether they would last. But it was irrelevant. "It's fine. It's over. I've moved on."

"I feel terrible that I upset you. That you transferred out of this department."

"You were the one who suggested a transfer. I had no choice. Either I moved voluntarily, or you'd assign me to some department where I didn't want to go." The air in the room was suspiciously disintegrating, and she contemplated flight. "So I made the decision. You are absolved of all guilt."

"I can't stop thinking about you. About what we

had. And could have in the future. I want to see you again, Alyssa. I was hoping you and I…"

She leveled in on his eyes to determine his sanity. His solemn demeanor was prevalent in the depths of his irises, in the set of his jaw, in the somberness of his face.

"You were hoping you and I could what? Start up another affair?"

He stepped back as if offended. "It depends on what you want. I'd consider leaving my wife if you were willing to take that step with me."

Was he serious? He'd consider? Was that really his proposition?

"Just to be clear. You want to get back together with me, and if I'm all in, you might leave your wife. Maybe."

"I'm not putting it exactly that way."

She placed her hands on her hips. "How exactly are you putting it?"

Of course, she had no intention of getting back together with Cole, but seeing him squirm to explain what he meant was priceless.

A laugh bubbled up in her throat at the ludicrousness of it, but she held it down. It was such an inappropriate reaction. Their whole situation had been absurd. She'd fallen for him when she'd sworn to herself that would never happen. It was only an affair. Then she'd shattered when he broke it off. What irrational world had she entered into with Cole? And now he was offering to bring her back into it.

She briefly thought that these words had been the only ones she wanted to hear a few months ago. She had prayed he'd leave his wife for her. But that hadn't happened.

Thankfully, she was in a better place, and this ridiculous proposal from her former lover now seemed farcical.

She inhaled, needing to put an end to this absurd conversation. "Never mind, Cole. You don't have to answer that. I've put you behind me. I won't go back there."

He took her hand in his and interlaced his fingers with hers. In the past, that gesture had driven her wild with desire. Almost anything he'd done had the same reaction. But that was lust. Sex at its best. And she had mistakenly equated lust with love.

She pulled her hand away. "I can't." Her voice was strong and determined to underscore the clear meaning of her words. His hand grazed her shoulder as she turned to go.

"Will you at least think about it?"

She would give him no room or inclination for hope.

"Absolutely not." Her voice was loud and clear so he wouldn't mistake her response. "As a matter of fact, I think your proposition is giving me the shove I need to leave this hospital and move on."

And with that, she left Cole behind.

For good.

****

Driving up the long entranceway to Glenn Pines was like coming home. Joy and happiness collided in Alyssa's being, and anticipation ricocheted from her heart to her soul and back. It was noon on Wednesday, two days before New Year's Eve. Mere hours before she'd be in Gabe's arms.

This time she'd packed strategically. No extra shoes, no jewelry. She knew where she was coming, what she'd be doing, and what was required. The only superfluous thing she'd packed was sexy underwear.

And she couldn't wait to wear it.

"Hi, Sharon," she enthused, seeing the same receptionist who'd worked there in the fall.

"Ms. Beckman. We're glad you decided to come back." Sharon still wore her signature long, blonde ponytail despite the twenty-degree temperature outside.

"Please call me Alyssa. Are there any messages for me?" She hoped not.

Given the lack of cell service once she arrived in the mountains, Gabe told her he would call the resort if his time of arrival changed.

"As a matter of fact, yes. Gabe Sutton called an hour ago saying he was stuck in Denver. Apparently, there's a snowstorm, and his flight was cancelled."

Alyssa's stomach sank. He was supposed to arrive back in New York yesterday. But when she'd spoken to him, he expounded on some problem with the shoot, of course, and his flight was scheduled for eight this morning. He'd never mentioned the possibility of a snowstorm. He probably hadn't paid much attention to the weather. Now it was too late.

"Did he say anything else?"

Sharon consulted her note. "Nothing else."

If she could have, Alyssa would have immediately checked the Denver weather on her phone app. Maybe having no cell service was a blessing. She would stay positive and not get bogged down in something neither of them had any control over.

"Okay, then. I'll go to our room and take a look at

the schedule of activities for today."

Right about now she could use some meditative yoga.

Once settled in, she donned her yoga pants, tank top, and sweatshirt. She scanned the schedule to fill in the rest of the afternoon, knowing Gabe would get here as soon as he could, even if he had to drive to a different airport to accomplish that.

The afternoon passed in a familiar rhythm, with some of the same instructors she'd had over the fall. She would have loved to have run into Edie or Missy and Conrad. But they were assuredly enjoying the Christmas and New Year's holiday with family and friends.

Surprisingly, Glenn Pines was crowded, and meeting new people came easily. She waited until seven thirty to go to the dining hall, hoping to hear that Gabe was able to book another flight. Stopping by the reception area to check for messages, she held her breath, hoping for the best.

"He just called again," said Sharon, a smile on her face forecasting good news. "He's still stuck in Denver. He'll probably be here tomorrow."

"What?" Her question assumed she hadn't heard her correctly, although she knew she did. Tomorrow. Probably. Not good on so many levels.

If all the planes grounded were vying to get out tomorrow, who knew what time he'd arrive? They would have lost a whole day of a five-day getaway. And what if the storm continued into tomorrow? She couldn't even contemplate that.

What she did realize was that this was what their life would be like. He hadn't managed to extricate himself from shoots outside of New York. He needed the extra money to put into *American Traveler*. How much longer he intended to travel, she didn't know. Further, his agent was a persuasive sort, and he clearly had not embraced Gabe's new path. So for the foreseeable future, Gabe would be off somewhere for days, he'd plan to come home on a certain day, something would prevent that, he'd plan on another day, an act of nature would interfere. And Alyssa would be waiting her whole life away.

That was not what she wanted in a relationship. She wanted to come home to someone, to share her day, to have dinner together, to sleep in the same bed. She wanted to have common interests, look forward to excursions on days off.

She headed to the dining room, a funk permeating her soul. What should have been a joyous reunion where they'd plan for their future was turning into a solitary reflection on why this would never work.

"Alyssa, over here." Mara, a woman she'd met in yoga class, motioned to an empty seat at a table of six. "These are my high school girlfriends, Janice, Margie, Willa, and Candace. We meet here once a year for a girls' weekend."

The women all talked at once, and Alyssa felt right at home, missing her girlfriends and wishing they were here to help her deal with utter disappointment. But this group would be a good temporary substitute.

In no time, Mara's friends dove right in and asked questions, provided advice, and made her laugh.

"So why are you all here on New Year's weekend?" Alyssa studied the group in their early thirties—her age.

"I'll start." Mara raised her hand, as if in class. "I recently learned my longtime boyfriend, Hank, had a girlfriend on the side."

Willa jumped in. "My boyfriend of a year decided he was gay. I guess I should have known."

Mara took Willa's hand. "We told you when you first started dating him, but you didn't want to hear it."

"I know." Willa shrugged. "I thought you were wrong."

Janice took the floor. "I can never find the right guy. I'm doomed to be single."

Alyssa nodded. "That's what I'm starting to think. I have bad judgment when it comes to men."

Candace jumped in. "My girlfriend's great."

Margie elbowed Candace. "Yes. And we're all jealous." She took a sip of her water. "I'm seriously considering trying a same-sex relationship."

Candace put her arm around Margie and gave her a hug. "It would never work out for you. You're too obsessed with men."

The conversation went around and around, and Alyssa bantered right along with them. She laughed and talked and bonded with these five strangers. The power of girlfriends, even new ones, still amazed. Yet lurking beneath was the sheer misery over the unambiguous evidence that Gabe's career would always come first.

They moved from the dining room to the game room and took over the ping-pong table, setting up a tournament amongst themselves. Their rallying cheers for each other echoed through the large room, and the laughter never stopped. They argued over close calls, made up a few rules here and there, and managed to garner an audience, making their games even noisier.

As they walked back to their cabins after ten, Mara took Alyssa aside. "If Gabe can't make it for New Year's Eve, there's a spot at our table for you."

Tears stung Alyssa's eyes. If Gabe didn't make it, she'd be devastated, their little getaway ruined. But to have five women looking out for her, just in case, touched her heart.

"Thank you." The words caught in her throat.

"It sucks that the weather isn't cooperating, but you know this isn't his fault." Mara gave her a sideways glance. "I'm sure he's suicidal, being stuck in Denver, when all he wants to do is be with you."

A tear slid down Alyssa's cheek, and she wiped it away with her glove. On some level, she acknowledged Mara's sentiment as true. But she couldn't help but think that Gabe should have known that a storm had the possibility of snowing him in. Storms didn't surprise people. They were forecasted. People prepared for them. Talked about them incessantly. Getting out of town a day earlier was what anyone who had something important to do would have done. A stark reminder of what life with Gabe would be like if she didn't let go.

When she awoke the next morning at six, she knew what she had to do. No use feeling sorry for herself. This was a good learning experience—as if she needed another one. If Gabe couldn't make it for a five-day getaway that he initiated, just like the one in Rome, he was never going to be aware of her needs and be there for her on a day-to-day basis. She would try to enjoy her time at Glenn Pines without him. If or when he showed up, she would listen to his defensive apology, but she intellectually knew this had to be the end. When she left here on Monday morning, she'd be leaving

Gabe behind—with amazing memories of a short-lived love.

A powerful sadness pounded against her heart. The only way to ignore it was to participate in activities. A nature hike was first on her agenda, and some fun classes with her newfound friends would make up the rest of the day.

She sidestepped the reception area, not wanting to know whether Gabe had left a new message because whatever that message might be, it would dictate her day.

And she wanted to be in charge.

****

Gabe's flight arrived in Philadelphia at two on Friday, New Year's Eve day. Plenty of time to get to Glenn Pines for dinner if no further transportation problems occurred. The car rental line curved around in loops as if he were waiting to board the most fantastic roller-coaster ride. If he hadn't already reserved a car, he would never even take the chance that one would be available. Everyone who stood in line was cranky, including him. Delayed travelers on a holiday weekend were a lethal combination.

He called Glenn Pines and spoke with Sharon for the sixth time in three days. He wanted to talk to Alyssa, but of course Sharon had no idea where she was, and a paging system at Glenn Pines was unheard of. Alyssa had to be furious with him, although he'd never seen her angry, except maybe on that second day at Glenn Pines when her kayak overturned and he'd teased her unmercifully. After that, their times together had been blissful, turning sad only when they had to part.

He'd make it up to her somehow. A two-hour drive would give him plenty of time to figure out how. Right now his sole focus was on getting a car and getting out of here.

When he arrived at Glenn Pines at five thirty, relief mixed with exhaustion and anxiety. He stopped at the reception desk to get an extra key in case Alyssa wasn't in the cabin and found his way to their designated haven. Inhaling for fortification, he unlocked the door and entered. Alyssa wasn't there.

Intending to go look for her, he decided to shower and change first. Two days at the airport and then flying and driving needed to be washed away. But the bed looked so inviting when he came out of the bathroom he didn't bother to exchange the towel around his hips for clothes. Only a few minutes to close his eyes. Refresh.

Soft lips brushed against his cheek, over his mouth, teasing, tickling. He struggled to open his eyes.

Alyssa sat on the bed beside him, her long hair pulled over one shoulder, her eyes shining, her lips smiling. What a sight!

"Hey, sleepyhead. I've been trying to wake you for a few minutes. You're dead to the world."

He reached up and slid his hands around her neck, tugging her toward him for more. He seized her lips and reveled in their taste, their touch. Tentative at first, Alyssa seemed to hold back. But he knew her body, her sensitive points. And he craved her, wanted her with his whole being. His tongue travelled from her mouth to her ear, and he circled her lobe, relishing the shivers that came with it.

His wandering hands caressed her shoulders, her

neck, her breasts, and a sigh escaped her mouth.

He pulled her sweater over her head, then started working on the zipper of her jeans. “Help me,” he begged.

Her laughter filled the room. And his soul. She stood and removed her remaining clothes, a striptease at its best. He yanked the towel from around his hips and pushed the covers down on the bed, making room for Alyssa, but not too much. He wanted her on top of him or under him, her choice, post haste.

This was no slow dance through foreplay. He was desperate to be inside her, and she met him with her own urgency. “Where are the condoms?” she asked, glancing at the nightstand.

“I didn’t unpack yet.” He jumped out of bed, rummaged through his suitcase, and produced the requested item.

As soon as he sheathed himself, she pushed him back on the bed and straddled him, positioning herself over him to invite him in. And he accepted that invitation with raw need.

He’d been dreaming of this since she left New York, but more so in the last few days. The anticipation had worn a path from his brain to his shaft, and he was more than ready to reach the pinnacle. But Alyssa wasn’t there yet. Too much meditation, no doubt.

He held her hips still. “Don’t move.” He inhaled, trying to control his runaway libido. He studied her face, her body connected to his. “You’re so beautiful. I missed you more than I can say.”

She leaned over to kiss him, as if to quiet his words.

He guided her hips in a gentle motion, allowing the

sensation to move through her core. He watched her face as her orgasm built from within, her hands grabbing tightly onto his forearms, her inner walls clenching around him before rippling outward. Her breath came in uneven, erratic gasps, and then she let go.

Seeing her fall apart, hearing her moans and sighs, feeling strong fingers relax their hold and stroke his chest, all had him reaching for his own release. But he wanted to draw this out, make their physical connection an emotional one as well. He needed her, wanted her. Loved her. And he wanted to show her that.

Lifting her off him, he then laid her down, stroking her neck with his tongue, filling his hand with her breast, rubbing his thumb over its hard peak before taking it into his mouth. She squirmed under him, her pelvis pushing against his hard shaft. He worked his way down her torso, silky flesh over strong abs, and he circled around her navel, eliciting a giggle from her.

"Ticklish?" he whispered, as he blew his breath over her moistened skin, sending other sensations over her body.

"I don't know what I am right now," she moaned as he continued his assault southward, nipping and laving her inner thighs before stroking the folds at her core, eliciting a shriek that spurred him on. He slipped in one finger, then two, as her wet heat coated them with raw sex.

"I want you back inside of me." Her hoarse demand was accompanied by frenzied hands pulling him up as she spread her legs to invite him in.

More than ready to comply with the lady's wishes, he entered her, slowly at first, calling on every bit of strength he had to make this feeling last. Until he could hold back no more. He drove into her, hard and fast, bringing her once again to that fabulous place.

And he was right there with her.

****

They arrived at the New Year's Eve dinner party at nine, a sexual glow connecting the two of them. Although deep down, Alyssa knew this was the end.

They'd lain in bed, tangled in each other's arms for a long time after they'd made love. Gabe apologized, but it came with the clichéd excuses she assumed his agent and the editors of the magazines continually heard. He wasn't getting the shots he wanted. It was too windy, too cold, too cloudy, too whatever. He tried again the next day. Same problem. He finally had to improvise and move the shoot indoors. She didn't ask if he'd known a snowstorm was coming. His work would have been his sole focus. It always would be.

Earlier, when she'd watched him sleeping peacefully, his face as beautiful at rest as when awake, she knew he owned her heart and soul. Claiming them back would be so painful. This weekend would be her gift to herself. When it was over, they'd go their separate ways. Only then would she allow herself to fall apart.

She introduced Gabe to her new friends. Their whispered comments in her ear as she kissed each of them spoke of how perfect things had turned out for her. How lucky she was to have her handsome, talented Gabe in her arms on New Year's Eve.

Only Alyssa harbored the imperfection of it all. She was not okay with leading different lives in a relationship. She'd done that with David, whose schedule never meshed with hers and who had his own hobbies, very different from her interests. People in a relationship should be in the same boat, or they'd be like two ships passing in the night. Cole was a whole other scenario—another different boat, another bad relationship. A third wrong move was not going to happen. She was done with bad decisions.

"You're quiet tonight." Gabe slid his arm around her waist and kissed her on the cheek.

To all outsiders, they must look like the perfect couple.

She turned toward him. "I guess I'm all talked out. I've spent the last three days with the five women from Cleveland. There is no silence with that group. Even on the nature hike, they barely stopped to listen to our guide."

"I was hoping we'd hike together."

She raised her eyebrow. "I was supposed to wait for you before I did anything?"

His face drooped. "Of course not. You do know how sorry I am, don't you?"

"Yes." Dragging him through the mud of accusations was pointless. It wasn't going to change anything, and it would only make him defensive and her seem unreasonable.

When the countdown began to midnight, he held her in his arms, swaying gently as if dancing with her. Alyssa relished the cocoon he'd spun her into, blocking out all the noise, the people, the scene. All she saw was Gabe, gorgeously handsome, with eyes that melted her insides and kisses that permeated her soul.

She let it all happen to her, loving the free fall and hoping for a cushion when she landed. Although she knew better.

The next two days passed in blissful harmony. They did everything together, enjoying outside activities in the crisp, cold air, as well as a few classes. And they more than enjoyed their time in bed.

Alyssa chose Sunday night at dinner to drop her bomb. They were both leaving Monday morning, and that seemed too limited of a time to deal with the fallout.

She steered them to a table for two, avoiding being too near any of the people they'd struck up friendships with. She contemplated having this conversation in the privacy of their cabin, but they could always retreat if need be.

"This was fun." She held his gaze for a moment before looking down at her plate.

"Fun? I thought it was amazing. We had two and half days to be with each other." He was pushing it with the half. He'd showed up after five on New Year's Eve.

"Is that enough for you?"

"No. Of course not." He reached across the table and took her hand, brushing her knuckles with his thumb. "I want to see you all the time. These few days together have brought us even closer. I was thinking that we should live together. Somewhere where I can get to the city easily and you can get to the hospital. Like you suggested the last time we were here."

Alyssa's heart hammered. He'd never given an inkling he'd even considered her suggestion before. But she had to stay focused on her decision. "You and I both know that living together doesn't mean we'd ever see each other. Your agent made it very clear that your schedule is booked for the foreseeable future. And you told Adam, as well as me, that you'd come up with the money needed for *American Traveler* by taking on more international jobs."

"Yes, but once I earn it, I can refocus."

"Won't there always be a need for more cash?"

"I hope not. The goal is to get more subscribers to cover the costs and make a profit."

She sighed. "I know what the goal is. But will it ever happen?"

They were no closer to resolving this dilemma as when they'd left Glenn Pines the first time. He couldn't rock his boat now and cut off the hand that fed him. And unfortunately, no real end date was in sight.

Alyssa knew how easy it was to stay stagnant, to avoid change. She had continued to work with Cole for over three months after they broke up. She probably wouldn't have made any change if he hadn't scared her into thinking he would transfer her out of the ER. And she wouldn't have her résumé at three different hospitals right now if he hadn't pushed to reignite their affair.

She swallowed her disappointment at Gabe's predicament. "Gabe, I…care about you. A lot." The word *love* was begging to escape, but she couldn't make herself more vulnerable than she already was. "But I can't do this. I know you couldn't get here on Wednesday because of the snowstorm in Denver. But if you had looked at the weather a few days earlier, you would have known it was coming. You could have left early if this meant enough to you."

"I couldn't leave early. There was a problem with the shoot."

She nodded. "I know. And there will always be a

problem that will come before me. I understand that's the nature of your job. It's your nature. But I don't want to be second or third or fourth. I want to have a real relationship where we don't only live together in name but on a daily basis. I want to share my life with someone who's around to share their life with me—not someone who's flying from Namibia to Egypt to Spain. I get that that's your life. You're an incredible photographer, and you should be so proud of where you are. But that can't be my life. Living alone. Waiting for you to come back."

His brow furrowed as if she were speaking a different language. "Are you saying goodbye?"

"Not until tomorrow." Tears swam in her eyes, and all she could see was a blurry Gabe.

He stood up from the table, his full plate of food growing cold. "I need to get some air." He turned and left the dining room.

Alyssa blinked her tears away as she stared through the window into the blackness of the night. She needed to get away from this place as well, but she didn't want to run into anyone who would demand an explanation. With eyes glued to the floor, she escaped, practically running back to the cabin.

The torrent came fast and furious, and she felt nauseous. Sobs reverberated around the room. She loved him so much the pain speared through her heart with a thousand blades. How could she have let this happen to her? And what thought process made her think coming to Glenn Pines was a good idea?

She should have left him in New York. But her imprudent heart kept hope alive. In the back of her mind, she played out the scenario that when Gabe arrived at the appointed time on Wednesday, he would sweep her off her feet with a plan that would work. He would have cancelled—or at least minimized—his fashion shoots in other countries, other states, and focused on working in the city. Maybe he'd have to travel a few days a month, but he'd be home most of the time—in New Jersey, not New York.

But that wasn't the reality. And although her optimism had kept her afloat until she arrived at Glenn Pines, the raw truth exploded in her face. Gabe was two and a half days late to a vacation she'd hung all her hopes on.

Worse yet, he'd showed up with no real plan to change his schedule—just a promise to try to refocus when he had enough money to protect his investment in *American Traveler*.

She looked in the mirror at her swollen, tearstained face and made a snap decision. She didn't want to drag this out. It hurt too much. Spinning on her heel, she quickly threw her clothes into her suitcase and grabbed her coat. But she couldn't simply disappear without a note.

After scrounging through her purse for a pen, she grabbed the small notepad on the dresser.

Dear Gabe,

I am truly sorry to say goodbye tonight. Although I told you at dinner it wouldn't be until tomorrow, I just can't stay. It's too painful. I can see clearly now that we, as a couple, will never work out. I wish you all the best in your career as a photographer and with your investment in American Traveler. *You're amazing.*

Alyssa

She wanted to tell him she loved him more than

life itself. But that might only encourage him to double his persuasive efforts. And she wasn't strong enough for that.

Leaving her key with the note, she gathered her things and left, her heart pounding and breaking at the same time.

Chapter Nineteen

Denise stood outside The Green Door Salon in Princeton when Alyssa arrived. Getting their group together all on the same day became impossible. One at a time would have to do.

She hugged Denise, whom she hadn't seen since right before Christmas when she returned her borrowed dress—over a month ago—although they did text and talk. Alyssa looked through the window into the marble and mirrored upscale salon. "I can't believe I agreed to a manicure and pedicure at this expensive place. I'm clearly not thinking straight."

"This is heaven for me. An afternoon to myself without any kids demanding my attention." Denise's smile split her face.

Alyssa followed Denise into the salon, taking in the elegant reception area. Not her scene on so many levels. Lacquered nails didn't quite go with her nurse's uniform, and within days the polish would be chipped and cracked. Besides, she was still saving all her money to buy David out of the house. With three months to go before the full amount was due him, she might just be able to pull it off—if she were careful with expenses.

But Denise had reached out to her, begging for company so she could tell her husband, Ben, she had plans with one of her Sworn Sisters. Those words were sacred, and Ben would assuredly accommodate her.

How could she refuse?

"How about hot pink?" asked Denise, holding up a bottle of nail polish from the rack of dozens.

"Not my color. I'd prefer clear."

Denise looked at her skeptically.

"Okay. Maybe nude. Something that doesn't stand out."

"Then why bother getting your nails done?"

"This wasn't my idea, remember? I had suggested lunch." With hand on hip, she speared Denise with a raised-eyebrow look.

"I know. I know. But now that you're here, couldn't you branch out a little? Try something bolder?"

Alyssa shouldn't spoil Denise's fun, so she perused the shelves before holding up a bottle containing the slightest hint of pink. "Better?"

"Barely. Why don't you choose something fun and edgy? Maybe navy blue or dark green."

Alyssa frowned. "I'm not fun or edgy. You do realize you're with me and not Nicki."

Denise laughed. "Maybe not fun today, but funny." Then she sobered. "I know you're upset about your breakup with Gabe. Have you heard from him since you left Glenn Pines?"

Alyssa's throat clogged with tears, but she refused to let them fall. "He's left me a few voicemails." Actually, more than a few. He'd been trying to contact her several times a week for the past three weeks. "I finally sent him an email this morning asking him to stop. It just makes things harder for both of us, and I need to move on."

Denise's voice gentled. "Are you sure you're ready

to pull the plug entirely?"

"Yes. Gabe's messages are killing me. He wants to talk out our differences, figure out a way to be together. I can't cave, and that's what I would do if I listened to his pleas in person. It's been hard enough hearing his voice through messages and emails."

"What has he been saying?"

"That he wants another chance to prove to me that we can make our relationship work." She shook her head. "But I already know it won't. In two short months, he disappointed—no, devastated—me. First when he cancelled our trip to Rome and then when he showed up days late at Glenn Pines. How many times do I have to be hit over the head to know that his career will always come first? I know what I want. I want someone who will move mountains to be with me."

Denise pulled her into a hug. "I'm sorry, Alyssa. I know how upset you were when you came back from your New Year's weekend. I was hoping the two of you would be able to work things out. But if you believe he's not the right person for you, then I agree with you. You should move on. You deserve to have exactly what you want." She stepped back but took her hand. "Now that you've cut the cord, maybe it will be easier to date others."

"Not a chance. I'm cutting myself off from men."

Denise's wry smile told her she didn't believe her, but at least she was ready to drop the subject. "Let's forget about all that for now. It's time to get pampered."

Alyssa couldn't help but give in to a little smile as well. "Let's do this." She grabbed a bright orange hue. "Maybe this will remind me of my new resolve."

They were ushered to side-by-side pedicure chairs

and soaked their feet in warm, swirling water. Denise practically purred. "Ahhh. I love this. It's so relaxing after a crazy week with the kids."

Alyssa had to admit it did feel good. And she could use a little relaxation. She'd been working her twelve-hour shifts at the hospital, plus overtime, all while learning a new field.

They spent the next hour chitchatting and being indulged, allowing her to take that first giant step in her resurrected life plan.

When they finished, Alyssa glanced at her watch. "Can we eat lunch now? It's almost two, and I'm starving." After she sent Gabe the email this morning, she'd run five miles in an attempt to clear her mind, heart, and soul. Now her stomach rumbled in protest.

"Sure. There are plenty of restaurants in this area."

They found an acceptable option in the next block. After ordering, Denise looked pointedly at Alyssa. "How's the job search going?"

"Good. I just interviewed at Mercer Health, and I think they're going to offer me a job. It's a bigger hospital, and there's more room for growth there."

"I still don't think you should have let Cole drive you out of Nassau General."

"He didn't. It was my choice. I feel good about moving on. I've been there for over ten years. I could use a change, a challenge."

"That Glenn Pines boot camp certainly worked wonders on you."

Alyssa smiled. "I agree. I'm a new woman." She paused and held her breath, waiting for the waitress to place their meals down before delivering her news. "I filled out an application for Cultural Solutions."

"What's that?"

"It's an organization that sends medical workers, college students, and teachers to impoverished areas where the people there could use help. I applied to go to Costa Rica for four weeks."

"What?" Denise almost dropped her chicken wrap. "Do you even know where Costa Rica is?"

Alyssa chuckled. "I looked it up. Of course, I knew it was in Central America, but it's between Nicaragua and Panama."

"And you think this is a good idea? What happens if you get a new job? You can't pick up and leave for a month, can you? And what exactly would you be doing there?"

"I told the director of nurses at Mercer, who I interviewed with, about my plan. She said the hospital gives leaves of absences for programs like that, and she said it wouldn't be a problem. Especially since I'll be working with cancer patients."

Denise slitted her eyes and stared at Alyssa with her mouth open. "Where did this come from? You've never even been out of the country."

"That's just it. I've never been anywhere other than a few northeastern states and Disney World." She grimaced. "My world is too small. I want to broaden my horizons. Start being a little adventurous."

"You couldn't have chosen a two-week vacation in Paris or Venice or Athens? You decided to go live in Central America for a month?" Denise's concern couldn't be missed. "Now I see what you're doing."

Alyssa cut her tomato atop her spinach salad. "Please share."

"You want to do things, go places that Gabe would

approve of."

"Wrong. I told you Gabe and I are finished. He will never know what I do or where I go."

"How can you go to a place to work for a month that you know nothing about?" Denise wrinkled her nose. "Is there running water?"

"Of course." At least she thought wherever she was going would have some basics. She'd better check into that.

"There are other ways to get away from a man without travelling two thousand miles."

"I'm not going to Costa Rica to get away from a man. He's already gone. I told you I need some adventure in my life, a new experience, something different. I'm boring."

"You are not boring, Alyssa. You never were. And you're saving lives here. In your hometown area. Not to mention the support you've been to your mom."

Alyssa heaved a heavy sigh. "I know. And it's been important for me to be there for her. Thankfully, her chemo is over." She moved her salad around her plate. "So next month is a good time." Placing her fork down, she turned her focus to Denise. "You've been to other countries before. And didn't you go away in August?"

Denise's face brightened. "We went on a river cruise in Europe. Without the kids. It was beautiful and romantic. I had Ben all to myself for ten days."

"See. You're seeing the world."

"We did not go to an impoverished village in Central America. We went to Europe on a very nice cruise ship."

"Maybe I'll do that someday, too. Hopefully with a man I'm in love with. I can't believe you and Ben have been together since high school. And married now for eleven years."

"I'm a very lucky woman." She gazed off into the atmosphere, an ethereal smile on her face.

Apparently their second honeymoon had done wonders.

"Maybe you should go on a real vacation with Gabe. To assure work doesn't interfere."

"I know you heard me. We are not together. There will be no romantic vacations. He's probably in Singapore or Bali or Miami, working his magic." Melancholy rose up in her, threatening to smother her heart, her soul.

"A few months apart may be the catalyst to make you realize how much you care about each other."

"I know how much I care about him. And I believe he cares about me. Time will not change our fundamental problem. We lead two different lives, and we will never be on the same timetable."

Alyssa pushed her plate away. No further comment was necessary. She didn't believe in fairy tales. Or hope. At least in this instance.

Denise came back to their earlier topic. "So I guess Costa Rica it is. Go. Experience. Just don't bring back any viruses. Illness is not attractive. Death even worse."

Alyssa dug deep for a smile. "Thanks for the advice. I'll do my best."

****

Alyssa collected her mail from the box. A large envelope caught her attention. No return address. Putting the bills on the counter, she tore open the envelope. A magazine, *American Traveler.* The magazine Adam published and Gabe invested in. Her heart galloped, and she forgot to breathe as she flipped through the pages, then stopped at familiar scenes. The article was titled "Finding Love at Glenn Pines" by Gabriel Sutton.

Tears blurred her eyes, and she blinked them away, trying to see the photos that accompanied the article. Several of her. They were exquisite—the colors intense, the light perfect.

She moved as if sleepwalking to the kitchen chair and fell into it while reading. It brought her back to that wonderful, magical place where she hiked, kayaked, played tennis, rode a horse, and it was all so much better because she had shared it with Gabe. He wrote about it all, starting with that first day when Missy fell and broke her wrist. A photo of Alyssa tending to her dominated one of the pages. Alyssa looked so caring, so capable. A tear slipped down her cheek.

Continuing where she left off, she read about Gabe's night of stargazing, first by himself, the next night with her. His words made her laugh through her tears. As she continued, she realized the article wasn't just about falling in love with Glenn Pines, which she assumed. He was talking about her. He referred to her as his muse and credited her with the beautiful pictures that went with the article.

When she finished, she sat back and closed her eyes, picturing herself lying beside him on a blanket, with him pointing out different constellations, recalling his musky scent, the feel of his shoulder beneath her head. The magazine slid from her hands and hit the floor.

She bent to pick it up, and a piece of paper slid from the pages. Leaning over to grab it, she discovered a letter. From Gabe.

Her hands shook as she held it before her, the wavy words appearing through the tears flooding her eyes. She swiped at them, desperate to read his thoughts.

Dear Alyssa,

I knew you would never see this if I didn't send it to you by mail. Travel magazines probably aren't your thing, and you specifically asked that I not email or call you anymore. I'm trying to respect that.

This will be the last thing I send you. Putting this piece together was so easy, so much fun, so bittersweet, because you were everywhere—every single place my mind took me. The photos also made it easy. Even the shots you aren't in, I knew exactly where you were standing, what you were saying or doing.

Although American Traveler *is all about the destination, how I felt being at Glenn Pines with you seeped into my writing. If we had been able to meet in Rome, I was going to follow up on this piece as a continuation of our journey, hoping you'd explore other places with me, too. I'm not joking when I refer to you as my muse.*

I understand why you don't want a relationship with me. My work has taken me away from home all too often. At first, that's what I wanted. A great way to see the world. Now I realize that this nomad life of mine is no longer the life I want to lead. I have you to thank for the many discussions we had that have opened my eyes.

I wish our relationship hadn't ended the way it did. I am more than sorry I ignored the weather and didn't get on a plane sooner. I ruined our weekend. And I ruined any chance of trying to convince you that I could change to make things work for us. You needed to see action, not just hear words.

I want you to know that our time at Glenn Pines was something very special to me. And now it's memorialized in writing. And photos. Thank you for being my muse.

Gabe

Her throat was so tight it ached, and her head pounded. She loved him so much. And he had loved her. They were meant to be together, if only the stars aligned. But she wasn't a photographer who could work side by side with him, and he wasn't a fellow nurse. Their career paths would never meet. Never even come close with the way things were now.

She folded the letter and placed it in the magazine where the article started. She'd want to read that article, that letter, over and over. But it wouldn't be good for her soul.

With determination, she crawled to the back of her closet and found her box of memories. In it was her diary from high school, pictures of her best friends, her family, programs from the school play, her nursing diploma. She untaped the box and laid the magazine on top. Then she took masking tape and laid it on thick, assuring it would be difficult to reopen it. She wound the tape around the box at least a dozen times, sealing her past away. Needing to protect her shattered heart.

She had a new life to forge, and the past was the past.

Chapter Twenty

Anxiety and excitement sped through Alyssa's system as the old van transported her and seven other volunteers from the airport to their destination—Cartago, Costa Rica. This was her first step in seeing a part of the world that didn't include the northeastern United States. Sure, she was only here for four weeks, and she had chosen a country that was known for its lush forests and friendly people. This being her first experience abroad, she avoided war-ravaged countries as well as the entire continent of Africa. If this worked out, maybe she'd do another tour and possibly even go to a country like Tanzania.

But she didn't want to get too far ahead of herself.

While initially looking into Doctors Without Borders, she wasn't about to sign up for an adventure that required nine months to a year. Cultural Solutions seemed a better fit for her first foray outside of her comfort zone.

Peering out the van window, she viewed living conditions like she'd never seen before. Many of the residences they passed were made out of rags hanging on poles. As they entered the city, people were everywhere, bicycling, walking, maneuvering around the cars to get to their destinations. Yet no one seemed in a hurry. Children of all ages ran through the streets, kicking a ball, playing with the many dogs that roamed with them, laughing. Bright colors were prevalent on the structures—turquoise, red, orange, yellow, blue. Very different from the neutral colors of the houses at home. But they weren't beautiful. Faded paint and crumbling cement prevailed.

Their driver, José, also their guide, was their source of all information as well as their translator. Friendly, laid-back, and with a toothy smile, he immediately erased some of Alyssa's fears. He pointed out where to buy groceries, a local bank, acceptable restaurants, and drove them by the beautiful Basilica. While most of their days would be spent immersed in their duties, they would have days off when they could explore the natural beauty of the country.

"Have you ever been here before?" she asked the young woman sitting next to her in the van.

"Not here. But I volunteered through this organization two years ago in Haiti. When I was in college."

"I was surprised to learn that Costa Rica was a destination through Cultural Solutions—but I guess poverty is poverty, and medical need is medical need—no matter the country."

"There's a definite need here. Many people who live in the rural areas lack access to basic healthcare, or they don't have the means to seek out medical assistance."

"It's like helping in the midst of paradise." Alyssa had read about the towering mountains, pristine beaches, verdant rainforests, volcanos, waterfalls, lush jungles teeming with wildlife. And she couldn't wait to see it all on her days off.

"This is definitely not a bad place to be. Although

it's considered a third-world country since the poor far outnumber the middle class and rich."

"What do you do now?" asked Alyssa, curious about everyone she'd be living with for the next month.

"I'm starting grad school in September. Getting my master's in social work. How about you?"

"I'm a nurse. Recently transferred from the ER after ten years, to oncology. My name's Alyssa by the way." She held out her hand.

"Julia. Happy to meet you." She shook Alyssa's hand. "It must be hard to switch fields after ten years."

Alyssa held her grimace. "It is. But I'm into the challenge. Where are you going for your master's degree?"

"Penn State. That's where I got my undergraduate degree. They have a good program, and it's affordable since I'm a Pennsylvania resident."

Alyssa thought back to her days in college. She hadn't strayed too far, deciding on Rutgers, forty minutes away. Although she had lived on campus, if a football game, basketball game, or frat party wasn't scheduled for the weekend, she went home. She really was boringly predictable.

"Why did you decide to come here?" Julia asked.

"I've never been outside of the country. I wanted to change that." Alyssa gazed out the window. "And this is quite a change."

"Who will you be working with?"

"Cancer patients at the clinic in town. What about you?"

"I'll be at the orphanage."

They turned into a residential street, and José pointed to their home away from home. "Here we are."

Alyssa took in the wooden structure surrounded by lush vegetation. Several hammocks were strung between trees. She whispered to Julia. "You don't think we have to sleep in those, do you?"

"Only if you want to. There will be bunk beds inside. A room for the women and a room for the men."

Alyssa had learned that home base had bathrooms. A sigh of relief. But communal living would be interesting.

They got out of the van, a total of four women and four men, although Alyssa would have called them kids. All in college or recently graduated. The snippets of conversation she'd heard on their ride told her they'd been to places like this before—and loved it. That gave her hope.

José provided a two-minute tour of their lodging, pointing out the large living room with lots of folding chairs and a few tables, the kitchen, the women's bedroom, men's bedroom, and two bathrooms. Everything was stark, simple. But the decorations on the walls would take days to enjoy—colorful handprints of all the volunteers who had been here before her with a message or inspirational quote. It was overwhelming and touching at the same time.

José explained where the closest bus was and showed them a map on the wall with routes to the different places they'd all be working. Alyssa hadn't been on a bus since high school.

Apparently, six others currently lived here, but they'd be leaving in two days. Julia and Alyssa chose a bunk from those available and found a drawer to call their own. The two other women from the van—Cindy from New Hampshire and Carol from Ohio—also claimed their accommodations.

For their first foray into town, the women decided to go to the market, food being a necessity. José gave them directions and a few hints on what to buy. The guys were going to sweep out all of the rooms in the structure, a chore that would be a daily necessity given the open doors and windows and lack of screens.

"I feel like I'm the dorm mom," Alyssa said to the three twenty-somethings as they walked into town.

"I think of you more like my older sister," said Cindy kindly. "I miss my sister, so you'll be a great substitute."

"Thanks. I like that." Despite the heat of the climate, an emotional warmth spread through Alyssa for the first time that day.

Their initial lesson was figuring out the local currency—their second, what some of the fruits and vegetables were. At least Carol liked to cook, making her the most interested in learning how to craft a decent meal from the offerings at the local grocery store. She was also the most fluent in Spanish and made friends easily at the market. Although Alyssa had taken Spanish throughout her school years, she rarely used it and had forgotten most of it. Hopefully, some of it would come back.

The heat of the midday sun had them perspiring on the forty-minute walk home. "Another lesson is to go to the market early in the morning," said Alyssa, wiping the sweat from her brow. "Clearly José wants us to learn most lessons on our own, since he didn't dissuade us from our mission."

"He's probably laughing with the guys right now," chimed in Julia. "I say we don't share our food with them."

"That's not very nice." Cindy was definitely the most charitable of the group.

Arriving back at home base, the women unpacked their bags and discussed what to have for lunch.

"I wish we had cell service here." Carol checked her phone. "I'd be able to pull up recipes and figure out what to do with some of these odd-looking vegetables."

The guys were out back, raking dead leaves off the dirt paths. Alyssa knew their names were Kevin, Ed, Norm, and Andre, but she wouldn't swear as to which one was which yet.

Carol and Cindy made sandwiches for everyone and called the guys in to eat. Suddenly inheriting a family of seven strangers—who would all have to figure out how to live and work together for the next four weeks—had her stomach knotting. The missing six would hopefully pass on whatever wisdom they could to this new group before leaving.

After lunch, Alyssa took a walk around the property, studying the different trees and plants. The familiar clicking of a camera had her spinning around.

Andre was crouched on the ground, photographing a leaf from a plant.

"You remind me of someone I know." She smiled at the memory.

"I hope to get paid for doing this one day." He adjusted his lens and took a few more photos.

"Taking photographs of nature? A job like that can take you all over the world."

"I can only hope to see the world like that." He stood and came closer. "Are you a photographer?"

She chuckled. "No. An ex of mine is." The stab of

pain twisted her heart.

"Sorry. A recent breakup?"

"Yes." She shrugged it off. "But I'm good." What a liar she had become—a necessary defense to protect herself. Dodging the subject also worked. "Where are you from?"

"Colorado. I'm heading to New York City after this. I have an internship at *American Traveler*."

Tingles rushed through her veins, and her mouth opened and closed. How could this be such a small world? "My…ex recently did a story for them. On Glenn Pines, a resort in the Pennsylvania mountains."

"Gabriel Sutton?"

Alyssa's heartbeat tripled before tripping over itself. Just hearing his name did crazy things to her insides. "Do you know him?"

"No. But I hope to meet him. I know all the photographers' names who contribute to the magazine. I make it my business. But his career is really in high-fashion photography. I'd love to get to know him and learn whatever I could." He paused, probably noticing her pale face and shaky hands. "Sorry if I'm fawning too much over your ex. I should just shut up."

She swallowed in an attempt to tamp down her racing heart. How could the mere mention of his name do that to her? "I haven't seen him in three months, since the beginning of January." Her voice cracked, and tears flooded her eyes. "I have something to do inside." She practically ran to the house, needing a moment alone to collect herself.

But that was not to happen. Kevin, Norm, and Cindy were sitting in the living room getting to know each other, Carol was in the kitchen with Ed, and Julia was in their bedroom writing in her journal—a snapshot in living color of what her immediate future would be. Escaping to the bathroom, she ran the water to cover up her confusing sobs, but the merest trickle came out of the spigot. Her astonished face reflected back at her from the tin mirror, and she started laughing. How was she supposed to wash her dust-covered face with a few drips? How was she supposed to fix her hair in a gray and rust reflection? Where was she supposed to go when having a meltdown?

The tears stopped in an instant, and Alyssa breathed in deeply, a recalled remnant from her meditation class. She counted to ten, then let out her breath slowly. Cupping her hands under the spigot, she let her palms fill before splashing the water over her face.

She'd come here to continue her journey of self-discovery and to start her exploration of the world. No more sad thoughts allowed. She was stronger than that. And if she didn't quite believe it right now, she intended to prove it.

****

The next day was her first on the job. They all woke at six, had fruit and yogurt for breakfast, packed a lunch, and headed into town as a group with the intent of helping each other get on the correct bus for their different destinations.

Alyssa was headed to a small cancer clinic across town. Nerves jumped in her stomach as they would on any first day on the job. Yet, in this particular case, compounding her anxiety was her lack of knowledge of the language and her fear that everything would be vastly different than her job at Mercer Health.

With only two wrong turns once she got off the bus, Alyssa arrived at her destination. Dr. Javier Benoit ran the clinic along with two long-term nurses and a handful of temporary workers like herself. To her joy, everyone welcomed her with open arms, and most of the staff spoke English. One of the nurses brought her to the reception area where she'd initially work with the intake receptionist to learn which procedures they covered before escorting each patient to their appropriate destination. That way, she'd learn the different areas of the clinic and what testing, diagnosing, and treatments they performed.

Unfortunately, the patients didn't speak English, so Alyssa paid close attention to the Spanish being spoken to them and concentrated on dusting off words she once knew and adding to them.

She studied each patient's chart, making sure she understood the treatments and medications prescribed or the therapies ordered. Many fewer people worked here than in a similar cancer center at home, so she filled in where she could by making the patients comfortable before their testing or treatments.

The ill children who were brought in, two of them babies, were particularly heartbreaking. So tiny and helpless. While she had dealt with some children in the ER at home due to broken bones, high fever, or scary cough, most kids were brought directly to Children's Hospital.

When she arrived back at her home base at around six, she was bone tired.

"How was your day?" asked Julia, who was in the kitchen with Carol making dinner, thank God.

"Exhausting, educational, wonderful." Alyssa

picked up a carrot and munched. "How about yours?"

"You'd think the kids at the orphanage would be depressed, longing for a family to take care of them. But most of them seem happy. They love to play games like kickball and tag. They were so excited to have a new face when I showed up, although they clearly love the workers who are already there. One of them was leaving today, and the kids clung to her like a koala on a eucalyptus tree." Julia followed Carol's direction to dice the lettuce. "I can't imagine how sad it will be for us when we have to leave them. And I've only been there a day."

Carol nodded. "I'm at the senior center, and the people there are similar to the kids. Happy to see new faces. Although I assure you we're not playing kickball or tag. Cards and checkers are more their speed."

Andre came in and snapped a photo of the three of them. "Perfect," he said.

"Perfect?" Julia pointed to her messy bun. "After a day of playing out in the dirt with five-year-olds, I hardly think this look is perfect."

Andre's smile was killer. Straight, white teeth flashed against chestnut skin, a day-old beard, and amazing blue eyes.

"I like candid shots of people doing normal things. The three of you are beautiful just the way you are."

"A man after my heart." Carol held her hand over her chest. "How does that line work for you, Andre? I know it works on me, but others may be skeptical."

He chuckled, then took a photo of Carol as she spoke to him.

Her green eyes smiled as did her mouth. "When you sell those to the fashion magazines, I want my cut."

"You got it."

Alyssa's déjà vu played havoc with her soul. What she wouldn't do to be back at Glenn Pines, giving Gabe a hard time about taking her photo. "Carol, don't sign a release, or you may end up on some gallery wall."

When Gabe asked her to sign one, she'd laughed, assuming her images would remain in his digital files with all the other photos he'd taken over the years. Alyssa still couldn't believe how beautiful the enlarged photos were with the right lighting and subtle frames at the gallery.

"Or *American Traveler* magazine," Andre added. "Did Mr. Sutton pay you for them?"

"Of course not," Alyssa stated. "We were simply taking a hike. I wasn't the focus of his pictures."

Andre peered around the lens of his camera. "Oh, you were the focus. The composition of those photos, the lighting, the foliage. They were all the frame for you. I looked at them again after you told me you knew Mr. Sutton."

Andre's words disoriented her. She grabbed hold of the counter to steady herself. "You have the magazine with you?"

He nodded. "My internship starts as soon as I leave here. I need to learn everything I can about that publication, so I packed the last few issues. Those photos were a love letter to you."

Alyssa swallowed the lump growing in her throat. "I met him at Glenn Pines." Her voice croaked. She cleared her throat. "We had a really amazing time. I'll never forget it." She inhaled and turned her attention to Julia. "Can I help with dinner?"

Alyssa needed to take her mind off Gabe. No use in

wasting one more minute feeling depressed, sad, or lethargic. She'd already done all that, and it hadn't changed a thing.

She should celebrate the memories of their time together and be thankful he'd shared a piece of himself with her. If not for him, she would never have signed up to come to Costa Rica—the first stop in her journey to see at least some of the world.

The next few days expanded Alyssa's heart tenfold. While communication was still difficult, she and the patients made up their own sign language. They learned from each other, and although the people in her care had to deal with their devastating illness, she was able to bond with them through a caring touch and doing everything in her power to make them more comfortable.

They smiled at her despite their condition, and Alyssa found herself teaching them English as they taught her Spanish. She took time to play word games with them in an effort to distract them from their treatments, especially those receiving chemotherapy. It reminded her of the hours she'd spent with her mom doing the same thing.

"You're very good with the patients," said Dr. Benoit. "Do you work with cancer patients at home?"

"I worked in the Emergency Room at a hospital for ten years. I recently moved to the oncology unit at a bigger hospital."

"Good. We'll be moving you out of reception, now that you know where everything is, and rotating you through the different areas."

This was the perfect placement for her to get great experience in her new field while taking her first foray into a foreign country.

Her first day off came six days later, and it coincided with four others' schedules. Alyssa, Julia, Carol, Andre, and Norm decided to go zip-lining at Manuel Antonio National Park. After a week of living together in very close, rustic quarters, they were becoming good friends.

"Andre, do you have to bring your camera with you?" Carol had been in Andre's lens for days. "You might enjoy it more if you aren't looking at everything through that tiny square."

"Not bring my camera? I don't think I could do that." He looked truly pained.

"Alyssa, help me out here," Carol pleaded.

She looked from Andre to Carol. A definite spark ignited between them.

Alyssa shrugged. "I don't think I can help you. Andre's camera is part of his makeup. It would be like cutting off his arm. But, Andre, it might be too clunky to hang around your neck while you're flying through the air on a zip line. And from what I understand, two people can go at the same time. You may want to hold on to Carol instead of your camera."

Andre's eyes sparkled when Alyssa dropped that possibility out there.

"I'll only bring my phone so I can take at least a few photos. But it won't get in the way."

Carol sent Alyssa a nod of thanks, and Alyssa smiled at her new friend.

If she couldn't have love herself, why not enjoy it vicariously through someone else's budding relationship?

Chapter Twenty-One

Two weeks into her tour of duty, as they all kiddingly called it, Alyssa walked Juan, one of her patients, to the bus stop a block away. "You seem a little stronger today than last week." His chemo was wiping him out, and she feared he'd fall without her arm for support. Although what help he received at the other end of his ride she didn't know.

On the way she played her word game with him and pointed out a food store across the street and said, "Market."

He repeated the word and said, "Bodega," which Alyssa repeated. They did the same with several other structures when Alyssa heard the familiar clicking of a camera. She spun around, almost expecting to see Andre.

It wasn't.

In the shadow of a large almond tree stood Gabe, his piercing green eyes focused on her. Was she hallucinating? She blinked. Perhaps the heat was interfering with her brain waves.

Afraid to say his name for fear it would disturb the air and make him disappear, she stood very still, drinking him in, one second at a time. *Please, please don't be a mirage.*

"Hi, Alyssa."

His words whispered around her.

Juan looked up and pointed to her. “Alyssa,” he said, affirming Gabe’s statement. Or maybe he said it to bring her out of her coma.

She refused to take her gaze from Gabe, who stood a few feet away. “Gabe. What are you doing here?” Her mind whirled, but no reasonable answer spun to the forefront.

A slow smile crept over his mouth. “Searching for you.”

“But why?” Although she understood his words, she didn’t comprehend their meaning.

“I miss you.”

Her heart jumped and danced an arrhythmic beat. She wanted to run and crash into him, feel his flesh and muscles against hers, know this was real. But her feet stuck to the ground, and all she could do was ask questions to unravel her confusion. “How did you find me?”

“I went to your house. You weren’t there, so I searched out your hospital. I learned you had transferred to another hospital. I went there and found out you had taken a four-week sabbatical to work in a clinic in Costa Rica.”

A smile tinged with surprise melted her soul.

He continued. “I remembered the name of your lawyer friend, Sam, and looked her up. She gave me more specifics after I begged, pleaded, and promised a photo session, even though she knew I wasn’t that kind of photographer.”

Alyssa nearly flew into Gabe’s arms, but caution held her back.

“Are you happy I came?” His smile ran from cheek to cheek, mirroring her own.

"Yes. But I'm in shock. I…I don't…" A rogue tear slid down her cheek. Why was she crying?

Gabe covered the few steps between them in a flash and wiped the tear from her face with his thumb in the gentlest caress. Then he raised her chin with his fingers and covered her mouth with his, hot and needy and delicious.

She wanted to glue herself to him, remain in his arms forever. But reality checked in, and she stepped back, glancing at Juan. He had the biggest smile on his face.

"I'm sorry, Juan. This is my friend, Gabe. *Mi amigo*. Gabe, this is Juan."

Gabe shook his frail hand.

"I'm walking Juan to the bus stop. It's at the end of this block."

"I'll walk with you."

Talking to Gabe in front of Juan was difficult, and she didn't want to ignore her patient, so she continued their Spanish/English lesson as her heart hammered a Costa Rican beat. Thankfully the bus was a minute behind them. Once she guided Juan onto the bus, she joined Gabe on the sidewalk, at a loss for words but with a dozen more questions.

"Do you have a job in Cartago? How long are you staying? Where are you staying?" Her mind tripped over more, but she left it at that. For now.

"I have all your answers, and we have a lot to discuss. Can you get off the rest of the day?"

Her heart dropped. "I can't. I need to get back." Here he'd travelled all this way to see her, but they'd have to wait.

Disappointment shadowed Gabe's face. "What

time are you finished?"

"Five."

"I'll be in front of the clinic when you get out." He raised his camera and took a photo of Alyssa, a smile twitching at his lips.

"I didn't say you could take my picture." Her raspy words held as much teasing lightness as she could possibly conjure up at this moment.

"I'll never be able to stop." Gabe's voice encircled and caressed her, despite the total mayhem colliding in her brain.

Back at the clinic, she gave him a quick wave and entered, fighting for control over heart and mind. Gabe must have combined this trip with a job. He'd never have time in his schedule to take a week or two off to track her down. What was his purpose? He said he travelled to Lawrenceville, went to two hospitals, located Sam. Then took a plane to Costa Rica. What was he thinking?

She'd find out. But not until five.

The afternoon couldn't pass fast enough. Alyssa tried with superhuman effort to keep her mind on her patients, but thoughts of Gabe kept interfering. Their bond was undeniably strong. So much so that she'd had to cut him off from communicating with her to bolster her resolve. Yet here he was, thousands of miles from New York City, to do what she wouldn't allow him to do back home.

On any other day, Alyssa wouldn't leave the clinic until well after five. She'd complete paperwork, finish up with a patient, and ask questions of the doctor or nurses to learn more about the services they provided. The hands-on experience she was gaining here in such a short time would aid her substantially at her job at home. Given the number of patients they treated, her days usually flew by.

But today, she watched the minute hand on the clock travel ever so slowly. And then it was finally five. She bolted from the building.

There stood Gabe, just as promised, looking as gorgeous as ever.

Alyssa walked over to him, controlling her breathing, wanting to pick up on that kiss she broke several hours earlier, but feeling so, so vulnerable. And scared. She didn't know what was happening, and she needed to know.

Gabe, on the other hand, had an advantage. He knew what was going on in that mind of his. He strode to meet her, took her hands in his, and gave her a tender kiss on the lips. "You're just as beautiful as I remember," he breathed.

"So are you." She connected with his eyes, emerald depths of intenseness.

She had to break the connection if she had any hope of having a conversation. They began walking.

"So what's the real reason you're here? Do you have a job in Cartago?"

He fell into step next to her, grabbing her hand as they walked. "As a matter of fact, I do. Once I knew where you were, I contacted Adam and suggested that I do a photo story down here for *American Traveler*. I researched the organization you're working for and put together a proposal. They both agreed."

Butterflies danced and collided in her stomach despite her instruction to simmer down. "Where are you staying?"

"There's a small hotel right in town. Originally, I was going to stay at your home base. The vice president in charge of public relations offered, but I knew that was overstepping the boundary. Especially if you didn't want me there. And if you did, it wouldn't give us much privacy." He yanked on her hand. "If you want privacy, that is."

She glanced at him, taking in the sparkle in his eyes, the half smile on his lips. "And if I don't?"

"I don't mind an audience if you don't." His half smile turned full blown.

"Funny man." Even the butterflies laughed.

"When's your next day off?" Hope peppered his voice.

"The day after tomorrow." She had planned a trip to the beach with Julia.

"Great. How'd you like to go to the Monteverde Cloud Forest? I understand there are howler monkeys, frogs, and a million birds."

Alyssa remembered their conversation about Audubon at Glenn Pines. "You're not going to kill any so you can take a photograph, are you?"

He tugged her into his side and kissed her temple. "Nope. I may find it hard to take any photos with you distracting me."

"So I'm a distraction?"

He stopped and turned toward her, cupping her face in his hands. "You're all I want to see." His eyes burned through to her soul, and she felt herself slipping into his orbit.

Her lips sought his, and she drank him in, thirsty for his love. Yet her niggling conscience whispered in her head. What had changed in the past three months that would make things work out between them? She needed to know.

She pulled away, lowering her eyes so she couldn't get sucked back in. "I'm really glad to see you, Gabe." She exhaled. "But I've been trying extremely hard to get over you. I could finally breathe without my heart splitting in two." That was a lie, but a necessary one. "Coming here was a huge step for me."

Gabe pulled her over to a bench on the corner. Cars whizzed by, and children ran through the streets and sidewalks laughing, tagging each other. They were in the middle of chaos, but the cocoon Gabe spun shielded and enveloped her.

"I've made decisions, too. All with you in mind. I hope you'll hear me out." He took her hands in his, forcing her to face him. "I've been extricating myself from international shoots and slowly transitioning to local studio jobs. I've been searching for my own studio space and have been pitching an idea to the magazine editors and advertising firms. Since I have literally thousands of photos from locations around the world, I've suggested blowing up photos of the location of their choice as the background for their particular spread. I could even do three-dimensional versions, but the shoot would be at the studio. It will save the magazines and advertisers thousands in travel expenses, and I could do the high-fashion shoots they want without leaving the city."

Excitement over his idea streamed from his pores and shone from his eyes. "Of course, renting studio space in New York is expensive, but I could charge more since I'd also be charging for my landscape photos. I've also considered saving some money by renting or buying space in New Jersey but close enough to the city to not be an issue."

Was this too good to be true? She didn't dare fall into it so fast. "That sounds wonderful, Gabe. Are they interested?"

"Of course. Saving money while still hiring the talent they want is music to their ears."

"I'm really happy for you." She smiled, feeling the contagiousness of his joy.

"There's more. I put my co-op on the market."

"What?" Confusion bumped up and erased her smile. Had she heard him correctly?

"Yes, I listed it. I figured I could use the money in the bank in case it takes a while for my new idea to take off."

"Where will you live?"

His eyes pierced hers, as if searching for something. "I'd like to rent a place near you. And once you're ecstatically happy with me being in your life, I'm hoping you'll consider looking around for a place for us to share." He studied her face.

Alyssa shook her head to realign her brain waves. "You want to move to Lawrenceville? There's no caveat that you're thinking about it?"

"Not if you'll have me. I'm ready to commit to you. Under your terms. I've been planning this for a long time. Ever since that last night at Glenn Pines. When you broke my heart." His face softened, and he brushed his knuckles over her cheek. "You need time to catch up. I didn't mean to storm you with all this, but you cut off all communication. While I wanted to come by to see you in Lawrenceville, I didn't know your schedule and was afraid you wouldn't let me in even if you were home." His eyes held all the sadness she felt deep in her core. "We have the next two weeks here to talk it out. You can process it. Change the plan in any way you want." He lifted her chin with his fingers. "This is all up to you, Alyssa. No pressure. If you need more space and time to consider my proposal, let me know."

"What about the cash you need to protect your investment in *American Traveler*?"

"At the time I didn't realize my father was giving me such a gift when he shared the gallery space with me in December. I sold all my photographs for a hefty amount. I was able to give Adam the cash he needed much more quickly than anticipated. Which reminds me—" Gabe unzipped his backpack and searched through his camera equipment. "I have something for you." He pulled out what looked like a check. "This is yours."

She took it and looked at the payee. *Alyssa Beckman*. A check for thirty thousand dollars. "What? What is this?" Her hand shook.

"It's your share of the profits from the photos of you from Glenn Pines that I sold at the gallery."

"But this doesn't belong to me. This is yours." She handed it back to him, but he didn't take it.

"You were my inspiration, my muse. Those photos were a huge hit at the gallery and, as I said, very profitable. People loved them, and I sold them all. At a very good price."

"But I signed a release. Those photos are yours."

He shrugged. "Even so, I wouldn't feel right not paying you."

"But…but we never talked money. You don't owe

me anything." She tried to push the check back into his hand.

"Why are you being so stubborn?" His smile went straight to her heart. "This can help you pay off your ex-fiancé. You won't have to work overtime." He folded the check and placed it in her palm. "I also made another decision. Since I'm heavily invested in *American Traveler*, I plan to do a few photo stories a year. To not only be a silent partner, but a contributing editor. It makes sense, Adam is thrilled to promote the magazine with my name attached, and I can make my own schedule for those stories."

Everything was falling into place. There had to be some catch. "You'll still be travelling some of the time, right?"

"Only for these stories. I'm hoping I can convince you to come with me on the trips abroad. For vacation, not work, where we can explore, take photos, and write the stories together. Just you and me."

"And that's why you're here for two weeks?"

"I'm here because you're here. I miss you. I want to be with you. And if it takes more than two weeks to convince you that you belong with me, then I will follow you to the stars and back."

Tears flooded her eyes. He had heard her. He had listened. And he wanted them to be together. "I…I don't know what to say."

Gabe's brow furrowed and his eyes dimmed. "I was hoping you had missed me as much as I missed you."

"I did. I do. With my entire being." She threw her arms around his neck and kissed him with all the passion that had been building with every word he said.

His plan excluded travel and included her. She held his face between her palms as she assaulted his mouth, reveling in their connection and not caring a whit that they were sitting on a bench in the middle of town.

A laugh bubbled up inside, and she shared it with him. "Is this real? Am I dreaming?"

He joined in her joy. "You are not dreaming. And neither am I. So is there an agreement in there somewhere? To some plan?" His gaze wound straight to her heart.

"Yes, yes, yes. I would love it if you moved to my town. And yes, we can look for a place to live together that works for both of us." She sobered as she caressed his cheek, his jaw, while fixating on his beautiful green eyes. "I love you, Gabe."

"I love you, Alyssa. I was miserable without you these past three months. I'm hoping that we can move forward now, with nothing getting in our way."

He captured her lips in his, a sweet, tender kiss that soon turned hot and needy, sending fireworks to every synapse in her body.

"How far away is your hotel?" she asked between breaths.

He chuckled. "A few blocks. Would you like to join me there?"

She jumped up. "Take me. Now."

"Yes, ma'am." He took her hand in his and led the way.

Epilogue

Six Months Later

"You finally made it to Italy. Cheers." Gabe held up his glass of champagne.

Alyssa couldn't contain her smile as she toasted with him. "It's not Rome. But I thank you for suggesting the Amalfi Coast instead of a big city. This must be one of the most beautiful spots in the world."

They sat in a private room at a restaurant high up in the hills near Positano, overlooking the steep terrain falling straight down to the Mediterranean Sea. Lights from houses and yachts twinkled against the dark evening sky.

"It's so good to relax after the crazy year we had." She and Gabe had strolled the streets of Positano today, meandering in and out of shops, galleries, and of course the church, before heading to the beach.

Gabe's hand covered hers, transmitting warmth and peace to her soul. "I figured you would like it better here. At least for your first European trip. But we'll make it to Rome one of these days." He paused, and a smile emerged. "It's hard to believe it was only eleven months ago that we met at Glenn Pines." Emerald eyes shone in the candlelit room.

"Being so busy has made the time fly. Opening your studio in New Brunswick, buying a house..."

"You getting your certification and landing a great job at the Princeton Cancer Care Center."

"We are awesome, aren't we?" Alyssa laughed at her self-congratulatory words.

They had been busy this past year putting into place their plans hatched while at Glenn Pines and cemented in Costa Rica. An unexpected result had been settling in her hometown.

"I will be forever in your debt for agreeing to buy a house in Lawrenceville."

"Once I met your parents and sisters and saw how close you were with your family, especially your mom, I understood why you stayed in the area where you grew up. And those adorable nieces and nephews can't get enough of Auntie Lys. How could I take you away from them?"

"I was afraid you'd run in the other direction once you experienced the chaos of our frequent gatherings."

"I love it. Mostly because I love watching your interactions—the teasing about who's the nicer sister, the arguing over what amount of mayo to put in macaroni salad, the borrowing of clothes, and then the debate about who wore it best. And I could never have moved you farther from your Sworn Sisters. It was clear that Sam, Nicki, and Denise would have made my life miserable. I never had those kinds of relationships in my family or with friends."

"I'm glad you mended fences with your dad. It's made your relationship with your mom and brother so much easier. And now you and your dad are partners at different gallery showings. What could be better than that?"

"It's taken some time, but I learned a lot from you.

First, that life can be precarious. I no longer take for granted that my parents will remain healthy and be there for me when I decide to show up. It also helped to see how important family was to you, even when you disagreed about something. At one point, my brother and I were best friends—until I put my career before him. Now that I've curtailed my travel schedule, work doesn't interfere with important events in their lives. Or ours."

Gabe reached across the table and took Alyssa's hand, sending sparkles fizzing through her blood. She loved that he could still do that to her.

"Alyssa…." His pause had her attention along with a tightening in his jaw.

"Is something wrong?"

"No." His serious gaze studied her. "Will you marry me?"

Her stomach bunched—in a good way—and her heart actually fluttered. Words were nowhere to be found.

He removed a velvet pouch from his pocket, which held the most beautiful emerald ring with diamond baguettes on each side. "I know the traditional engagement ring is a diamond, but this seemed more special, just like you." He stood, then knelt beside her. "Will you?"

Her hand flew to her mouth as she focused on the deep green gemstone that reminded her of the color of his eyes when he was about to kiss her. "It's beautiful. Perfect." She connected with his gaze, the question he had asked reflected therein. "Yes!"

Her smile broke free as did his, and he placed the ring on her third finger.

Her hand shook with emotion as he held it before saying, "I love you."

She leaned into him and kissed his perfect lips. "I love you, too."

He deepened their connection as he stole her breath along with the last piece of her heart.

A word about the author…

Maria Imbalzano recently retired as a divorce lawyer, and while she loved writing legal memorandums and briefs, she now writes romance and women's fiction full time. She also speaks on the topics of perseverance and motivation to local groups. When not writing, she enjoys spending time with her husband, two daughters, granddaughters, and friends at home or at the Jersey shore.

~*~

Visit Maria online at:
http://www.mariaimbalzano.com
If you enjoyed this book, please consider leaving a review at your favorite vendor or book site.

www.ingramcontent.com/pod-product-compliance
Lightning Source LLC
Chambersburg PA
CBHW070045030726
47506CB00002B/349
9781509236985